I

Praise for #1 Bestselling author
John Michael Hileman

Praise for *UNSEEN*

"As a United States Air Force Pilot in the middle of training, I have very little time for anything outside of flying and family, but I eagerly made an exception when hearing about this book and was truly rewarded with each turn of the page; suspenseful, thrilling, and thoroughly engrossing until the very end!"
~U.S. Air Force Pilot Kyle Bradford

"This heart-pumping story grabbed me, forced everything else away, pulled out my tears and stole my sleep from the fascinating beginning to its conclusion. Satisfied? NO! I want more!"
~Ruthie Burke
Director of First Step Pregnancy Resource Center

"This book powerfully touched every raw emotion within from the moment it began till the very end."
~Amazon Reviewer Stephanie Dunn

"A fascinating plot that grabbed my attention from page one, a great pace that kept the pages turning, and a deep richness that still has me thinking."

"John Michael Hileman has done it again! Unseen delivers, with engrossing characters and a story line that will capture your heart."

"...not only a great riveting read, but one that shakes you to your core with a purpose."

Praise for *MESSAGES*

"*Messages*, by John Michael Hileman, is a high-energy, fast-paced work of fiction, packed with grit and substance. This edge-of-your-seat suspense thriller will entice readers from the first page to the last."

"If I could make it more than five stars I would. What a fantastic story! The pace never slows down, just picks up speed all the way. And it's amazing how one little thing from the beginning is a huge tie-in at the end. Phenomenal! Very well done!"
~Reviewer Donna Snow

"This book has many great twists and turns. It is a very well written suspense. For once, I di+d NOT have it totally figured out until the author wanted me to. To me, that's great suspense ... There are strong Christian themes in the book, but they don't overpower the storyline. I think if I were in David's shoes, I might ask many of the same questions. "
~Karen Baney, author of *Nickels*

"From the very first page, I was swept away. The characters are well developed, the plot is masterfully woven and the subject is entirely fresh."
~Dianna Young, author of *Muted Grey*

"Hileman is a genius at developing suspense, giving enough breadcrumbs along the way to satisfy, but pleasantly surprising me near the end to find that he'd been holding the truth close to the chest, waiting for that right moment to spring it on me."
~Rosie Cochran, author of *A Murder Unseen*

Praise for *VRIN: ten mortal gods*

"I don't even like science fiction/fantasy, but once I started reading *VRIN*, I wanted to keep reading it till I was done. It was deep enough to really make me think ... but not so deep that I couldn't understand it."
~Amazon Reviewer Hope Buswell

"Since I'm not much of a pleasure reader, I have to thank John for writing a book that I could actually enjoy. The book was appropriately cerebral and completely accessible. I was hooked within the first ten pages. When John releases his next book, I'll definitely read it."
~Amazon Reviewer Greg Bingham

"After reading *Messages* I decided to give this author another chance, and, WOW, was I impressed! Every reader of fantasy, sci-fi or spiritual fiction should find something delightful in this book. As a fan of all three, I found it highly satisfying on every level."

~B.F. Spink, author of *After Midnight In Savannah*

"I've read the author's suspense/thriller, Messages, so I should have known that this book would be no less enthralling. Be ready for a rollercoaster that will shake you up and dump you off at the end feeling dizzy."

~P. Creeden, of SpiritFilledKindle.com

Books by
John Michael Hileman

UNSEEN
MESSAGES
VRIN: ten mortal gods

By
editor Joanie Hileman

Miracles: 32 True Stories

A NOTE FROM JOHN

If you would like to be put on my reader list, drop me a
line at **johnmichaelhileman@gmail.com**.

A special thanks to author Dianna Young
for inspiring this book.

CHAPTER 1

There was a disorientation in not knowing where or who she was, but Abigail Atwater waited patiently for it to sort itself out; it was her nature to be forgiving. She wiped the sweat from her forehead with a wrinkled hand and squinted at the sun glinting off the windows of the tan brick building across the street. It had been a high school in years past, but now was an apartment building for the lower to middle class. This was her destination. She was sure of it. But the reason had not yet solidified in her mind. She shrugged internally and wiped more sweat from her upper lip. Though it was early, the temperature had already reached a blistering eighty-eight degrees, but a smile stretched out on Abigail's face. She didn't mind the heat. In fact, she quite enjoyed the feeling of warmth enveloping her body.

She gripped her cane and put weight on it as she looked back at the building looming behind her. It was shiny black, and covered in scaffolding. Construction workers crawled like ants upon the rigging while the noise of heavy machinery filled the air of downtown Sunbury.

Sunbury. The name instantly gave birth to images and feelings. She knew this place with its normally quiet streets and friendly people, but it looked different than she remembered it, more cluttered and busy.

It had not yet grown into an adult city with all the troubles that come along with it. Not that it was absent of troubles, but Sunbury was mostly country folk turned city folk. Therefore, its residents had not yet learned the dangers of smiling and saying hello when passing each other on the sidewalks.

Abigail looked down at the shriveled hand resting on the simple wooden cane; she lifted the other to touch her face. The ridges of skin felt soft as silk— and droopy around the chin. By all indications she was old, but she didn't feel old.

A car door slammed, and she looked up like a startled cat. Across the street a pot-bellied cab driver walked around the side of his cab to meet a beautiful red-headed women at the trunk. He flipped the trunk open and hauled three suitcases out onto the sidewalk. There was confusion for a moment, followed by an exchange of words. Abigail could not make out what they were saying, but, whatever it was, it was fiery— and exciting! The woman shook her head furiously, the man's arms raised into the air, and boisterous shouts were heard above the noise of the construction. There was so much heated emotion and passion that Abigail wanted to wave her hands around, too, and shout loudly with great conviction. What fun it would be to well up with emotion and energy. What rapture to allow it to explode into sharp words and demonstrative motions.

But as she stood smiling, her mission began to take shape in her memory.

She had not come to this particular street and this particular building by chance; she had been sent to deliver an important message.

Inside the old high school, beyond the angry woman and the fat-bellied cab driver, was a door with a 203 on it. Behind that door was a handsome young man who needed to hear the message she had been sent to deliver. But was it time yet?

She craned her neck and looked up the street. A dump truck had stopped in the middle of the road as a man with a sign stood holding back traffic. She turned carefully and looked down the street. A group of men in orange vests were directing cars to take a detour up the hill. The downtown street, which was normally streaming with traffic, now sat barren and devoid of life, save for the cabby and his regrettable cargo.

By all indications, it was time.

Abigail stepped off the curb, adjusted her sapphire flowered dress, and made her way across the hot pavement. The woman and the cabby paid no attention to her as she passed. They were having far too much fun talking loudly and waving their hands about. Well, mostly the woman. A look of apathy had settled on the man's face. The right corner of his mouth was stuck in a pinched expression, as if to communicate his boredom and lack of interest in the matter.

Abigail climbed the granite steps, but before she reached the double wooden doors, they flew open, and an attractive brown-skinned woman stepped out. Abigail froze mid-step.

"Girl! You coming in or are you gonna hassle that poor man all day?" Her tone was playful; Abigail immediately liked her.

The redhead looked up flabbergasted. "He only grabbed three of my bags and won't go back unless I pay the extra fair!" She stabbed her finger at him. "Which I'm NOT gonna do!"

He remained silent, and crossed his arms.

"Let him go! We'll go get it later," she called, holding the door open farther.

Abigail took advantage of the extra space and shuffled past the woman into the building. The entrance room was spacious, with a wall of metal mailboxes to the left, and to the right, a brushed metal communication box with buzzer buttons. Abigail scanned down the slightly crinkled list taped to the inside of the glass compartment next to the buttons. There it was: 203. And the name: Jake Paris.

Abigail stiffened slightly as the two women fumbled through the door behind her, banging the luggage and making enough racket to wake the whole building.

"I told him there were four," said the redhead.

The brown-skinned lady dug a key card out of her pocket and swiped it on the door. "We'll call the airport when we get upstairs and make sure they still have it."

"They better, Jackie. If my bag gets stolen, I'm suing that cab company!"

The ladies pushed into the hallway beyond, and Abigail slid through behind them.

12

"So—how was your trip?" Jackie said, as Abigail tagged along, unnoticed behind them.

"It could have gone worse, I guess. It was the red eye, but at least I didn't have to sit next to a fat guy or some chatter box."

"No, I mean the trip to Houston, you know... Everything?" She emphasized the last word.

"Oh. Did I see Blake?" Her voice sparkled when she said his name. "He came up from Galveston; we spent some time together."

They stopped in the T-shaped intersection at the end of the short hall, and the redhead pressed a glossy white-tipped thumbnail to the elevator button.

"And?" said her friend with a brilliant white smile.

"I don't think it is going to work out."

Precisely when the ding of the elevator sounded, a frown flashed on Jackie's lips. "Why? What happened? Is he another dirtbag?"

"No. It's just that—he loves his job traveling around Texas. He doesn't want to move to Maine."

They filed into the elevator and leaned against the back wall. Abigail stepped on and turned to face out. Neither woman paid any attention to her.

"Why don't you move there?"

The redhead shook her head. "My family's here. You're here. I can't move to the other side of the country. I- I just don't know him well enough."

Jackie put her hand on her hip. "Is he worth holding on to?"

"Well... I... Yeah. I mean, he's really sweet, he's gorgeous..." She shook her head. "But—it's complicated."

"Girl, you need to call him and set something up."

"I can't impose on Sarah again. She has enough mouths to feed."

"I don't mean go to Houston, ask him to come here, you know, for a visit."

Ding.

Abigail stepped out. The ladies brushed past her and headed up the hall. Now it was Abigail's turn to frown; she wanted to hear the rest of the story, how they'd met and fallen madly in love. But it was time.

Each floor in the old high school looked the same, with the main hallways shaped like a T and ending with a bank of tall windows or double doors. Carpeting helped to make it feel more like an apartment building and less like a school—but not much less.

She gripped her cane and waddled forward down the hall. The ladies conversation grew fainter behind her, but, before they were completely out of earshot, Abigail heard something that made her stop and listen intently.

"I think I'm pregnant, Jackie," said the redhead.

"What?"

There was a sound of a door opening. "And it's his..." Then the door shut.

Abigail smiled.

She continued on to the end of the hall where a paint-chipped bank of windows let light in through double-paned glass. There were two doors, one on each side of the wide hallway. Abigail tapped her cane on the one marked 203.

CHAPTER 2

Jake Paris stood by the kitchen table his girlfriend, Jenna, had considerately placed near the large bank of windows in their apartment. They afforded him a view of the beautiful courtyard in front of the building as well as the network of streets that threaded through the hillsides of Sunbury. She knew he enjoyed watching the city come to life, so it only made sense that the table should live there. Just like the nightstand needed to be on his side of the bed, because he liked to empty his pockets into the drawer after a long day. He didn't ask her to cater to him, it was just her nature to bring harmony into everything around her. Not just harmony in her relationship with him, but in every aspect of her life.

When she'd decided to buy a carpet for the living room, she had taken snap shots of the brown sectional couch, the tannish-red wallpaper, and the slightly cherry colored table upon which their television was perched, so she'd be able to find a carpet that matched perfectly. He loved that about her. His life before her was a chaotic mess. Jenna offered him a harmony his heart desperately yearned for.

This harmony was only mildly disrupted by Jenna's emotional temperament, which by some was considered a little volatile, but he didn't mind. He understood that it was a trade off. Her hyper-emotional sensitivity was the reason why she felt so strongly connected to everything, and why she always worked so hard to bring unity. He could deal with the occasional outburst of tears, both happy and sad, if it meant stability in every other aspect of his life.

He sipped his orange juice and looked at her sitting on the couch, her blue eyes fixed on a couch cushion. She slid her fingers down a long strand of chestnut hair, listening intently to whoever was on the other end of her cell phone, oblivious to his contented stare. Her naturally red lips were curled into a smirk, and her soft brown cheeks lifted as she smiled in response to what was probably a joke. She had no idea how beautiful she was, or how much he loved her, and needed her.

Jake glanced at the clock and quickly finished his orange juice. But as he turned to leave, the television caught his attention. The local news anchor was running down the news for the day. "Local authorities warn residents to keep close watch on their children, on this, the fifth anniversary of the Cape murderer, named for the location of his first murder in Cape Cod, Massachusetts four years ago. Officials say the killer could strike anywhere and that residents should be vigilant to watch for any suspicious..."

A loud cracking knock startled him. He set the glass on the bar between the kitchen and the living room and looked over at Jenna. She continued to twirl her hair and stare at the couch cushion. It must have been a good conversation for her to have missed that knock.

Jake went down the short hallway and looked through the peephole in the door. In the distortion of the glass, he could see a tiny old woman with bright green eyes, horn-rimmed glasses, a festive flowered hat, and a broad smile encased in wrinkles.

Who on earth?

He opened the door to reveal the rest of his odd guest. "Can I help you?"

She continued to smile as she gazed at his face.

Jake looked up the hall. "Do you live in the building?"

"She was right, you are very handsome," said the woman, her words jiggling out of her throat.

Jake's eyebrows rose. "Ah, I'm sorry—who are we talking about?"

"Shorter than I thought." She cocked her head and looked him up and down. "But not much."

"Look," said Jake, checking his watch, "I have to get to work, is there something I can help you with?"

Her pretty green eyes lit up. "Oh, yes! There is indeed. I was so excited about being here I almost forgot."

Jake flinched slightly as she shoved her hand into her crocheted pocket book. He wasn't sure if he thought she had a gun, or mace... but the action made him uneasy. He was relieved when she pulled out a single white rose.

"I'm supposed to give this to you," she said, holding it out.

"I think you have the wrong..."

"Here," she said, clutching his wrist. She spoke gently. "Take it, take it. You're supposed to take it." She placed the stem in his palm and closed his fingers around it. Her soft cold hands enveloped his, and she looked up with such compassion he could almost feel it pouring from her eyes into his heart.

"Don't let the flower die, Jake." Her voice cracked. "Don't let the flower die."

He looked at his big hand encased in hers.

"Right," he said with an incredulous grin. "Don't let the flower die." He gave a knowing nod, as if this was a secret they alone shared. And followed it with a wink.

She reached up with her right hand, gripped his tie, and slowly tugged him down. Her face scrunched into a wrinkled smile, and her eyes struggled to focus on him. "And be nice to the children, Jake." She closed her eyes and nodded gently.

"Yeah," he said knowingly. "Got it." He pulled gently on his hand, but she wasn't ready to let go.

Her eyes opened as if she had just been awakened. Still holding the tie, her left hand reached up and patted him lightly on the cheek. "You're such a nice boy." The grin stretched out on her face, and she let out a soft sigh. Her grip loosened, and Jake stood upright, nonchalantly fixing his tie. The old woman pointed to the flower. "You're going to want to put that in water."

"Yeah. I'll do that right now," he said, hoping she would be satisfied and scurry off on her merry way.

But instead, she stood in the hallway, smiling her wrinkled smile and gripping her wooden cane.

"Is—there anything else I can help you with?" he said, slowly.

"Oh, no. I'm done." She stood with stiff confidence, her head wobbling ever so slightly.

"Then, ah, I'll just go and put this in some water, like you said?"

She nodded enthusiastically.

"Okay. Well, have a nice day." He backed up into his apartment, closed the door softly, and set his eye to the peephole. The old woman still stood in the hallway, smiling, apparently oblivious to his departure.

"Is she blind?" he muttered. No, just crazy, he decided.

He hung his head, his hands still straddling the tiny glass portal. He could feel the stem of the rose pressed between his palm and the door. This was all he needed today. It wasn't enough to have a day of boring sales calls. He had to add to it the annoyance of some crazy old woman making him late to work.

He tilted his head back up and peered through the hole; his heart skipped a beat. Though he could see quite a distance down the hall, the old woman was nowhere in sight. His hand snapped to the doorknob, but he didn't twist it. His desire to avoid talking to the old woman was stronger than his curiosity. He pushed off the door and went back to the living room, tossing the flower onto the kitchen counter as he passed.

Jenna pulled the phone from her ear. "Was someone at the door?"

"You wouldn't believe me if I told you."

She shrugged. "I didn't hear the buzzer."

"She didn't buzz," he said, checking his tie in the mirror, "she must have slipped in."

Jenna fumbled with the phone, "Yeah. Hold on, Jake's talking to me."

"We can talk about it later."

"You sure?"

"Yes. I'm sure." He leaned over the couch and gave her a kiss. "I'll see you tonight."

Her brow furrowed. "I might be late."

It was easy for him to guess why. Jenna had worked hard to secure the understudy position for a major musical production at the Sunbury Theater, and today was her day to run lines with the cast. She'd heard rumors of a talent scout stopping by, so this was a big day for her.

"Knock 'em dead," he whispered.

"They're as good as dead." She smiled.

Jenna went back to her conversation, and Jake grabbed his briefcase off the counter. His eyes fell on the beautiful white flower laying in the grout between the rose colored tiles. He wanted to just throw the thing in the trash, but it was easy enough to fill a glass from the sink and plop it in. Besides, Jenna liked flowers. Perhaps he would even score a point or two. The little flower fit perfectly in the tall thin glass, and Jake admired his handiwork, for a fraction of a second, before heading out to work.

To his relief the old woman was nowhere to be found.

CHAPTER 3

Jake ran down the granite steps of his apartment building, cell phone pressed firmly against his ear. "Yes. I have three pages of leads. I plan to be at it all morning... Yes, I know there's a deadline." His mind was so lost in the conversation, he missed the little girl hopping on the sidewalk and almost slammed right into her. She hopped backwards, lost her balance and toppled to the ground.

"Are you okay?" He juggled his briefcase and phone. "I'm sorry. Can you hold on a second, Bob? What? Yeah. Okay. I'll see you in a sec." He flipped the phone closed and bent down. "Are you hurt, honey?"

The little girl seemed dazed at first, but quickly recovered and climbed back to her feet. "Ah'm okay. Nuthin' ith bwoken."

He looked her over anyway. All he needed was to start the day off with a lawsuit. "I'm really sorry, sweetheart. I didn't see you there."

She looked up with big eyes. "Don't wowwy. Thumtimes ah'm gwothed in thtuff, too."

He squinted down at her. "Gwossed in stuff?"

She squinted back, and pursed her lips. "You know, in-gwothed."

He stared at her blankly, trying to translate in his head.

She put her hands on her hips. "Not wookin' weyer ah'm gowin."

"Oh!" He laughed. "Yes. I need to watch where I'm going."

"With all that mutho math, yaw gonna huwt thum-one."

He gave her a quizzical expression. It was odd to hear one so young using the term muscle mass, and the way she stood facing toward him, engaged in the conversation, reminded him more of an adult than a child.

She held her hands clasped in front of her pink ruffled shirt. "But ah fawgive you." Her eyes were trained on his as she spoke. "It hoppinth."

He smiled and shook his head. "Well—I will try harder to watch where I'm going."

The little girl shrugged. "Okay. Thee you wound."

He looked at her amazed.

"Unless theyor thumpin elth you wanna thay."

"No," he blinked. "Ah, hey..." He looked behind him, realizing for the first time that he was talking to a toddler. "Where's your mommy? You shouldn't be out here alone."

"In dayor," she said, pointing to the apartment building.

Jake remembered the news piece about the Cape murderer, and a nervous snake curled in his gut. "She lets you play outside by yourself?"

"No, sheeth right dayor." The little girl pointed to the front of the apartment building. Jake could see the profile of a very pregnant woman sorting through a handful of mail just inside the glass doors.

"That's your mommy?"

"Yup, lookin' at mayol."

"Well you better catch up before she misses you."

The little girl smiled up at him. "It wath nithe to meet you."

"It was nice meeting you, too." Jake smiled down at her. "I'll see you around."

She began climbing up the granite steps. Jake turned and jogged down to the parking lot and got in his car.

The ride across town was uneventful. But the time he normally would have spent rehearsing sales scripts was spent watching the scene with the little girl play out over and over in his mind. He couldn't believe how mature she'd acted. Most of the children Jake knew were loud and full of energy. They definitely didn't know words like muscle mass or engrossed. And, they certainly wouldn't have recognized the subtle cue that a conversation was coming to an end.

Jake slammed on the brakes, only narrowly avoiding a collision with a sandy-haired boy with freckles. His mom and two freckly sisters had already reached the other side, but he had stopped in the middle of the road and was looking up at something of interest.

A horn bleated behind Jake's car, then sounded again.

"Lady, do you mind!" Jake yelled out the passenger window at the woman on the sidewalk.

She looked around, then gave him a puzzled look. The girls glared.

Jake glared back.

Was she his mom? She had the same fair skin and freckles and sandy blond hair.

"Hey! The light's green!" screamed the driver behind him, followed by another beep.

Jake gripped his steering wheel and leaned toward the passenger window again. "Lady! You want to get your kid under control?"

"Are you talking to me?" she hollered back.

Jake shook his head in frustration. What was going on with these people and their children? Parental neglect was running rampant in Sunbury. He rocked back into his seat, and stared out at the sandy haired boy, who was now staring back.

Jake tapped his horn, and scowled. At this point there were multiple horns going off, and every pedestrian in sight was looking in his direction—as though he was the problem. Were they all blind? Did they not see the boy in the middle of the intersection?

His hand shot to the door handle, but, before he could open the door, the boy turned and started hopping toward the curb.

Jake stabbed his foot on the gas pedal, and the tires screeched as he peeled off down the road. He slammed the stick shift into second, then third, but forced himself to refrain from punching the gas pedal a third time. He didn't need to add a speeding ticket to his list of irritations for the day; his finances couldn't handle one more shred of debt. In the end analysis, there was simply no money to float a temper tantrum at this time.

He pushed on through traffic, staring numbly at the bumper of the car in front of him. In his mind he could see the mother and the other pedestrians with their judgmental stares and frowns of disapproval. Why were they looking at him? Why weren't they looking at the child obstructing traffic?

None of it made any sense.

CHAPTER 4

Jake stared at the papers littering his desk, then slid the phone in toward him. There were enough names to keep him busy for several days, but he didn't have days. He needed to finalize at least two contracts before the close of business, or there were going to be cutbacks. Last year it was a week of vacation time. His boss, Bob Miller, had gathered everyone in the conference room and explained that the company could not sustain four weeks paid vacation time, and that he was deeply sorry, but something had to be cut. Jake believed him. Bob had introduced health insurance initiatives, 501ks, and in-work fitness programs to help relieve stress and make the team more productive. There was no law requiring him to do these things, and it wasn't a corporate tactic to draw employees from other software firms. Data Tech was the only software company within eighty miles of Sunbury. Bob was just a good guy, and a great boss.

Jake considered himself the luckiest man on earth to have snagged a job straight out of high school. It was a data entry position and didn't pay much, but it got his foot in the door. In four short years he'd been able to triple his salary, hopping between jobs within the company, and now he was on the short list for junior programmer. But he had to run sales calls first. It was a right of passage within the company because every programmer had to know the software well enough to convince someone else they needed to buy it. It was also Bob's personal philosophy that a programmer hungry enough to make a sale is a programmer hungry enough to make a program the client wants to buy.

"Hey, Jake."

He looked up.

Debbie Jones, Bob's secretary, stood sideways in the entrance to his cubicle showing off her enormous belly. She looked like a snake that had just swallowed a hamster.

"You need to cut back on the brews, Deb." He pointed. "You're getting a pot belly."

She scowled playfully. "Bob wants to talk to you in his office at nine, okay?"

"Did he say why?"

"Nope. He probably just wants to go over sales prospects with you."

Jake looked at the papers on his desk again. There wasn't room to add more prospects, but maybe Bob had some closers. It would be a relief to work on a couple that had already been primed. He leaned back in his chair with a squeak and smiled up at Debbie. "So, when you gonna have that thing?"

She rubbed her belly, and her eyes sparkled. "Three more weeks, end of July."

"Do you know what it is yet? I mean, other than a baby?" He froze, as if something startling had just occurred to him. "It is a baby, right?"

She ignored his joke. "Jack and I want to be surprised, so we didn't find out. I thought everyone knew that."

"We-ll, I don't get up to the fourth floor very often. I think they're afraid I'll lead an insurrection."

"He really has you busting your butt, doesn't he?"

"Yeah, but it'll only be for awhile. Soon this will all be nothing but a fond memory, and I'll be coding with the big boys."

"I bet you will," she said, backing into the aisle and disappearing behind the partition. "Nine a.m. In Bob's office."

He saw the top of her head bobbing away.

"Yes, ma'am."

Jake looked at the clock. He had fifteen minutes, enough time to make one call, if all went well. He slid the pages around, searching for the most promising lead. It would be nice to go to the meeting with something already in the can.

As he scanned the sales documents, he gradually became aware of a low steady thumping coming down the aisle. Jake turned and looked, but there was no head above the office dividers. The stomping got closer. And louder. Soon a little blond boy appeared in the entrance to his cubicle.

"Amazing," said the little boy, panting. "This is definitely my favorite part. I don't know why you guys don't do this all the time."

Jake blinked.

The boy bolted off down the aisle, his loud stomping heard clearly as he circled the entire outside of the sales office. Jake stood and looked over his divider. He could still hear the stomping, but couldn't see the boy. He looked around. A few co-workers were talking on their phones in nearby cubicles, and Debbie was standing near the elevator with someone from accounting. No one was paying any attention to the running boy. No one. Where was this child's mother? And why didn't anyone care to stop him from making this unholy racket?

Jake stepped out of his cubicle just as the boy rounded the corner, stomping even more loudly. How was that not bothering anyone?! Jake put his hands up. "All right, slow down. Slow down."

The boy came to a stop. "You know," he said, catching his breath. "When I run, it makes my skin all tingly." He held his arms out. "I love that feeling."

Jake gave him a stern look. "You can't be running around in here like that."

"This is the best place to do it!" His eyes glowed. "Listen," he said, pounding his sneakered feet against the hard wood floor. "It makes noise underneath, and off the walls, too!"

Jake stared, dumbfounded, then looked around the office. "Can no one hear this?!" he asked, loudly.

Three cubicles down his co-worker, Amy, poked her head up over the divider. "Hear what?"

"This!" said Jake, thrusting his hands toward the little boy. Jake leaped backwards. "Wh- whoa!"

Amy's brow rose sharply. "You okay, Jake?"

He dropped to the floor and looked under the dividers. The boy wasn't there, only the feet of his co-workers. "What on earth...?" he muttered.

"Jake?"

"Yes?!" He said with a groan.

"What are you doing?"

He got back to his feet and looked around. "I think I'm losing my mind."

Her head cocked to the side. "Well, if you find it, let me know. Maybe mine's sitting next to it." She gave him a crooked smile. "Well, gotta get back to work." And with that, she ducked back down behind her office wall.

He wished he could do the same, but there was something bizarre happening, and there was no ignoring it. Children didn't just vanish from a busy office, or show up out of the blue for that matter.

Jake heard the elevator ding and turned to see Debbie stepping though the doors. Next to her, with the broadest grin he had ever seen, was the little boy.

"Deb!" he blurted.

She was still talking to the accountant who was standing outside the elevator, but she looked up and acknowledged him.

"DEB!" he shouted again, and took off down the aisle.

She glanced again and gave him a look as if to say, whatever your game is, I'm not playing.

"No, Deb! Hold the door!"

Both of them were looking at him now, but that didn't stop her from letting the elevator doors close.

Jake rounded the corner and stopped. "Really? Really, Deb?"

The accountant laughed.

Jake ignored him and ran to the stairwell. Bob's office was only two floors up. If he pushed it, he might be able to get up there as she was stepping out. He took the stairs two at a time, gripping the rail and swinging himself around at each turn. In seconds he was on the fourth floor, pushing through the door and down the hall. Debbie was just stepping out of the elevator, the doors stood open behind her. As Jake barreled down the hallway, she turned toward him. Her arms crossed on top of her belly, and a look of irritation formed on her face.

Jake slowed himself and thrust his hand between the closing elevator doors. The bumpers squeezed against his flesh, and the doors reversed direction.

"I've never seen someone run up two floors to catch an elevator," she said. "You know it does go back down."

Jake scanned the inside, but the little boy was gone.

"I have a lot of work today, Jake. I'm about to go on maternity leave..."

"Do you believe in ghosts?" he said, still staring into the hollow innards of the elevator.

He could feel her eyes probing him, noticing the sweat on his temple, the tightness of his jaw, the intensity of his expression.

"You're serious." Her voice broke when she said it.

He swallowed. "Something strange is going on. I could have sworn I saw a little blond boy in here with you."

"You ran up two flights of stairs because you thought there was a little boy in the elevator with me?"

He turned toward her, realizing by her expression, that he had probably said too much already. If he didn't implement some damage control soon, he might find himself the subject of endless water cooler discussions, or worse, fired. It was too late to deny what he had said, and there was no way to shrug it off as a joke—his only hope was to allow her to shrug it off as a joke.

"Do you believe ghosts can haunt a building?" he pressed.

"Yeah." Her eyes got big. "Ghosts of little blond boys are haunting Data Tech."

"I've heard about some strange things around here: doors opening by themselves, shadows on the stairwell wall, noises coming from empty rooms..."

She pressed her lips together and glared.

"Now ghosts on the elevator." He shot her an intense look. "Did you feel his presence?" He secretly hoped she would give him a straight answer, but knew her well enough to know she wouldn't.

"You dope." She punched his arm. "I actually thought you were serious."

He grinned, and rubbed his arm.

"You think it's funny scaring pregnant women?"

He shrugged sheepishly, "It's kinda funny."

"I hope Bob buries you in leads."

Bob! Jake had completely forgotten his meeting with Bob! He took off down the hall, scooted through Deb's office, and knocked on Bob's door.

Bob's voice was muffled. "Come in, Jake."

Jake stepped into the office. Bob sat behind his desk motioning for Jake to have a seat. Where were the sales papers? Jake noted the somber look on Bob's face, and fear clawed at his heart. This wasn't a sales meeting. It was something far worse. Jake took a seat and attempted to mask his nervousness.

Bob took his glasses off and set them on his desk. "Jake, as you know, money has been tight, and we've all been working hard to make up the difference." He looked Jake in the eye. Then looked away. "But we just haven't been able to pull out of this downward trend." Bob's defeated expression spoke volumes. This wasn't about the ping pong table or the cafeteria incentives. Jake was about to lose his job.

"I'm sorry it's come to this. You're a hard worker, Jake." He paused. "Truth is, you're a great programmer, but I need great sales guys. I need guys who can squeeze blood from a stone."

Jake stared out the window. He didn't believe his day could get any worse—but he couldn't have been more wrong.

"I have to let you go until things pick up."

There it was. He knew the words were coming, but they stung anyway. Four years he'd spent building a career in software development, and now what was he going to do? There was nothing in Sunbury. Data Tech was the only software company in the area. And he didn't have the resources to move to a larger city. His credit was maxed. How would he ever match his current salary working at a retail outlet? A smothering heaviness settled on his chest.

"I'm sorry, Jake. It's beyond my control."

Jake looked at his lap, then at Bob. "If things turn around, can you give me a call?"

"You'll be the first one."

Jake stood up and offered his hand. Their eyes met as they shook, and Jake hid the fact that his world was crumbling around him.

CHAPTER 5

The cramped downtown apartment was alive with activity, but Holly Paris was utterly alone. Everything that mattered to her in the world was gone. Six years ago, she couldn't have imagined her life with a child in it. But now, she couldn't imagine living without one.

Her little boy was the only person in this whole God-forsaken world who saw her as more than white trailer trash. There was no judgment behind his beautiful green eyes. There was no condemnation in the creases of his lips. And there was no expression of pity. That was the look she hated most. Poor pitiful Holly—can't get her life together. It was the same look the slightly overweight blond FBI agent was giving her now as she spoke with a neighbor in the doorway. Holly scratched her wrist compulsively. She'd hated this world before Gabe entered it. Now the horror of living without his hugs and his smile was more than she could bear.

The officer she knew as McConnell came out of the kitchen and whispered something into the ear of the agent. The agent nodded, checked her notepad, then looked at Holly while still speaking to the neighbor in the doorway. "Thank you, Mr. Jackson. If you see or hear anything, you have my number."

The man produced a set of uneven yellow teeth that still seemed bright against his dark leathery skin.

"Yes, ma'am, I do. And I'll let you know, because I'm like that. I'm a law abiding citizen. You ask people. They tell you."

"You're free to go, Mr. Jackson."

The old black man bowed several times in jerky motions, then backed his way out of the apartment. Holly wished she could do the same. She dreaded the attention she was getting. There was no way she could have covered all her tracks; they were bound to stumble onto something she didn't want them to see. Then it wouldn't matter if they found her son, because the same people who came as rescuers would turn on her without hesitation and rip her child from her desperate hands. They wouldn't see how much she needed her son, or how much he needed her. They would only see an unfit mother and a child in need of protective services. It was all rules and regulations with these so-called "civil servants." Her thumbnail dug into the already torn skin on her wrist. She never should have called them. She should have handled this herself.

Sergeant McConnell turned toward her. "Holly, this is Special Agent Grant. She is here to help you get your son back. Please give her your full cooperation."

Agent Grant slid aside the flipped tips of her retro bob hairstyle, and produced a smile. Her hazel eyes didn't feel as piercing and judgmental as Holly had expected, but she was still not comforted. She was beyond comforting. The shock of losing her son had left her a hollow shell.

"Agent is so formal. Please, call me Angela." She offered her hand. "I know you're scared, but I need you to be brave."

Holly nodded.

"As you know, your son is not the first to be taken. Sergeant McConnell told me you've been watching the news."

Holly swallowed.

"You have to get that out of your mind. Each of these cases has been different, and you're already off to a good start. You called us right away, and we were able to respond quickly. We've learned some things about how this kidnapper works and are going to do everything we can." She looked Holly in the eye. "I believe we can get him. Do you understand this?"

Holly scratched her wrist and nodded.

Agent Grant took a seat in a kitchen chair that had been moved into the living room, looked at her watch, and waved to one of the officers waiting patiently behind her. He placed a laptop on the old wooden coffee table between them, turned it toward Holly, and stepped back.

"I'm going to ask you to do something now, Holly, something hard. You don't have to do it. But, if you do, you could help us get your son back. You do want to get your son back, right?"

A shiver caused Holly's body to quake.

Agent Grant looked up at the officer. He pulled out a plastic evidence bag with a large piece of brown paper bag in it. He laid it on the coffee table and slid it across. Glued to the paper bag was a photo from an ink jet printer. It was a picture of children's blocks, two sets of two numbers stacked on four sets of three numbers.

Holly's eyes widened. "What's this?"

"This note was tucked between your fridge and the wall."

"Yes. That's where I keep my paper bags. I wasn't hiding it. I've never seen this before..."

"We're not implying that you have." She pointed to the plastic bag. "Do you see those numbers? Do you know what they are?"

She looked around at all the faces staring at her, then down at the note. "I don't know." She paused. "Sh- should they mean something to me?" As she stared, a terrifying thought pecked its way through the fog of shock surrounding her brain. Why would this image of blocks be glued to one of her grocery bags? Her eyes flitted up. "Did the person who took my son make this? Was he in the grocery store?" The thought of him stalking her and her son sent a streak of terror rippling through her gut.

"Stay calm, Holly."

"Has he been following us? Has he been watching us?"

"I know this is hard, but I need you to answer my question."

Holly struggled to reign in her thoughts. She had to be strong. "I don't know. I don't know what the numbers are."

Agent Grant pointed with her pencil. "The top two numbers are a time. The bottom four are an IP address, a location on the Internet. The man who has your son is going to post something there at 9:00 a.m. And..."

Holly's eyes shot reflexively to the clock on the living room wall. It was ten till nine. "What's he going to post?" Her eyes snapped back to agent Grant's. "What's he going to post on the Internet?"

"If he does as he has the last three times, he will post a video of your son."

Her belly tightened, followed by an involuntary groan of despair.

"We need you to watch it with us. We need you to look for anything..."

"No. I can't. I can't do it."

"We need you to look for mannerisms, speech patterns..."

"I can't. I can't watch it."

"Your son is counting on you, Holly. You need to do this for him."

Her eyes lit with fire, her hands clenched in desperate fists of rage. "I CAN'T WATCH HIM BUTCHER MY SON!"

Agent Grant's voice was even and tender. "He won't. It's not like that."

A tear trickled down the side of Holly's nose as she gripped her gut. Her voice was barely a whisper. "I can't... I just can't."

"We've seen this before. He's just going to talk to you. He isn't going to hurt your son on the video."

The room was eighty degrees, yet she couldn't stop the shivering in her middle.

"We'll let you leave if he does anything. I promise."

Holly rocked. The tears were flowing and she couldn't stop them. The thought of seeing that man with her son—what he would say. How could she watch it? How could they ask her to watch it?

Officer McConnell interrupted. "We only have a few minutes."

Agent Grant lifted a hand to silence him. "You can do this, Holly." She looked at her notepad. "Do this for Gabe."

Holly struggled to compose herself.

"If you give in to your fear—he wins. Help us get this guy."

Anger boiled in Holly's heart. She wanted this man to pay for what he had done. She wanted to hurt him with her own hands. What kind of monster preys on little children? Who could slaughter a child?

"Help us, Holly. Do it for Gabe."

She bit her lip and wiped her tears with the back of her hand. Gabe needed her to be strong. If ever she had a reason to be strong, this was it. This was not a problem she could run away from. She sat up straighter, and, with the little strength she could muster, gave a firm nod.

Officers flooded into the room, and a laptop was turned so all could see. One of the officers placed a small mounted camera in front of the laptop to record the message.

Holly looked confused. Why? She thought. Why make me watch this if it's going to be recorded anyway? Do these people lack the compassion to at least view it first, to shield me from the worst of it?

After what seemed like an eternity, the black video box came to life on the screen. In the middle of a nondescript room stood a lean man wearing a white prom tuxedo with ruffles on the chest. His bow-tie was bright red and the jacket pocket had a handkerchief of the same color poking out. Dark black eyes peered at her through a white porcelain mask. The emotionless expression made Holly feel sure she was looking into the face of a cold and calculated killer. No sympathy, no remorse, only emptiness. The sight made her recoil.

"This is not the first time we have spoken," said the man in a digitally-effected voice.

It was unlike anything she had ever heard in movies or on television. The sound sent tremors of terror through her bones.

"I have told you before. You are not allowed to tape these broadcasts. You know what happens when you tape them."

Holly looked at Agent Grant with pleading eyes. "What happens when you tape them?"

Grant held her hand up. "It's okay. He's bluffing."

"Am I bluffing?" said the man on the screen.

Holly's eyes grew wide. "He can see us?!" Her hands shot toward the camera. "Shut it off! Shut it off!" she screeched.

An officer grabbed her by the arms and held her back.

"Shut it off! You're killing my son!"

Agent Grant reached out and grabbed the camera. "All right!" she said, with an intensity Holly had not yet seen in her. "All right," she said again, with less emotion. "But you need to watch! You hear me? You need to remember. Without that camera, we only get one chance."

"Yes," said the man on the screen, "remember."

Officers scrambled in the background, searching for the wire tap, but Holly kept her eyes rooted on the screen.

"I want you to remember," said the man in the porcelain mask, "remember who it was that saved your son's life."

Saved his life? What did that mean? Would he spare Gabe?

"I want you to see something, Holly."

Agent Grant leaned toward her. "Remember how he says your name. Watch how he walks. Study it all."

The man disappeared from view, and the camera wobbled.

"Watch and listen, Holly," said the agent, her voice almost a whisper.

An open door came into view, and just beyond was a bright room with primary colors. As the camera entered the room, terror gripped Holly's chest. In the corner Gabe was playing with action figures on the floor. Children's music played in the background.

"You see," said the man from behind the camera, "he is safe."

Holly screamed at the screen. "Gabe! Gabe!"

"He can't hear you, Holly."

"Please don't hurt him!"

"Do you see how happy he is?" A hand reached out and the door closed. "You know, I find it ironic that you are worried that I will hurt him."

Holly tried to wrap her brain around his words. Again he was implying that he would let her son live. Was her son different from the others?

The camera was returned to its original perch, and the man reappeared in the frame. "How could I possibly hurt him any more than you?" Even with the digital effect, she could hear the contempt in his voice. "What kind of life did you have planned for him, Holly? Oh, that's right, you don't have a plan. How many years will he suffer because you decided to bring him into the world? If I were to butcher him in cold blood, he would suffer less than what you have in store for him."

The words sliced at her heart like a hot knife. It was true. What kind of life was she giving him? What kind of mother was she? Gabe deserved more—but she needed him.

"Look at you, Holly. You can barely take care of yourself. What made you think you were fit to raise a child? What made you think you could be a good mother?"

Tears flooded her eyes. He was right. Everything he said was true. She had considered not having him— saving him from a life of poverty and shame. She knew what life she was bringing him into, but she chose to have him anyway.

"You had your chance to make the right choice. Now I'm going to do what you were unwilling to do, I'm going to make the choice for you."

What choice? She struggled again to unravel his riddles, but her brain was numb with panic.

"Fortunately," he said, "I will be more humane than you have been."

His words bored their way into her head like a worm, cutting through dead tissue until they found a nerve. He would do what she was unwilling to do? Kill her son! Holly lurched forward. "No! Please don't kill my son! I'll do anything you want, anything!"

But even as she said it, she realized—she had nothing to offer, and no one to turn to for help. She had burned every bridge and broken every promise she had ever made.

"Will you still be selfish? Even now? Look at yourself!" said the digitally warped voice. "Do you want me to tell the nice police officers what a fine upstanding mommy you are?"

"Please..." she whispered. "Don't." Tears poured down her nose and cheeks. He was right. Everything he said was true.

"Do you want me to tell them that you are only one hypodermic needle away from exiting this world and leaving your son alone in a filthy run down apartment, wondering when his mommy will return? How does a six-year-old recover from something like that? I'll tell you how. He doesn't!"

She quaked as his words resonated through her. Since Gabe, she'd managed, for the most part, to stay off the hard drugs, but recently she'd come close to giving in to the temptation again.

"Or better yet, maybe he'll grow up. Maybe he'll have the fun of hiding his dirty little secret from all the kids at school for fear they will discover that his mommy sells her body for drugs."

Holly's eyes pleaded with the officers in the room. "It's not true. I would never..." She could never do such a horrible thing. It would never get that bad. She would give him to the State before she ever let that happen.

"I'm not the criminal here. It's you who should be locked up for bringing this poor creature into the world. He didn't ask for this life. What did he do to deserve this life of pain?"

"Please, just let my son live. I'll find a home for him—a better home."

"Do you know how they put down sick animals?"

The imagery was more than Holly could bear. She wanted to retreat, but where could she hide? She felt the agent's hand on hers and looked up. Agent Grant's face seemed like the face of an angel in the refracting light of her tears. "I know this hurts, but you must be strong—for Gabe. Try to remember every detail."

"They stick them with a needle, and the animal drifts off to sleep. One pin prick and their suffering is over. What is the greater evil? One pin prick, or years of horrible suffering?"

Holly could not respond.

"I promise you, your son will not suffer. He won't even feel the prick of a needle. He will simply go to sleep and never wake up."

She grabbed her ears. "Noooooo! I can't listen anymore. I can't!"

The figure stood silently staring, as if he could see Holly rocking back and forth—her eyes squeezed shut—her hands clutching her ears. He waited for her. He watched her like a lion watching its prey, waiting for the moment when it is most vulnerable.

Holly gasped for breath and slowly lifted her eyes to the screen.

"You don't have to be strong, Holly. I'll be strong for you." He leaned forward, and the screen went black.

"Nooooo! My BABY!" she lunged toward the screen, but was stopped by a muscular officer. "My baby! He can't kill my baby!"

Agent Grant grabbed her firmly by the wrists and stared into her eyes. "Listen to me! Listen! He won't. You can stop him! You can do this, Holly. You're strong enough. You won't let him kill your baby, and we will help you. Do you understand me?"

Her body went slack and her voice shivered. "He's going to kill him. He's going to kill my son." Her eyes froze into a dead stare.

"No. He isn't. You're going to stop him. You're going to help us nail this guy."

CHAPTER 6

Jake climbed the steep narrow stairs to the door of his friend Dan's apartment. It never smelled good in the small apartment house, but today a new odor offended Jake's nostrils. It smelled like a stack of diapers in the middle of a redemption center. Jake pounded on the door marked by a gold 3 that was hanging upside down on one screw. He listened.

"It's open," came Dan's voice, distant and muffled.

Jake removed a plastic bag hanging from the handle and opened the door. Dan's collection of empty diet soda bottles lined the left side of the even steeper stairs that led up to his living room. They were not the source of the redemption center smell from the hallway, however. Dan was a strange mix of clutter bug and neat freak. He was too lazy to return the bottles, yet his obsessive compulsive disorder forced him to rinse them thoroughly and place them back into their cardboard containers.

Dan kept everything clean, even the piles of clutter that seemed to encircle every room in his apartment. He was the only person Jake had ever known who kept ordered piles of clean junk lying around on the floor. But for Dan it wasn't junk, they were milestones—shrines to past television, movie, or music conquests. To Dan—it was all treasure.

48

Jake crested the top of the stairs and saw Dan in the middle of his living room, bathed in the light bouncing off the wall he used to project his computer screen on. He could afford a projector screen, but he liked having one wall covered with images from his desktop, while the other walls were covered in posters.

Jake saw that he had caught him in the middle of his morning routine; he was still wearing his workout clothes, and the bar on the weight bench still had weights on it.

For the two years he had known him, it always struck Jake as odd to see Dan in his natural habitat. He was a decent looking guy, dark hair, dark complexion, muscular. He would have no trouble finding a girl, if he was interested in pursuing such a thing. Instead he was like a child who never grew up. He lived in a dumpy apartment house and every penny he made was spent on creating the most sophisticated media system on the eastern seaboard. When he wasn't working at the Sunbury Savings and Loan, he could be found in his living room surrounded by the things he loved: television, movies, music, and his weight bench.

"Here," said Jake, tossing the bag at Dan.

Dan peeked in, and an evil grin lit his face. "Oh, yeah, just in time for lunch!"

Jake plopped down in a chair next to Dan's desk. "What is it?"

Dan reached in and pulled out a post card with a picture on it. "You'll love this," he said, handing the card to Jake.

It was a photo of a fat pasty-white man with a hairlip. The inscription said, Willy Packard, Guitar Wizard, and there was a signature.

Jake handed the photo back, "I don't get it."

Dan laughed. "This guy's been hanging bags of bread on my door for over a week now, and leaving his calling card."

"He leaves bread on your door? Who does that?"

"Willy Packard, Guitar Wizard." Dan let out a full belly laugh and slid the bread out onto his desk. It had a homemade look to it, but was packaged in a plastic bag, complete with bread tie.

"Does this guy have a crush on you or something?"

Dan laughed again. "I don't even know the guy."

"Then why is he leaving bread on your door?"

"I don't know! I think he thinks I'm someone else —probably some girl he met at a club or something."

"Well, why don't you leave him a note? Let him know he has the wrong apartment?"

Dan's face went blank.

"Dan? Hello?"

He shrugged. "It's good bread."

It was Jake's turn to laugh. "Dan... There's something seriously wrong with you."

Maintaining the same blank yet slightly comical expression, Dan ripped off a piece and held it out. "You want some?"

Jake pushed it away. "I don't want any of your ill-gotten bread."

Dan got up and went to the kitchen. "It's good bread," he said again, as if repeating it would make it less wrong.

"Yes, and I'm sure Willy baked it lovingly with his own two hands."

Dan appeared with a plate, some butter, and a knife. "He ain't much to look at, but he'll make some girl very happy some day."

"Not if you keep stealing her bread. The love of his life is probably eating some old stale bagel right now, while you devour Willy's freshly baked bundle of love."

"Yeah, but you're forgetting something. He's a guitar wizard. He can get any girl he wants."

Jake wanted to laugh, but he couldn't help thinking this Willy guy was probably head-over-heels in love with a girl who probably wouldn't give him the time of day. And to add insult to injury, some stranger was eating the bread meant for her. He was probably slow mentally and had enough struggles in life without someone making fun of him, and stealing his bread.

"Your mom would be proud seeing you make fun of the mentally handicapped."

"Really? That's the angle you want to take? You don't know he's mentally handicapped. He might actually be a guitar wizard—with a gift for baking."

"It's on you, man."

"All right, all right!" he said, raising his hands in the air. "I surrender to the moral police. But..." He bent over and coddled the loaf. "I'm keeping this one."

Jake shook his head in feigned disgust.

"So, what brings you here to oppress me with your holiness this lovely Monday morning?" he said, releasing the bread and turning his attention back to the computer screen. "I thought you had a ton of sales calls to make today."

"I would have, if Bob hadn't let me go."

Dan sat up straight in his office chair. "Oh, man. Really?"

"Yeah. First thing this morning."

"I'm sorry to hear that, man. How are you taking it?"

"I don't know. I'm still in shock."

"I bet." He held the loaf out to Jake, "Want some comfort bread?"

Jake swiped it away. "Are you emotionally stunted?" he said, only half joking.

Dan's face drooped as he poked a piece sheepishly into his own mouth.

"I don't know how I'm going to tell Jenna. Things are already tense between us, she's been dropping hints about marriage and kids and stuff. I'm just not ready for that."

"Have you been down to the job center?"

"Yeah. I grabbed a business card with their website on it. I guess you can file online now."

"Do you want to do that right now?"

"No. I need more time to process." He shook his head. "This has been the weirdest day ever."

"What do you mean, weird?"

"I mean like Twilight Zone, weird."

"Is this before or after you lost your job?"

"I'm not having a psychological break, if that's what you're implying."

"No. I'm just saying, stress does crazy things to the mind."

"I don't know why I'm even telling you this."

"Look," he said, jutting his hands out toward Jake, "just tell me what happened. I'll shut my mouth and listen. I promise."

This was possibly the biggest mistake in the history of mistakes, but Jake didn't know who else he could tell. Dan was the closest friend he had, besides Jenna, and there was no way he was telling Jenna.

"All right, I'll tell you. But if you breathe a word of this to Jenna, or anyone else for that matter, it will be open season on all the skeletons in your closest."

"My lips are Fort Knox," Dan said, pretending to lock his lips with a key.

Jake took a deep breath, then let it all out. He told about the old woman and the flower, his encounters with the children on his way to work, and ended with the boy on the elevator. Dan listened intently, making no reaction. When Jake finished, he leaned back in his chair, and said, "Now tell me that's not weird."

Dan rubbed his unshaven chin. "It's weird. I'll give you that."

"So you believe me?"

His face soured. "Are you kidding? Mr. Goody Two-Shoes? I think you're genetically incapable of doing wrong. Heck, you can't even indulge in a tasty loaf of bread without feeling guilty."

"Cut it out. I'm far from perfect."

53

"You're like a nun trapped in a man's body."

"Look, this is serious. Something really freaky is going on."

"I'm sorry, you're right, I shouldn't joke. Clearly, this whole thing is rattling you. I'd be messed up too if some old woman visited me and then ghost-children started showing up."

"You think they could be ghosts?"

"Well, I don't know why I said that. I've never heard of ghosts walking around outside in broad daylight. I would think that kind of thing would draw some media attention."

"But they didn't look like ghosts. They looked real."

"Did you touch any of them?"

"No."

"Did anyone else see any of this stuff?"

"No- I don't know. It seemed like just me, I think."

"Maybe you're hallucinating. What have you had to eat today? Or maybe someone slipped something in your drink?"

"No. It's not drugs. I don't feel any different than I normally do."

Dan brought a web browser up onto his projected screen.

"What are you doing?"

"I'm Googling it."

"Googling what?"

"I don't know, phantom children, daytime ghosts, creepy old ladies with flowers."

"Seriously?"

"Why not? This is the digital age. If you had this experience, maybe someone else had it, too."

Jake's phone buzzed in his pocket. He slid it out and looked at the caller I.D.

"It's my mom. I have to take it."

Dan acknowledged him and went back to his search.

Jake took the phone into the kitchen and flipped it open. "Hello?"

There was silence on the other end.

"Mom?"

"Jacob." His mother's voice sounded frail and vulnerable. He had heard this tone before, many times, usually when she was about to shatter his world—again.

Jake was the older of two unwanted children, the product of a drug-addict mom who was too wasted most of the time to remember to use protection. His little sister Holly was the other, but not the second. The second had died during child-birth in the cellar of some guy his mother had known only a month. That guy turned out to be Jake's second step-dad. But after his mom had caught him cheating on her, twice, she had taken Jake and Holly, and moved to Maine.

At nine years of age, Jake had thought his life would have new birth in the city of Sunbury, like a phoenix rising from the ashes, but his mother had not changed her ways. She fell right back into drugs, and the list of male companions grew longer than Jake cared to keep track of.

55

The last five years had been the most stable his life had ever been, mostly because he was no longer under his mother's roof, but partly because she had made a real effort to change. She had managed to stay with the same man for five years and had, as far as Jake knew, stopped using drugs. He'd even started calling her Mom again.

But hearing her voice like this and remembering the many times she'd let him down before... A flood of emotion came back to the surface. "Mom." His voice grew cold. "I really can't do this right now."

"Jacob," she said again, in that familiar voice of weakness, "...something's happened."

He dreaded to hear her next words. What would it be this time? What crisis could she come up with to affect him now that he was no longer dependent upon her to take care of him? He didn't know, but if there was a way to make this day any worse...

"Something's happened to Gabe."

Her words drove a knife into his gut. Why did it have to be Gabe? If there was still a tender place left in his heart for family, that place was strictly reserved for his little nephew.

At seventeen, Jake had been there when Gabe took his first breaths and opened his big beautiful eyes for the first time. Jake had changed his diapers and taught him to walk, while his sister was busy rebuilding her reputation with her high school entourage. It had been a couple years since he had seen him for more than a few brief moments, but his love for Gabe had never diminished.

"What happened?"

She could barely get it out. "He's been taken."

Jake's heart constricted. "What? Wh-what do you mean? By who?"

"That killer on the television, the one who takes children."

"Are you kidding? In Sunbury?"

"Your sister called me this morning in a panic, talking about his bed was empty and she couldn't find him."

"Where is she now?"

"At her place, with the police."

"I'll head over."

"I don't know if they'll let you in. They're calling it a crime scene, like he's already dead." Her voice broke. "I told Holly I would try to find a way to get there. I feel so..." She struggled to keep her voice. "Jacob... Do something..."

"I'm heading over now. I'll call you."

She couldn't respond.

And Jake had no words left to say.

CHAPTER 7

Holly Paris sat curled up on her couch, cradling a cup of mocha iced coffee that one of the police officers had brought in for her. Her gaze sat fixed on the cup. The room had been cleared except for her and the ever-intrusive Agent Grant. Holly wanted to see the gift as an act of kindness, but she knew better. These people had rules and regulations for everything. Everything was by the book. Somewhere, in some government big-wig's filing cabinet, was a list of procedures for every possible circumstance. What to do if the killer calls. What to do if they find something dangerous. What to do if the phone rings and it's the pizza guy. There was a process for handling every conceivable situation. There was even a procedure for handling people. They didn't care about her or her son. They were just doing their job, and their job, at the moment, was to befriend her, break down her walls, and extract information. What better way to do that than with a cup of mocha iced coffee with cream on top?

She gripped the plastic cup and let the cold sink into her fingers. It was painful to the touch, but feeling something was better than not feeling anything at all. The shock and helplessness had emptied her insides, leaving a dark hole of deadened nerves. But she had to fight the numbness, she had to let the pain in, or her son was as good as dead.

She rolled the thought around in her head. If he intended to kill her son, why had he not done it already? Why show her a video and draw things out? Did he get some kind of sick pleasure from it?

"Why is he doing this?" She spoke in a low voice without raising her eyes.

Angela Grant looked up from her laptop. Holly could feel her eyes probing as she searched for the calculated response. "Why is he doing what?"

"This," said Holly, still looking at the cup.

"He is a disturbed individual. We don't know why he is doing this."

Holly looked up. "No. I mean—he already has my son, why doesn't he just kill him? What is he waiting for? Didn't he kill the first two right away?"

The subtle hesitation and slight stiffening of Agent Grant's posture revealed her unwillingness to answer the question. It probably went against some rule in some handbook somewhere. "This isn't productive," she said in her gentle yet commanding way, dismissing the line of thought as one might discard a poorly chosen blouse. "Let's focus our energies on finding your son."

Holly resented the way they all protected her like mother hens, as if it was anything more than another procedure. The agent did an impeccable job of hiding it behind her friendly smile, but Holly knew her mind was busy figuring out the next acceptable move in their elaborate game. Even her concern for Holly's emotional well being was a choreographed play. Agent Grant was merely an actress playing her part. Her lovely angelic face set Holly at ease, but she detested her calculated mind with its rules and processes.

Holly glared. "Why won't you answer my question? It's a simple question. Why doesn't he kill my son like he did the first two?"

Agent Grant's eyes rested on Holly, the clickety click of her mind was almost audible. What was she allowed to say? Would she get in trouble for talking about the deaths of the other children with the distraught mother she was instructed to keep calm? She looked at her laptop screen, then casually at Holly. "How about we go over his mannerisms again and see if we can find a match. Can you think of anyone who has come into your life in the past year?"

Angela Grant was a machine. Holly was sure of it.

"I already told you. There's no one. No one talks like him. No one walks like him. Why won't you answer my question? This creep has my son. I want to know why he's doing this."

Angela remained silent.

"Is he toying with me? Does he get some kind of sick pleasure out of watching me suffer? Or is there..." She stopped herself.

Angela's eyes leveled on Holly. "Is there what, Holly? Hope?" Her eyes grew warm. "There's always hope."

Holly pressed her back into the couch cushion. "I just want to know if my son is different from the others."

"This man never strikes the same way twice. He leaves the children's blocks as a calling card, and in each case there is a video, but beyond that there is no pattern. We have leads we're following, and we have a ton of data on this guy. But now it's up to you; you can help us fill in the blanks. What you know will help us take this guy down, and rescue your son."

Holly almost believed her.

"You need to tell us who you know, and how they might have access to your apartment. Your son was not bound or in distress. That leads us to believe that he's had contact with this man in the recent past."

Holly hadn't thought of that. She remembered Gabe playing peacefully with his toys on the floor. He wasn't taken by force. He'd been lured out of his home by someone he knew. Holly set her drink on the coffee table, and put her feet on the floor. "He goes to daycare, and I bring him to the park sometimes."

"We have an agent checking his daycare. Do you remember seeing anyone with the same size and build interacting with Gabe at the park?"

"I don't remember."

She tapped on the keys of her laptop. "What about the other residents in your apartment building, do any of them have regular access to your son?"

"Mark does. He lives down the hall. He watches him sometimes, but he would never do this. He's always volunteering at places downtown, helping people in need. He would never do this."

"What's Mark's last name?"

"Phillips."

"Would you say he's the same size as the man in the video?"

Holly stammered. "He's maybe... I don't know. I couldn't tell how tall the man in the video was."

"Does he move like him?"

"I don't know."

"How long has he been your neighbor?"

"I don't know, six or seven months." As the words came out, a chill ran down her back. If he was the killer, he would have had time to finish his business in the last place and travel to Maine. There would have been plenty of time for him to get Gabe in his sights and to hatch a new plan.

She didn't want to believe it was Mark, but how well did she really know him? She did know that he volunteered with needy people—but he could have made that up. She had left her son hours and hours with a man she hardly even knew. How could she have been so careless?

"Do you know where he is now?"

"At work, probably. He does construction. I don't know where."

Agent Grant flipped her phone open and pressed a few buttons. "We have a lead on a suspect. I want you to find everything you can on the neighbor, Mark Phillips. Yes. Then we'll go have a chat with him. Bump him to the top of the list. He works construction, find out where. Okay. Thanks." She closed the phone and slid it back in her pocket. "Is there anyone else like Mark, someone Gabe felt comfortable with, perhaps a relative or a friend?"

Holly felt so helpless. She wanted to spill her guts, because if anyone could save her son, she believed Agent Grant could. But the truth was a minefield. Her friends were not the type of people who would exactly appreciate a visit from the FBI.

"I can't think of anyone," she said, disengaging from the conversation.

"No one at all?"

"No." She looked out the window with cold, dead eyes. "Do you mind if we take a break? I need a smoke."

Agent Grant quietly assessed her chances of successfully continuing the questioning. The result must have been a low percentage, because she set her laptop on the coffee table. "Go ahead, take a break. Clear your head."

Holly stood awkwardly and shuffled to the front door. A uniformed officer stood guard in the hallway, and there was one on the front steps of the apartment house as well. Three cruisers and two dark blue government cars lined the street.

Holly crouched down on the stairs and lit up. She wanted something much more powerful, something to make it all go away, but she couldn't leave her son when he needed her most—not like her mother had done so many times. It disgusted Holly to see how much she was like her mother. But she was not going to run away this time. She would fight the ache in her head and stomach, and bear through the sweats, to turn over every rock to find her baby. He was all she had left to live for.

When Jake pulled onto his sister's road, he saw her sitting on the stairs with a police officer looming behind her. She looked like their mother: dirty blond hair dangling down in coils, fair skin, dark eyeliner used generously around the eyes, and a black silk choker with a silver cross. Her dark clothes made her look like an off-work prostitute: a short skirt and two torn black t-shirts.

To see her like this grieved him. She had been his sunshine for most of their childhood. When she was little she used to wake him with a kiss on the nose, and had always been the first to hug him when he was sad. She was his golden-haired angel—until she fell from heaven.

Jake parked on the street, and he and Dan headed up the sidewalk toward the apartment house. She saw them from a distance, but kept smoking her cigarette and staring at the ground.

"Mom called me," he said when they reached the stairs. "How are you holding up?"

She looked up at him and scowled. "Why did you bring him?"

"Nice to see you, too, Hol," said Dan.

Jake got between them. "Dan came because he wants to help."

Her laugh sounded more like a spit. "Yeah, I bet he does."

Jake grabbed Dan by the arm and pulled him away. "Do you and my sister know each other?"

Dan looked over his shoulder, then whispered to Jake, "I may, or may not, have sent your sister a love letter extolling my unending love and adoration for her —in the eighth grade."

"And you didn't think this was something I would want to know?"

His face scrunched up. "It was a non-event, Jake."

"It doesn't feel like a non-event."

"Why? Do you think she likes me?" he said, raising his brow.

Jake punched him in the chest. "This is serious, Dan. My nephew has been kidnapped."

Dan rubbed the spot. "I'm sorry I had a thing for your sister in the eighth grade. I didn't think she would even remember it. Do you want me to go sit in the car?"

"I want you to be serious for once in your life."

"Humor is my self defense mechanism. I didn't mean anything by it."

Besides his weird compulsion to clean and order junk, Dan also had a peculiar need to make light of stressful situations. His own family had once disavowed him for making an insensitive remark at his aunt's funeral. He was asked to say a few words and had taken the opportunity to note that the body in the casket could not possibly be his aunt's—because her makeup was on straight.

Dan's problem was not a complete lack of empathy but an uncontrollable compulsion. Jake understood that and, under normal circumstances, was quicker to forgive, but today was anything but normal.

Jake stabbed Dan in the chest with two fingers. "Just keep your crazy thoughts to yourself and be helpful. Okay?"

Dan nodded solemnly.

Jake turned back to his sister. "Do you want Dan to leave?"

Dan piped in with, "I'm sorry about the whole undying love letter thing in eighth grade, in fact, I'm sorry about eighth grade in general."

She took a drag off her smoke. "What letter?"

His eyes darted left and right. "You're not mad at me about the letter?"

Her mouth pinched at one end. "I'm just not in the mood for your weird sense of humor. It's been a rough morning, Dan."

"Fair enough," he said, shoving his hands into his pockets.

Jake put a foot up onto the bottom step. "Look, we just want to help. Is there anything we can do?"

She shrugged.

"Have you heard anything positive?"

"Not yet, it's been mostly interrogations."

On cue a slightly heavy, blond, blue-eyed woman in a white dress shirt and dark blue dress pants stepped out onto the front porch. On her belt was a holstered gun and in the center of her chest hung her FBI credentials. She was looking directly at Jake. He acknowledged her with a subtle nod of his head.

"I'm Special Agent Angela Grant. You must be Jake."

"Yes ma'am." He climbed to the top of the stairs, shook her hand, and stepped back. "FBI, huh."

"Yes. We're brought in on cases like this when incidents occur in several states."

"Is there any news about Gabe?"

"We're working leads, but no arrests have been made."

"Is there anything I can do?"

"You haven't been around in over a year, is that correct?"

Jake glanced at his sister. "Yes, ma'am. My sister and I don't see much of each other—because of our schedules."

"Then we're all set for the moment." She handed him a card. "Call my office if you see or hear anything suspicious."

He took the card and stared at it. The weight of her words, and her posturing, made it clear that his presence was not required. He was an absent brother, and as far as the government was concerned, he could continue to stay absent—even though he was here now, willing to be available for his sister in her time of need. He had made the effort, but it didn't matter.

A revving engine caused everyone on the porch to look up and watch as a television news van stopped in front of the building.

The uniformed officer climbed down the stairs and met an attractive woman hopping out of the passenger side. Her voice had a timber of urgency. "We have a few questions we'd like to ask."

The officer blocked her way, and Agent Grant swung open the door to the apartment building. "Why don't we step inside where we can all have a little more privacy?"

"Are you investigating the Cape murderer?" the reporter hollered. "Miss! Miss! Has he taken your son?"

Jake saw the fire in Holly's eyes. "Come on," he said, "you don't need this right now." He gripped her arm. She resisted for a moment, then stood and turned toward the door. As fate would have it, he was going to get to be a big brother after all.

Agent Grant guided them down the old worn out hallway to Holly's apartment. The way was made narrow by stacks of old tools, banana boxes filled with junk, and a rusted ten speed. There was also the lovely odor of cat box hanging in the air like a cloud.

Agent Grant opened the apartment door. Inside were men and women, some in suits, some in uniform, and all gathered around an official-looking man with a dress shirt and black vest with the letters FBI in white.

The noise of the debriefing simmered to an awkward silence when they entered; and Dan was quick to pick up on the awkwardness of it. He scanned the room, and the hint of a grin bowed his lips. "Looks like I picked the wrong day to go on the lamb."

Jake shoved him.

"What?"

The officers stood like the statues of Easter Island, observing them silently as they passed. Agent Grant guided them through to the kitchen and gestured for them to take a seat around the kitchen table which was covered with a table cloth Holly had picked out of the trash when she worked at the Ramada Inn. The spots where she had sewn up the holes were only noticeable to someone looking for them.

It had been awhile since Jake had been at his sister's place, but not much had changed. For a ratty two-and-a-half bedroom apartment with wallpaper dating back to the seventies, and kitchen cabinets missing all but one handle, she kept the place surprisingly nice. She had a knack for making old things look less like junk and more like antiques. It might have been the way she decorated the place with dried flowers and old trinkets, but the absence of anything modern, apart from the television, gave the mystique that the grunge of old age was a purposeful art decision, rather than a regrettable financial constraint.

The only room in the apartment that looked even remotely modern was Gabe's half bedroom, which was really just a large closet off the living room. His twin bed sat on stilts above a sturdy dresser and brightly colored toy box, and the floor was usually littered with cheap plastic toys.

Holly did a masterful job of separating this breach of visual continuity from the living room with a door made of thick beads threaded on strings. She never had to worry about him leaving the door open, and having the two eras collide in a distasteful fashion. Entering or exiting the room was only a temporary disruption of the bead barrier. As gravity quickly returned it to a sheet of brown stained wood, the living room was thrust, once again, to its proper place in the past.

The debriefing in the front room started up again, but the officer spoke lower, and Jake could only catch every few words. They were discussing evidence and plausible suspects to track down. Jake struggled to listen, but Agent Grant's voice drowned them out. "Please have a seat. We'll go over things again and then get out of your hair." She leaned her back against the kitchen counter.

"Are you leaving?" said Jake, sitting down.

"Yes. We'll leave an agent to keep watch out front, but we've gathered all we can at this location." She looked at Holly. "Here's what we know so far. There are no signs of struggle in your son's room, which leads us to believe he left his bed willingly, for what purpose, we don't know. It could have been to grab a glass of water or use the bathroom, anything really. All we know is, he wasn't dragged from his bed."

Jake studied his sister. Holly's eyes were fixed on Agent Grant, but her eyelids drooped. There was also a trace of perspiration on her forehead and temple.

"We don't know if he was taken in the apartment or outside, but there are no signs of forced entry. Who else has a key to your apartment, besides you?"

Holly blinked. "Just me, the landlord, and Amber."

"That's your roommate, correct?"

"Yeah. But she's hardly ever around. She works for the airline—as a flight attendant."

"When was the last time you saw her?"

"Maybe a week ago."

"When do you expect to see her again? We would like to speak with her."

"I don't know her schedule. She just comes and goes whenever."

Agent Grant looked at Jake, "Do you have a key?"

He gave her a surprised look. "No."

"Where were you last night, between eight p.m. and this morning?"

"I was at Dan's last night, then I went home to my apartment."

"Do you live alone?"

"No, I live with my girlfriend. What are you getting at?"

"I'm not getting at anything. I'm trying to eliminate you as a suspect. It sounds like you had an alibi all night. That's good."

As Agent Grant questioned him, Jake noticed a movement out of the corner of his eye. He glanced over to the door and was surprised to see a little curly blond-haired girl standing half in the doorway. She looked like a life-sized Cabbage Patch Kid, pudgy build, round cheeks. She wore a yellow sun dress with matching shoes, and dangling from her hand was a white stuffed rabbit. She stared at him, emotionless, her piercing blue eyes steady and unblinking.

Who did she belong to? His sister didn't have a little girl, and, as far as he was aware, she wasn't watching any other children; she could barely take care of her own. Was she a ghost? The thought of it sent a shiver down his spine, and he immediately launched into denial mode. How could it be a ghost? That was stupid. Ghosts didn't just appear in physical form in the middle of the day in a packed house. But—he looked around—why didn't anyone else seem to notice her standing there glaring at him between the two rooms?

The Cabbage Patch girl stepped fully into the doorway, still staring. Jake squirmed in his chair.

"Holly?" he said, in a cracked voice—not realizing he had interrupted Agent Grant. He looked around the table. Everyone was staring at him like he had ketchup on his shirt. "I ah, don't mean to interrupt, but, do you watch any children?"

Her face scrunched up. "No. Why?"

Now that the question waved through the air like a red flag, he wished he could take it back. He was hoping she would say yes, and he could laugh at how silly he was acting. But now, not only was it possible that the little girl was actually a ghost, but all eyes were on him. How was he going to explain such a strange question?

"I'm sorry. I was just thinking out loud," he stammered.

"Do you want to share it with the class?" said Dan.

He shot Dan an irritated look. "It's nothing. I don't know why I said it. Forget I said anything."

They all took a moment of silence for the death of Jake's reputation, and the agent continued with her analysis as if nothing had transpired.

"We need to know everyone who has access to this apartment, or access to Gabe during the week. This was not the act of an outsider; he is someone you know, perhaps someone you all know. He's likely been preparing for this all year, so there have to be traces of his planning. We are looking into any scheduled visits from the utility companies in the area to look for more wire taps like the one we found in your lamp."

Jake struggled to pay attention, but the eyes of the Cabbage Patch girl bored into the side of his neck. Was she real? Did she belong to one of the officers in the other room? Why would someone bring their kid to an investigation?! He wanted to yell at her, ask her what she wanted from him. But he couldn't risk exposing his delusional state to the dozen or so law enforcement professionals who all had the authority to toss him in a rubber room and throw away the key.

Jake stood up, feigned a stretch, and took two casual steps toward the door. He stood quietly watching the conversation. No one appeared bothered by his standing, so he took another step toward the doorway and looked around innocently.

The little girl looked up at him. Her eyebrows tightened slightly, and her right foot made a hop backward as her body wobbled to regain its center of balance.

Jake held his position and watched to see if the little girl relaxed. She had stopped looking at him, because he now towered over her. Her eyes were on Agent Grant instead.

Jake's eyes danced from face to face in the kitchen and then the living room. All eyes were off him. He peeked down again and, as he did, bumped the little girl lightly with his thigh.

"Hey!" she shrieked, backing into the living room.

The sound of her voice startled him. He hadn't expected to feel her shoulder against his thigh, never mind the sound of her scratchy little voice. For a second he believed she had to be real, but a quick check of both rooms made it clear that she was not. Her voice was certainly loud enough, yet no one showed any indication that they had heard her.

He turned casually in the door, and looked down. She tracked him with accusing eyes and pulled her rabbit to her chest. "Kawa doesn' wike dat! My bunny eeder."

Their eyes locked onto each other in silence as Jake's mind buzzed to understand what he was looking at. She wasn't a real child, but how could she be a ghost? She felt real, and sounded real, but how could she be real?

He wanted to speak to her, ask her any one of the many questions exploding in his head, but was forced to only stare in stunned disbelief.

"Are you all right, Mr. Paris?" The voice of Agent Grant dragged him back to reality. "You look like you've seen a ghost."

"Yes," he said, spinning in the doorway. "I mean, not yes I've seen a ghost, but yes I'm all right, here, standing here. Ma'am."

He felt a smack on his leg and glanced down without moving his head or neck.

"You shouldn't posh peepoe. Is not powite."

He withdrew from her.

Agent Grant spoke in an even tone. "Would you like to rejoin us? Or would you like me to have someone escort you to a more comfortable location?"

"I'm sorry," he said, taking his seat again, "I was curious about what they were saying in the other room," he lied, hoping that would explain his trip to the doorway, and save him from getting kicked out of the apartment for acting suspicious—like eves dropping on official business didn't look suspicious.

"You can relax, Jake. We're not keeping anything from you. They're doing the same thing we're doing, covering all that we know so far and determining what has to happen next. You're not going to hear anything in there that you wouldn't hear directly from me."

Jake nodded.

"Now, the person we're looking for probably has military training of some kind; he has access to technology that is military grade. We think, because he spends months placing roots in a new location, he may have let his guard down and mentioned things he shouldn't have. He might have shown a knowledge in military weaponry, or tactics..."

The Cabbage Patch girl walked into the kitchen, dragging her stuffed rabbit on the cigarette-stained linoleum. She stopped, firmly erect, two feet from Jake, and said, "Um posed to tell you sumpin."

Jake looked down at her discreetly.

Apparently, this irritated her, because her body stiffened and her voice raised. "Um posed to tell you sumpin!"

Jake's head snapped up, expecting a response from the others at the table, but all eyes remained on Agent Grant.

The girl folded her arms and stared at him again with her piercing blue eyes. What did she expect him to do? He wasn't about to have a conversation with an invisible child and reveal to the world that he had completely lost his mind.

Had he lost his mind? It was beginning to look like a real possibility. Jake squirmed in his chair, preparing himself for her complete and utter meltdown, but it didn't come. Instead, she let out a huff, and left the room.

He wanted to chase after her, but Agent Grant had probably dealt with enough craziness for one day. So he sat, immobile, watching the door, hoping she would return and tell him her message. Who was she? What was she supposed to tell him? Who sent her? If she was a ghost, then whose ghost was she? A realization occurred to him. Could she be the ghost of one of the Cape murderer's victims? Was he seeing their ghosts? He waited for an opening in the conversation.

"Agent Grant?"

"Yes, Jake?"

"What did the other children look like? The other victims?"

Her eyebrow raised. "You think there might be a physical connection between the children?"

He followed her lead and made his questions sound as though he was curious about what traits the children shared. "Were they all the same age?"

"No. The first little boy was six, like Gabe, but the last was five. The two girls were two-and-a-half and five."

This little Cabbage Patch kid, Kara, looked to be around two-and-a-half.

"Gabe has blond hair, did the others?"

"No. The first boy had brown hair, and one of the little girls had brown hair. There is no commonality between the five of them."

"Which girl had brown hair?"

"The older one. The little one was blond. But there are no common traits they all share. It's a good theory, Mr. Paris, but I'm afraid it's a dead end." She turned back to her notes.

"Was she chubby?"

Agent Grant looked up; her eyes narrowed.

"The little blond girl, was she chubby?"

"How is this relevant to the case?"

Jake struggled to find a reason she would accept, but found nothing. He had to let it go. Besides, the information was probably online.

"Yes, Mr. Paris. She was chubby."

His eye flitted up. Did she actually say what he thought she'd said? One of the victims was a chubby, blond, two and a half-year-old girl. Jake looked back toward the living room.

Agent Grant folded the top down on her laptop. "Well, I guess we're done here. If any of you can think of anything else that will help in the investigation, you have my card. Call the office and file it with the agent on duty. In the meantime we'll work with what we have."

Jake got up and walked to the living room. Only three officers remained.

And there was no trace of the little girl.

CHAPTER 9

After the law enforcement officers had all left, Holly excused herself and went into the bathroom. She didn't look well, and Jake knew why. She had gotten back into drugs in the last couple of years. It was one of the reasons he hadn't been around to visit. He couldn't bear to see what she was doing to herself, and it had been nearly impossible for him to resist the urge to start a fight and take Gabe home with him. Instead of being strong and doing the right thing, he ran from the situation, like his mother had so often done. He had not been the big brother he should have been, but now he was hoping to correct that course.

While she was in the bathroom, hopefully evacuating her system of toxins and not digging out some hidden stash, Jake seized the opportunity to bring Dan up to speed.

"Dan, I saw a little girl while Agent Grant was talking."

"I thought you were acting weird."

"She looked around two-and-a-half and was blond and pudgy." He paused, waiting for a look of comprehension to descend upon Dan's face. But of course, none came. "It's her!" he whispered hoarsely.

"Who?"

"One of the victims!"

There it was, the look of comprehension. "Yeah, she did say that! Are you kidding me? That's awesome!"

Jake looked through the kitchen toward the bathroom door, which was still closed. "Keep it down. I don't want my sister in on this. This is crazy people stuff, our relationship is strained enough."

"What did she say? Did she tell you who he is? Who the killer is..."

"No, well, she said her name was Kara and that she was supposed to tell me something. That's pretty much all I got."

"That's it?"

"Yeah."

"What was she supposed to tell you?"

"How would I know?!" He glared at his friend. "This thing is getting weirder by the minute."

"Weird left the building with Elvis, man. This is way beyond weird."

"Maybe these—ghosts—are being sent to me as messengers to lead me to the killer." A hint of relief passed over him. "What else could it be? That has to be it."

"It's as good a theory as any."

Even if it wasn't true, Jake allowed himself to believe it. Hope, even misplaced hope, had the effect of a healing balm on the heart.

"Where is she now?" Dan got to his feet.

"I don't know. She came in here, then went back out there, then she was just gone."

Dan looked in the closet and behind the couch.

"I already looked for her, she's gone. And besides, you can't see her anyway."

Dan bolted to the door. "Maybe she's in the hallway." He was gone for several seconds, then returned with a sullen face.

Jake wanted to get frustrated at the thought of her being unreachable, but something deep inside reassured him that these ghosts were here to help. It couldn't be a coincidence that they started showing up the day his nephew went missing.

Holly returned from the bathroom in a more recessed mood than when she'd gone in.

Jake attempted to comfort her, but knew it would not be well received. "You okay, Holly?"

She gave him a cold look. "Save your big brother act, it's just us."

"I came over because I care."

"I saw you while we were talking to Agent Grant. The last place you wanted to be was here. You hardly looked at her the whole time she was talking."

"I was trying to hear what they were talking about in the other room."

She tilted her head. "Why are you here, Jake? Is this your chance to take Gabe from me? Are you waiting for your chance to swoop in and be his hero?"

"If that were my goal, he would already be living with me."

"Oh really!"

"Do we have to do this, Holly? I'm here for you, I've always been here for you. You're my sister. I don't always like how you behave but..."

"Well I'm sorry I haven't lived up to your exacting standards, Jake! We can't all be perfect like you."

Dan stepped in. "Guys! We don't have time for this. We have to figure out what we know, and get Gabe back. We should be thinking about him right now."

Whether it was exhaustion or an overwhelming surge of emotion, Jake didn't know, but Holly started to crumble to the ground. He reached out and pulled her into his arms. They fell against the couch and Holly began to shake and cry uncontrollably. Her voice was desperate and weak. "I'm sorry, Jake. I'm sorry. I'm sorry I'm such a screw-up..."

He held her tighter. "We're okay, Holly. We're going to be okay."

"I break everything I touch." She shivered. "And I don't know how to stop. I don't know how to stop being a screw-up. I don't know how to be strong for him. What is wrong with me?"

"We're going to get through this."

"I'm not strong enough to save him, Jake. And I'm afraid. I'm so afraid I'll never get him back. Even if they save him, I'll never get him back."

"We'll get him back, Holly. Shhhh, it's okay." He rubbed her back.

Her voice became a whisper, and tears poured from her eyes. "I need him so much, Jake. Don't take him from me. Please don't take him from me."

He held her and let her cry. There was nothing else he could say. He couldn't make her believe that he was not there to take Gabe away. That was something Holly would have to figure out on her own. His words were empty. Only actions would prove his love was real. Despite all her flaws, she was still his sister, and he loved her, unconditionally.

He had tried to be a good brother, but her destructive behavior seemed to always pour out into his life. That was why he'd started pulling away. It wasn't a lack of love, it was self-preservation.

Once he started getting his life on track, it seemed wise for him to not be around at all. He couldn't stand to see her and Gabe surrounded by the destruction of her bad choices, and she'd refused to listen to him. He thought it was pride and stubbornness, but he could see now that it was simply weakness. Holly was just like their mother. She didn't have the strength to face life, so she ran to drugs to numb the pain. She ran to men to rescue her, but they weren't men, they were boys controlled by their own appetites. They offered easy access to the drugs she craved but lacked the moral fiber and willpower to be the hero she needed. She needed someone faithful, someone honest, someone stable.

Jake looked at Dan perched on the edge of the couch like a stone gargoyle, watching patiently for an opportunity to help, like a hero, waiting to swoop in and save the day. Jake had never considered it before, but Dan was a stand-up guy, in spite of his quirks. He was good to his family, held down a steady job, and kept a clean lifestyle—even with the decay of western society all around him. How different would both their lives have been if she had responded positively to that letter? Maybe he would have done anything for Holly. Maybe she would have been his inspiration, challenging him to do more with his life; find a house, get a better paying job, come out of the cocoon of his living room and breathe fresh air once in awhile. Maybe he would have been the stability she needed to raise her son right, living a clean, happy life.

Jake looked down at Holly, and his chest puffed out slightly as he choked back his own emotion. The wrong man was holding his sister. She didn't need a big brother, she needed a hero, and, even with his mild quirks, Dan Clark was the man for the job. All Jake had to do was get Holly to stop loathing him.

CHAPTER 10

Holly was spent, so Jake left her on the couch with a cold compress. He turned the television on low in case there were any updates, then went into the kitchen to talk with Dan.

"She going to be okay?" asked Dan, looking past him through the door.

"Yeah. She just needs some time."

"She having withdrawals?"

"Yeah. That's definitely part of it, but I think mostly she's just been through the ringer emotionally. There's a lot going on in her head right now. She doesn't know how to process it."

"Is there anything we can do?"

"We just need to keep pumping the water into her and let her rest. When she's ready, she'll come out of it." Jake got a cloth from under the sink and wet it down with cold water. "These will help, too. Go swap this with the one on her head."

Dan's eyes widened. "Me?"

"Yeah. Why not?"

"She hates me, Jake."

"She doesn't hate you. She just doesn't get your humor."

"I'm pretty sure I saw hatred when she saw me on the steps. She won't admit it, but she saw that letter. She saw it—and she hates me."

"That was a million years ago, she doesn't hate you."

"She caught me staring at her one time in gym class. She told me then she hated me."

Jake stared at his friend a moment, then stuffed the cloth into Dan's hand. "Just do it. Maybe she'll hate you less."

Jake watched as Dan took the cloth into the living room and replaced the one on Holly's forehead. Holly's eyes opened to slits, and her face tightened. Jake's best guess was she didn't like having anyone see her like this, least of all Dan. But somewhere in there, there had to be a twinge of gratitude.

Dan returned with a told you so look on his face.

Jake grabbed the cloth from his hand. "Hey, Rome wasn't built in a day."

Dan circled him and leaned on the counter. "What are you up to, Jake?"

"What do you mean?"

"Rome wasn't built in a day?" He pointed at the cloth. "And the whole put a cloth on her forehead thing? Are you trying to—you know—get me and Holly together?"

"Don't you like her?"

"Yeah, in the eighth grade!"

"Shhhh. Keep it down."

He leaned in close. "Jake. A lot has changed since the eighth grade."

"Look. I'm not thinking straight, okay? I lost my job, my nephew has been taken by a serial killer—I'm seeing ghosts. I'm a little messed up right now, just trying to play damage control. If that freak kills Gabe, he'll be killing Holly, too. She needs someone stable, someone strong."

"No offense, man, but I don't think I have what it takes to put a reign on your sister. She's about as wild as they come."

"You could use some excitement in your life."

"My life has plenty of excitement thank you very much."

"You work at the bank all day, and you sit in your living room all night, every night, like you've given up on life."

Dan folded his arms. "I like my life."

"You need to get out of virtual reality and step into the real world, and Holly, my friend, is as real as it gets."

"I'm not gonna lie, Jake, I think she's beautiful, I mean really beautiful, but I can't be with someone who does drugs. And she has a kid." He brought his hands up apologetically. "A great kid I'm sure, but he doesn't even know me."

Jake looked at his sister curled up on the couch, and his heart ached for her. "This isn't my sister, Dan. This is not the life she wants, but she feels trapped. She needs someone strong who can show her the way out."

Dan's eyebrows rose. "There's only one problem with your plan, Jake. She..." he gestured dramatically toward the living room, "hates my..." he pointed at himself, "guts."

"Never-mind. Forget I said anything." Jake went over to the kitchen table, slid a chair out, and slumped down into it. His sister wasn't the only one struggling with the stress of the day, but he couldn't afford to take it out on Dan.

Dan took a seat across from him, and they quietly waited for the heaviness to leave. Dan was the first to speak. "So, what do we do now? Just wait?"

"Well, Holly is no condition to brainstorm with us, so I guess waiting is all we can do. The FBI has a list of leads. Maybe something will pan out."

"What about the ghost kids?"

"I don't know if I even want to think about that. If they are ghosts—and I don't think I'm ready to believe that yet—but if they are, and if they *were* sent to help, then why didn't they help? And where are they now?"

"Why don't you go look for them?"

"How am I going to do that?"

"Well, you know what they look like, right? The girl at your place, the two boys, and the girl here."

Jake looked up. "You're right. There were four of them, the same as the number of victims. The girl here looked like the two-and-a-half-year-old Agent Grant talked about. Do you remember what she said about the others, what they looked like?"

Dan rubbed his thick neck. "I don't remember. She didn't give much of a description. Just ages and hair color." His hand fell to his side. "But I could look online."

"Holly doesn't have a computer."

"We could go to my place."

Jake looked into the living room again. "No, I don't want to leave Holly alone, and there's no way I am ever bringing her up to your place."

Dan frowned. "Yeah, it is kind of a mess."

"Ya think?"

"Hey, how about I go get my laptop. I'll plug it into my cellphone and run off the cell signal."

"That's actually a good idea."

Dan scowled. "What? I don't have good ideas?"

Jake ignored his wounded look. "Listen, *I'll* go, that way I can also stop by my apartment building to see if I can find that first little girl. You watch over Holly and call me if you hear from the FBI, or if there is a news update."

It wasn't much of a plan, but it was something.

CHAPTER 11

Angela Grant and Agent Perez pulled up in front of a commercial construction site on the eastern edge of Sunbury in a black sedan. Agent Grant shifted into park and surveyed the possible exit points. "How sure are we on this intel?" she said.

"He's in there," said Perez in his hoarse Mexican accent. "He's been working on this job for the last two weeks, every day till six."

Angela grabbed her binoculars and made a quick scan of the grounds; it would make matters less complicated if she could locate Mark Phillips before stepping on site.

There were only eight men visible inside the hollow ribcage of the building. Three of them were pouring cement near the back. The one who had his back turned was of average height, with a lean build. His pose resembled the slight leaning stance of the serial killer while his white work helmet gave the appearance of a mask.

"I think I see him," she said. "He's pouring cement near the back." She set the binoculars on the seat and got out of the car. Perez came around and joined her.

"As soon as we step inside, the foreman is going to make a beeline toward us and tell us we need a helmet. I want you to play interference." They started across the street. "I don't want Mark to know we're coming, so let's enter through that right door where the plastic is." She pointed.

They crossed the dirt parking lot, keeping an eye on the three men at the rear of the building, and entered through the right door. The smell of dust and dirt filled Angela's nostrils. In the surprising quiet of the construction site, she could hear the dirt crunching between her shoes and the cement floor. Some of the men were eating lunch, and two others were poring over a blueprint laid out on a piece of plywood between two sawhorses.

One by one heads turned toward them and soon all eyes were watching. Angela kept her eyes fixed on Mark Phillips. He set a bag of cement down in front of him, wiped his forehead with the back of his dirty grey hand, and looked up. His first expression was one of confusion, but when she held her badge up, it changed to fear.

"Mark Phillips, I'm Special Agent Angela Grant with the FBI. I need to ask you a few questions." Her voice reflected off cement and metal.

Mark took a step backwards, and Perez said under his breath. "He's gonna run isn't he? Tell me he's not gonna run."

With that, Mark bolted toward the rear door. Angela and Perez took off after him.

"I hate it when they run!" shouted Perez. He was a muscular Mexican with a little extra meat around the midsection; great for breaking down doors, but not so great for chasing criminals. Angela's full bodied figure wasn't ideal for chasing down criminals either, but she tended to surprise her colleagues by how quickly she could move.

Angela cut through the center of the building in a dead sprint, then slowed at the rear door opening. The way was clear. Mark was sliding down the embankment directly behind the building.

"Stop! We just want to ask you some questions!"

He continued to slide, so she slid down after him. The sharp gravel bit through her pants and into her hand. Perez ran along the bank and headed down to cut Mark off. There were only two choices, head toward the parking lot on the other side of the road that skirted the embankment, or run down the road and enter the residential neighborhood.

Mark Phillips got to the road and looked back. Agent Grant was halfway down the embankment. There was no way he was going to make it to the houses, so he jumped the guardrail and ran across the parking lot. At the far end was a fitness center, and beyond that a tree line. If he got to the tree line, he might lose them.

Angela hit the bottom of the embankment hard and regained her footing. As she ran, her hand ripped the radio from the velcro on her belt and she brought it to her mouth. "Suspect is fleeing on foot to Boyd's Gym! We need backup!" She leaped over the guardrail. He was only one row ahead of her. If she dug in, she might be able to catch him.

Her heart pounded in her ears, her nose and lungs burned with each breath. Slowly the gap between them closed. But it wasn't enough. He made it to the gym and ran up the stairs and through the door.

Angela followed. She cut right and ran up two flights of stairs to see Mark running down a wide hallway with a Plexiglas view of racquetball courts on his left and tanning rooms on his right.

"Stop him!" she yelled as she pursued him past the check-in counter and down a tight stairway beyond. At the bottom she lost him briefly at the convergence of three large rooms and a hallway lined with lockers, but picked him up again after passing beyond a divider wall. He was headed to the back of a workout room, straight toward a red door with a glowing exit sign above it.

"Stop that man!" she screamed.

A burly Italian man in spandex pushed backwards from his treadmill and slammed hard into Mark, sending him flying into the wall. He scrambled to get his footing, but the muscle builder was on him.

Angela gulped for air as she helped the Italian turn Mark onto his stomach. "You have the right to remain silent. Anything you do or say can be used against you in a court of law..."

CHAPTER 12

Jake stopped by Dan's and grabbed the laptop before heading over to his apartment building. There was no sign of the little girl out front or in the east wing of the old school house, so he headed back over to the west and caught the elevator just as it was starting to close.

Inside was a red-haired woman he recognized from his floor and, at her side, a strawberry blond girl with the greenest eyes Jake had ever seen. She smiled up at him.

He smiled back.

"Hi," she said, blinking up at him. "I'm Abby, and this is my mom."

The woman looked up briefly and offered a weak wave. "Hey," she said.

"Hey, how's it going?" said Jake.

He stepped on the elevator and stood sideways to them. There was an awkward quiet for a moment as the doors closed and the elevator launched upward.

"I've seen you around," said the redhead. "You're on my floor, right?"

"Yeah. Just up the hall."

Again there was silence. The elevator came to a stop.

"Well, maybe we'll see each other around." She was trying to be upbeat, but Jake could tell something was bothering her.

"I imagine we will," he said.

"Bye," said the little girl.

Jake gave her a little wave. "Bye."

They went left, and Jake went forward.

Rounding the corner, he saw that the end of his hallway was filled with household items and moving boxes. The door across from his apartment was open, and a man with a box disappeared inside. Sitting near his door, on a milk crate, was an eight- or nine-year-old brown-haired girl, drawing on a tablet in her lap.

"Moving in?" said Jake as he approached.

She looked up from her tablet. Her eyes twinkled. "Yup. Just moved in."

Jake fished in his pocket for his keys. "What are you drawing?"

She tilted the pad to give him a better view. It looked like a bird rising out of the water, but it was unfinished, so he couldn't be sure. The details were impressive. She had blended the pencil marks with her fingers, creating gradients in the feathers, which gave them a beautiful three-dimensional look.

"You drew that?"

"I'm going to be an artist," she said, matter-of-factly.

"Well, you're on the right track. That's beautiful."

"Thanks." She turned the pad back and continued to blend the colors.

Jake found his key and put it in the door. "Well, it was nice to meet you."

"Nice to meet you, too," she said, scratching and rubbing the thick drawing paper.

95

"I'm Jake, by the way."

She glanced up. "I'm Aiyana."

"That's a pretty name."

"I'm named after my great grandmother. She was an Indian."

He chuckled at the blunt manner in which she said it. "Well, I'm sure I'll see you around."

"I'll probably be right here," she said. "I like the way the sun comes through the windows and makes a pattern on the rug."

Jake had never noticed before, but Aiyana was right. It was rather spectacular how the dozen-or-so tiny windows laid a pattern of shadows and light on the dingy maroon rug. In spots, the sun warmed the color to a bright red.

"You notice things," he said.

She looked up sheepishly. "I see more than I like."

It was an odd answer, but he didn't have time to pursue the questioning. It wasn't chance that brought him to his apartment, but rather nature reminding him that this might be his only chance to take care of business.

He entered his apartment and almost knocked Jenna over.

"I thought you were going to be at the theater all day?"

"There was an accident."

It took him a moment to digest her words. He was well past his quota for freak occurrences.

"Nothing bad," she added. "Mina rolled her ankle. The doctor thinks she has a fracture."

Jake could see the mixed emotion waging war on Jenna's face. She felt bad for her friend, but Jenna was Mina's understudy, and this accident could mean a huge opportunity for her. She needed Jake to give her happiness his stamp of approval. "It's okay," he said, "you can be happy."

Tears welled in her eyes. "I'm sorry. This is just so overwhelming. My life is changing so quickly, and I don't know how to process."

"Just take a deep breath, and tell me what happened." He was always playing damage control when it came to anything emotional.

She took a deep breath, as instructed, and said, "Mina came in this morning, and there was a lot of discussion about the scout showing up today, and the director decided to run lines with Mina instead of me. I was bummed of course, but happy for Mina. This scout is from a major touring company, and I would be happy if either one of us got called up.

"I stayed back stage and helped in every way I could. It was so exciting, Jake. We were all trying to get a peek out the curtain and get a glimpse of the scout. She was sitting with the director in the eighth row.

"Anyway, at the end of act one the director asked me to run lines for act two. I couldn't believe it, and Mina was so supportive. She helped me get dressed and prepped. She really is an incredible friend."

Jenna stopped for a second to regain her composure and wipe tears from the corners of her eyes. Mina was the closest thing Jenna had to a best friend, they hung out quite a bit, and Jake liked her, too. The last time the three of them were together it was for dinner and karaoke at the pub downtown. They'd all laughed so hard his side ached the whole next day.

Jenna continued: "After act two we took a break and Mina and I went into the dressing room. That's when we met the scout face to face! She said we both did a wonderful job, and that we were way better than anyone she had seen this year, and if it were up to her, she would offer us both a contract but she only had one contract to give." A conflicted look flashed in Jenna's eyes. "She offered it to Mina. She has more experience than I do, and the scout was looking for someone who had shown the ability to handle the rigorous hours and crazy travel schedule. But..."

She stopped to catch her breath.

"But—she tripped over a prop and rolled her ankle in the third act. If the doctor says she needs a cast, not only will I get the lead in this production, but the scout says she'll draw up a contract for me this week!" Jenna's shoulders slumped. "I'm so conflicted. I don't want to hope Mina broke her ankle!"

"It's not like you broke it." He lowered his eyes. "You didn't break it—did you?"

She smacked him. "No. I didn't break it."

"Then be excited for her if she recovers, and mourn with her if she doesn't."

"This is what I've always wanted, but I didn't want to get it this way, and what about..." She stopped and looked away.

"It is okay to be excited." He shook her by the shoulders, "This is a good thing. Super good."

"It's just such a big change in our lives. How will our relationship change?" The floodgates were threatening to open.

"Whatever happens, we're in this together. I'm not going anywhere."

"This could be the biggest thing we've ever had to face."

"We've had challenges before, we'll work through this one, too."

She nodded stiffly. "You're right. I'm worrying for nothing." She dabbed the sides of her watery eyes. "I'm glad you were here. I feel so much better about this whole thing." Her eyes flicked up. "Aren't you supposed to be buried in sales today?"

He avoided the topic of his job, figuring that pill would go down a lot smoother if she were to get the contract with the traveling theater company. He went straight to the crisis with his sister. "My mom called this morning. It's about Gabe."

She gave him a fragile look.

"You know the killer, the one on the news?"

She gasped.

"They think he has Gabe."

Her eyes looked like they were going to explode out of her head. "Why didn't you tell me? Here I am going on and on..."

"It's okay, Jenna. You didn't know."

"How? How does that even happen in Sunbury?"

"That's what I thought, but it's happening. I spoke with the FBI agent running the investigation. They're trying to piece the clues together and talk to suspects."

"Holly must be devastated."

"She's well beyond that."

"So—what are you doing here?"

That question threw him off, but he recovered quickly. "I grabbed Dan's laptop from his apartment and stopped by here to use the bathroom and grab a couple things."

"Is there anything I can do?"

"Not really. Are you done with the theater for the day?"

"We're supposed to go back, but this is way more important."

"Well, why don't you go, and if anything comes up, I'll call you."

"Are you sure? I wouldn't feel right abandoning you..."

"You're not abandoning me. There isn't much we can do except wait for the FBI to catch this guy."

"You're sure?" Her lip trembled.

Jenna was not as good at suppressing emotion as Jake. Her body's response to everything was to cry. She cried when she was happy. She cried when she was sad. She cried when she was frustrated. Jake wasn't sure why she started crying now. It could have been a feeling of helplessness, he didn't know, but he knew better than to ask. Jenna could never make sense

100

of the plethora of emotions swirling around inside her. The best course of action for Jake was to wrap his arms around her and let her work through whatever emotions she needed to process.

So that's what he did. He held her tight, and looked toward the kitchen. On the counter, still sitting in the water glass, sat the little white rose, a stark reminder of what had happened that morning, and of what the mysterious old woman had said to him. Her words echoed in his mind. "Don't let the flower die, Jake. Don't let the flower die."

A single question formed in his mind.

Was Gabe the flower?

CHAPTER 13

Jake pulled out his phone as he got to the elevator at the end of his hall. He thumbed in Dan's number and put it to his ear.

"Hello?"

"Hey, Dan. Have you heard anything new?"

"There was a special news break on channel five a few minutes ago, but they didn't say anything we don't already know."

"What'd they say?"

"You know, standard stuff. On his fifth anniversary the Cape murderer strikes in Sunbury, Maine, blah blah blah. They mentioned Holly, but it was obvious they don't have a clue about what's going on. You should see all the activity out front. It's a circus."

"How's Holly doing?"

"She's been making calls. It sounds like she's trying to figure out if any of her friends know anything." Dan spoke low into the phone. "She keeps calling this one girl, Stacy. I get the impression she knows something."

Jake didn't know much about Stacy, but what he did know wasn't good. Stacy was plugged into the drug scene. She was one of Holly's suppliers, and for a high school drop-out, she sure knew a lot about chemistry.

The elevator made a ding, and the doors opened. A man stepped out with a box. Jake gave him a nod and stepped on the elevator.

"What do you think she knows?"

"I don't know for sure, but I get the impression from Holly's side of the conversation that there are a lot of people who have hung around Gabe in the last year. She's trying to figure out who he would trust enough to go somewhere with."

Jake looked up. The red-haired woman was stepping onto the elevator with her little girl trailing behind. Both had somber looks, and the woman was red around the eyes, like she'd been crying. Her daughter clung to her leg.

"Well, tell Holly to be careful what she says on that phone. If you know what I mean."

"You think it's tapped?"

"I'm sure it is. That's probably the first thing they do."

"Hold on a sec, she just got off." Jake listened.

Ding. Slowly the elevator doors crept open. The woman moved quickly, pulling free of her daughter's grip, and headed off down the hall. The girl quietly chased after her. Jake thought it was odd, but he had enough on his plate to think about.

He stepped off and looked down the hall toward the east wing of the building. He decided it would be wise to check one more time for the ghost-girl before heading back over to his sister's apartment.

"Jake?" That was Dan.

"Yeah, I'm here."

"Your sister's not happy."

Jake heard her screaming in the background. There was a shuffle with the phone, and Holly came on. "They tapped my phone?"

"I don't know, Holly. I'm not a police officer, but I think it's standard procedure for them to tap the phone in a kidnapping case."

"What am I going to do, Jake?"

"Well, who did you call, what did you say?"

"I called everyone I could think of that's been here in the last year, everyone I had a phone number for."

"Did you talk about anything illicit?"

"No. I told them what was going on, and asked if they'd seen anything—or asked for phone numbers."

"You told them Gabe had been taken?"

"Yeah. I wanted to see what their reaction was. I wanted to see if they acted suspicious. They're going to kill me. The FBI's gonna break down their doors and dig through their stuff. I'm dead, Jake, dead!"

"Calm down, Holly. It's okay. These guys are careful. You told them Gabe was taken. They know what that means. They're probably covering their tracks as we speak."

"You think they knew about the tap?"

"I don't know what they know, but since the feds are in town, they're probably being extra careful."

"You're right, Jake. Now that I think of it, some of them did sound weird, like they were being careful what they said." Her exhale of relief was noticeable.

"So you're okay, Holly. Just hold tight and don't make any more phone calls."

"I wouldn't say I'm okay. They may be able to cover their tracks, but they're still not going to be happy about it."

"Yeah I know. It's an ugly mess. But just stay low until I get there. I won't be long."

"Okay. I'll stay off the phone, but hurry."

"I will, Holly."

He pressed the cancel button and slid the phone back into his pocket with more emphasis than usual. As far back as he could remember, his sister had always had a way of making every situation worse. The only reason either of them still had a relationship at all was because Jake continued to forgive her. It wasn't always immediate, as was the case now. Sometimes he allowed himself a brief moment of bitterness, but that was all. As quickly as the fire rose up inside his heart, the waters of forgiveness were already beating it down.

Jake came to a stop at the bottom of the stairs. In the distant echo of the staircase, he heard the muffled cry of a baby. He froze and listened. The crying persisted. Slowly he climbed the stairs, listening intently. The sound was growing louder as he went, it was definitely inside the stairwell.

He rounded the turn to the last flight and looked up, expecting to see a mother with her baby, but there was no one. Where was the sound coming from? It was very loud now, filling every square inch of space at the top of the stairwell. He continued climbing, and, as his eyes crested the top of the last stair, he saw it, a baby, lying on the floor, wrapped in a blanket. As he approached, the baby's cries dwindled to a coo. It's large round eyes locked onto his face, and remained fixed.

"Hey, little—guy?" Jake said, checking to see if the child was hurt. "How did you get here?"

The baby stared through the droplets still clinging to his lashes. Jake decided it was a he. The male traits were distinct in his face, and he was wearing blue.

"Where's your mommy? We need to find your mommy."

Jake heard a noise beyond the stairwell door. When he got to his feet to check it out, the baby began crying again.

"It's okay. I'm not going anywhere, buddy. I'm just looking for your mommy."

This did not appease the baby in the slightest, and he let Jake know by taking a deep breath and letting loose a howl.

Jake opened the door and looked down the hallway just in time to see a woman reach the elevator. There was no possible reason why she could not hear the baby's crying, yet she ignored it and pressed the button. Jake started to call out, but when she turned sideways, he froze. Judging by the size of her belly, the woman in the hallway was at least eight months pregnant. How could she be the mother of the child in the stairwell? But still, even if she wasn't the child's mother, why was she ignoring his cries? She stepped on the elevator.

Jake called out, "Hey!"

He took two steps forward and looked back at the door closing behind him. When it sealed, he could still hear the baby clearly. This solidified his assumption. The woman on the elevator may not have been the baby's mother, but she had to have heard him crying. He started running for the elevator. He thought to call out again, but if she was ignoring him, he didn't want to give her warning that he was coming. He heard the ding and saw the doors beginning to close. Five more feet! If he could just get his hand into the door, he could prevent it from closing. His feet slapped against the rug as he slowed himself down. His hand reached out for the crack that had almost sealed, but there was no way to reach the rubber bumper inside.

"Hey!" he screamed, slapping on the elevator door. "Hey!"

He jogged back toward the stairwell. There was no way he would make it to the bottom floor in time. What was he going to do with a baby? He had to get back over to his sister's apartment. He had to find Gabe. He didn't have time to track down this baby's mother.

As he approached the stairwell door, he noticed the baby had stopped crying. He creaked it open.

The baby, and the blanket, were gone.

CHAPTER 14

Holly's head pounded, and her tongue felt like a foreign object in her mouth. She watched Dan with weary eyes as he brought a tray of food for her. She hadn't really seen him in over two years. He was more muscular than she remembered, and his boyish face now had a growth of thick dark hair on it. Was this the nerd she remembered from high school, the gangly class clown who sat in the back corner of the room reading comic books? His eyes looked darker, and his brows thicker.

A news break came on, and Holly's attention shifted to the television. A horrible picture of her was being shown in a tiny box above the newscaster's left shoulder. He spouted off details of the kidnapping as one might list items they need at the grocery store. As usual, there was nothing helpful to glean from it. It was the same story repeated for those who had missed it the first ten times.

There was a knock at the door and Jake pushed through with Dan's laptop tucked under his arm. "What'd I miss?" he said.

Holly looked at the tray Dan had brought, sandwich, chips... She reached for the Pepsi. "We haven't heard anything."

"How's the mob out there?" Dan asked.

"There's a lot more of them, it's kinda creepy. They're just milling around chatting. I expected more

108

drama." He handed the computer to Dan. "Let's get this set up."

Dan took it into the kitchen and set it on the table. Jake and Holly followed.

Holly leaned against the wall, even though she needed to sit. Her legs felt like they were going to buckle, but she didn't want to miss anything on the computer screen. "Dan said you went to get this so we could look at some websites? Figure some things out?"

Dan gave Jake a weird look. It was so brief, she wondered if it had happened at all.

"Yeah," said Jake. "We want to look up information on this serial killer, maybe see something the FBI missed. I know it's unlikely, but we have to do something."

Dan sat down, plugged the laptop into his phone, and clicked some buttons in rapid succession. The desktop appeared on the screen. "Let's start with a search and see what we get for hits." He brought something else up and searched for "Cape murderer."

"The top hit," said Dan, "looks like a site dedicated to serial killers."

Jake leaned in. "Let's see what they have on this guy."

Dan clicked some things and scrolled down a few pages. "This is perfect. There are articles and photos from dozens of serial killer cases in here." He scrolled down another page. "Here we go. The Cape murderer."

Jake looked at Holly. "You sure you want to see this?"

She was caught off guard by the question. A hidden barrier had gone up inside her, protecting her, shielding her from thinking about Gabe directly, but this question chipped away at that barrier. If she viewed these pictures, she would be forced to remember that her son could already be dead like these children. She would be forced to remember that horrible emotionless white mask, those dead, evil eyes. Did she have the strength to see the possible end her son may yet face?

She gripped the cold soda can. "I have to, Jake. I have to know if there is anything here that will save my son."

"All right, Holly, but you tell us if you need to stop." He looked down at Dan. "Go ahead."

Dan clicked through several pictures before Jake stopped him. "Which one is this?"

Dan read from the description of the photo. "Carmen Thomas, victim number three."

"She's the chubby blond one?"

Holly noticed the look again. It was as if Dan wanted to ask her brother a question, but stopped himself. She might have missed it if she was watching the computer screen with them, but she could only bear a few quick glances at a time.

Jake squinted at the screen. "Are there better pictures of the children? Like home photos?"

"Why?" asked Holly. "Why are you so interested in what the children look like?"

Jake looked up at her, and there was a fraction of a pause. "Just curious. Why?"

"Curious," she parroted. He was hiding something. She didn't know what, but the two of them knew something and were keeping it from her. She wasn't blind. She could see their non-verbal communication. She could see Dan's hesitation and Jake's reassuring hand moving to rest on his shoulder.

Jake spoke in an even tone. "Let's take a peek at the children and see if there are any physical similarities."

Holly squinted at him. He'd said that before during the meeting with Agent Grant. Did he have a lead? If he did, why would he hide it? She folded her arms. "Okay, what are you two up to?"

Jake masked a guilty look. He was such a terrible liar. "We're just looking for clues. If you have a better idea, I'm all ears."

"Agent Grant said there were no physical similarities between the children. Why are you still on this? Do you know something?"

He grimaced. "What do you mean? Why would I hide anything from you?"

"Jake, you can't lie to save your life. You've always been bad at it. You two know something and you're keeping it from me."

Dan twisted around now to add his look of indignation to the pile.

"Fine," she snapped. "Keep your secrets." She leaned back against the counter and let them know, with no uncertain body language, that she was not happy with whatever game they were playing.

Jake and Dan gave each other a look, as if they were wondering what her problem was, then promptly returned to scanning the webpage. With each image of the children, Jake's face grew more and more perplexed.

"I'm guessing you didn't find what you were looking for," said Holly.

Jake put his hands on his hips. "Agent Grant was right. There's no similarity."

"Now what?" said Dan.

Jake slumped down into a chair. "I don't know."

Holly fumed. "That was your plan? Look at pictures of the other victims and then give up? Don't they have bios or something? Let's find out where they lived, who their parents were, where they went to school. There has to be some connection between them."

"The FBI would have already done that."

"Well let's do it again! Maybe they missed something!"

Dan clicked through more pages and read what he found. All the children had a single mom who collected welfare. The kids were all between two and six, which they already knew, and the author noted that each of the mothers had sought counseling from their local women's clinic.

Holly remembered the haunting accusations of the killer, and how they centered on the choice she had made to keep Gabe. He assumed she had made the choice out of weakness, but it wasn't. It was the hardest thing she had ever done. It would have been so easy to make the problem go away. She was told by the State-funded clinic that it would be quick and discreet.

No one would ever know—not even her mother. Anyone above the age of thirteen was considered, in this circumstance, to be an adult; no parent signature was needed. Her mother didn't need to know. Her boyfriend didn't need to know. Her friends didn't need to know. Her reputation would have remained unscathed by the scandal of a teen pregnancy. But she'd made the hard choice and gave up everything to have Gabe.

How odd it seemed to her now that the sweet middle-aged woman at the clinic and this cold-blooded killer would share the same ideology. The woman at the clinic never once suggested that she should keep her baby. Instead, she took every opportunity to reinforce Holly's doubts about herself. She wasn't ready to have a child. What kind of life would she give a baby? What kind of mother would she be? Sure, she said it in a sweet gentle voice and with great compassion, but they were the words of a killer.

"Are you okay, Holly?" Jake had noticed her mood change.

"I think there is a connection with the clinic. I don't know how, but I think there is."

"What are you thinking?"

"I don't know. It's just a weird feeling I have about that place. The killer obviously has a real problem with mothers who aren't ready to be mothers. You should have heard him. It was like he was angry at me for choosing to have Gabe, like his life with me was so horrible it wasn't worth living—just because I was his mom. He said it was better to kill him than let him live the life I chose for him."

"Don't let him get in your head, Holly. He's a whack job."

"He knew exactly what to say."

"Have you shared those thoughts with anyone? A boyfriend maybe?"

She shrugged.

"You must have said something to someone."

"I didn't even know I had those thoughts until he started accusing me."

"What men have had contact with Gabe in the past year? Has anyone new come into his life? Anyone who might be connected to the clinic?"

"I don't know, Jake. I know a lot of guys. But I don't believe any of them are capable of something like this. Sure, they're a bunch of losers, but they're good guys."

Jake remained diplomatically silent.

"I know you don't approve of my friends, Jake, but they're good people."

"I'm not saying they aren't."

"But you're not saying they are, either."

"Let's not get into this again, okay? Gabe is out there somewhere in the hands of a very bad man, and we need to figure out who this guy is."

She wanted to be angry; she needed someone to lash out at. It hurt to keep the emotion inside. But Jake was right. She had to get hold of herself and concentrate on finding her son.

114

"What else is on that website?" she said.

Dan turned back to the screen and scanned through more articles and more photos. Some of the images were from the crime scenes. Holly had to turn away twice to recompose herself. It was desperately hard to look at the dead bodies of the other children. One shot in the head. One found in a dumpster wrapped in plastic. But she forced her eyes to return to the screen each time, if only for the briefest of moments.

"Wait!" She pointed. "Go back to that last picture." She came in and gripped Dan by the shoulders. "I don't believe it!"

Jake scanned the photo on the screen. It was a police barricade with one of the victims, a little boy, lying on the ground. Professional men stood around the body as bystanders watched with intense expressions.

"What do you see, Holly?"

She stabbed at the screen. "There! The man in the yellow shirt. I know him. That's my roommate's boyfriend!"

CHAPTER 15

Angela Grant stood when the detective came out of the interrogation room. He set his coffee mug on one desk and his butt on another.

The edges of his mouth disappeared into his bushy mustache. "If this is the guy, he's the best actor I've ever seen, and the most nerved up basket-case I've ever seen. He's already confessed to three crimes unrelated to this case, and I'm sure if I pressed him, he'd confess to a dozen more, even if he didn't do them."

"So what'd he do?"

"Well, he thought you were after him for driving migrant workers up from Boston."

"He's helping illegals? That's why he ran?"

"Yup, and he confessed to possession of marijuana."

"So he's not the guy."

"Not unless your killer is a nervous spaz with a trust fund and entitlement issues."

Perez came in from the break room. "This isn't the guy?" he said in his husky voice.

She pursed her lips. "Nope. He ran for other reasons."

"So what's next?"

"Did you talk with Holly's roommate, Amber, yet?"

"Yeah. She didn't have much to say. Her job with the airline keeps her away most of the time, and when she is here she's usually in Dedham with her grandmother."

"Has she brought anyone home in the last year?"

"She couldn't remember bringing anyone back to the apartment except a guy named Gary Carter. She's been dating him for a little over a year. He's lived in Sunbury for twelve years at an apartment complex called The Schoolhouse. So unless the serial killer has come home to roost, he's not our guy."

"Talk to him anyway."

"We're already on it."

"How about that list of Holly's friends, how far have we gotten with that?"

"It's like shining a flashlight into a sewer. The rats don't like the light."

"O-kay. Well, we have a lot of ground to cover, and a lot of people to talk to, so let's get on it." She looked at the detective. "Thank you for your assistance."

"Anytime. You have the complete cooperation of the Sunbury police department. Let us know if we can be of any further help."

She gave him a salutatory nod and left out the door with Agent Perez.

CHAPTER 16

The blurry man in the photo wore sunglasses and a baseball cap, and his body was hidden from the chest down. His expression looked neutral, but Jake didn't know for sure because of the harsh lighting and the poor quality of the photo. It could have been anyone with a mustache, beard, and baseball cap.

Jake pulled himself away from the screen. "Are you sure?"

"It's him," she said.

"It's kinda blurry."

"It's definitely him. I've even seen him wear that cap."

Jake looked again. "A lot of people have a Yankees cap."

"Jake. He's been here a dozen times. That's him. Same beard, same round face, same sloping shoulders. That's Amber's boyfriend, Gary. I'm sure of it."

"Then we need to call Agent Grant."

Holly stepped back, crossed her arms, and bit her lip. Jake knew his sister well enough to pick up on her nervous ticks. She was clearly unhappy about the FBI coming back.

"It's all right, Holly."

Her eyebrows shot up. "What?"

He didn't bother to pursue it. Half the time he was either flat out wrong about how she was feeling, or she twisted things to make him think he was wrong. He shrugged it off. "I'll call Agent Grant and let her know what we found." He pulled out the card the Agent had given him. It was a switchboard number, but they transferred him to her cell phone.

"Special Agent Grant."

Jake pressed the phone tighter to his ear. "Agent Grant, this is Jake Paris."

"Hi, Jake. How's your sister holding up?"

"Pretty good, considering."

"That's good to hear."

"Um. We found something we think you might want to know. It's a photo on the Internet from one of the crime scenes. Holly's swears one of the guys in the crowd is her roommate's boyfriend."

"The roommate's boyfriend?" There was a tone of interest in her voice. "Which child was it?"

"The fourth. The little five year old blond boy."

"Okay. Well, we talked with Amber this afternoon and she did mention him, but we haven't spoken with him yet. We appreciate you bringing this to our attention. We'll bump him up on our priority list."

"Have you heard anything about Gabe?"

"I wish I could say yes, Jake, but unless our guy makes another move, all we can do is follow the bread crumbs."

"Have you seen anything that leads to this guy Gary?"

"I'm not at liberty to discuss case details with you, but I assure you, we have our best people working on this. If you come up with anything else, let us know, okay?"

"Yes, ma'am. Thank you."

"Thanks for the lead. We'll be talking again soon."

"Okay." He closed the phone.

Holly's eyes probed him. "What did she say? Is there a connection?"

"They're not allowed to discuss the case with us."

"Why not?"

"I don't know, but she said they have their best people working on it."

"So what are we supposed to do, just sit on our hands and wait for them to find my son?"

"I don't know, Holly."

Dan interjected. "Why don't we go to this guy's house and ask him some questions."

It was clear Holly didn't like that idea. "If Gary's the killer, then it would be stupid to show up on his door step and say, excuse me, are you holding my son?"

Jake handed the phone out to Holly. "Why don't you call Amber and ask her about him."

"Are you kidding me? What if they're in on this together?"

"I don't think serial killers work in teams. It takes some heavy psychosis to kill little children. I doubt someone like that would be confiding in his girlfriend."

She ran her fingers nervously down her long blond curls and stared absently toward the floor. He couldn't tell if it was his comment about serial killers killing children that had caused her to leave the building, or if it was the nervousness of talking to her roommate about something so emotionally taxing, but he held the phone out toward her and waited patiently for her to return.

"What do I say to her?"

"Just tell her what you know and see if she can help."

Holly took the phone and stabbed some numbers into it, but didn't immediately put it to her ear. It was only when a voice could be heard buzzing in the earpiece that she responded to it.

"Amber, this is Holly. Yes, yes, I'm okay. I need to talk to you about something."

Jake motioned for Dan to follow him into the living room.

Once they were out of earshot, Dan said, "I've been waiting to talk to you. What's going on?"

"These ghost-kids aren't the killer's victims, they're something else."

"What do you mean? They don't look the same? Jake nodded.

"So what are they then?"

"I don't know, but I found a little baby on the stairs at my apartment building a little while ago, and when I went back, he was gone."

"Wow."

"Vanished. Into thin air. I checked the stairwell all the way to the first floor. There's no way anyone could have taken him so quickly."

Dan's expression changed; it looked as though he was beginning to second guess his decision to trust Jake. It wasn't a look of unbelief, but more the kind of look one might give someone who just started swatting at imaginary flies.

"I'm not crazy, Dan, this stuff is real."

"Well ghosts I get, but babies on stairwells..."

"Hang with me, man. I can't have you flaking out on me now."

"Me? Flaking out on you?"

"Look. Forget I said anything about the baby on the stairs."

"Maybe you're hallucinating. I saw a thing on the Discovery Channel about a woman who had a brain tumor that caused her to see all kinds of weird things, like spiders and bugs and stuff."

"I don't know what's going on with me, but this is real. And I think these kids know something. I need to track one of them down to find out what they know."

"So you're gonna go back out?"

"What else is there to do? The FBI is hunting this guy, and I don't imagine they're going to come asking me for help."

"What about your sister? What are you going to tell her?"

"Are you two talking about me?" Holly stood in the doorway.

Jake dodged the question. "What did Amber have to say?"

"Are you two talking about me?" she said, with more emphasis.

122

"No, we're not talking about you, we were just discussing how you'd feel if I stepped out to check on Jenna."

That caught her by surprise. "Jenna? What's wrong with Jenna?"

"Her friend had an accident today at the theater. Jenna thinks she may have broken her ankle. I figure if the FBI is searching for Gabe, and we don't have any leads to follow, I might see how things are going—if you can live without me for a couple of hours."

"I don't get you, Jake. You were all gung-ho to turn over every rock an hour ago. Now you want to take a break and go check on some girl with a broken ankle?"

"Plus, he lost his job," said Dan.

Jake turned in shocked amazement. "Really, Dan? You thought that was the right thing to add?"

Holly's demeanor shifted. "You lost your job?"

"It's nothing. I'll find another one."

Holly shook her head. "I'm sorry."

"Yeah, well, I just figured I'd check in with Jenna. I was on my way to do that when I got the call from mom about Gabe. You think you'll be okay with Dan a while longer?"

She looked over at Dan and shrugged. "Yeah. Whatever."

"All right, well, just call me if anything comes up, okay?" He turned to leave. "Oh." He turned back. "Did Amber have anything new?"

"All she had to say was she didn't think it could possibly be him, and she wants to see the photo. She's coming home in a couple hours."

"Where is she?"

"At her grandmother's farm in Dedham."

"I thought she was in another state."

"She got back this morning and headed straight to her grandmother's. She's been sick a lot."

"Did she see Gary before she went?"

"She said they've only talked on the phone in the past few weeks. Her schedule has kept her away. And now her grandmother needs her. But the FBI spoke with her today and she wants to come back and see if she can help."

"Okay. So we're at a dead end."

"I don't know about that. I'm gonna keep reading that webpage and see if I can figure anything else out."

"All right. So, Dan, do you mind staying again while I go check on Jenna?"

"Yeah, I can stay, if you're sure you don't mind, Holly."

She bit the corner of her lower lip and gave a weak shrug.

Dan shoved his thumb toward the door. "I'll just watch T.V. And guard the door."

"Whatever," she said again, then rolled off the door jam and into the kitchen.

Jake and Dan shared a look.

Then Jake made a quick exit, before anyone changed their mind.

CHAPTER 17

Jake drove through downtown Sunbury, past the Greyhound bus station, up to the Dunkin' Donuts, and back down to the courthouse, looking carefully at every child he saw along the way. There weren't many, and the few he saw didn't look in his direction.

He found a parking space near the intersection at the center of downtown, parked his car, and got out. The sidewalks were moderately littered with pedestrians, most heading toward the waterfront because there was a concert going on, but some were enjoying a little shopping at the local stores and open-air market behind the museum.

He started up the sidewalk then slowed. On the other side of the street, standing at the crosswalk, was a tiny Asian girl with a long black ponytail blowing in the breeze. A man stood nearby but, by his positioning, it was clear he wasn't with her. She turned and looked in Jake's direction. Adrenaline surged in his chest. Was she looking at him? He increased his pace and crossed over.

Her eyes stayed locked on his. Her thin arms dangled at her side and her flip-flopped feet turned inward toward each other.

Jake ran up the sidewalk and came to a crouch before her. "Are you one of them?" he asked abruptly.

She stepped back, and gave a tiny smile.

He almost reached out to touch her to see if she was real, but remembered that he could feel them even if they weren't. It wouldn't prove anything. How on earth could he find out if she was real without looking crazy? Or was it already too late for that? If she was only visible to him, it wouldn't take long for people to start staring at the weird man crouched down talking to himself on the corner.

He shoved his hand in his pocket and pulled out his phone. "Hello?" he said, still looking at the little girl. "Are you supposed to tell me something?"

The girl cocked her head, clearly confused. "Ah you talkin' ta me?"

"Yes!" he blurted, "Do you have something to tell me?"

Her face was a blank canvas, and her answer a simple, "No."

He couldn't help but wonder why the sender of the message had decided it was a good idea to have children deliver it. If the message was so important, why not send someone who could articulate their purpose?

"Can you at least tell me where you're from?"

Her chin jutted out. "Why ah you hoedin yaw phone?"

Jake struggled to keep his voice and expression from revealing his frustration. "The other little girl said she had a message for me. Do you have a message for me? I need to know."

A woman came swooping in. "What are you doing? I thought you were behind me! Don't ever do that to me again!" She grabbed the girl by the wrist and gave Jake a suspicious look.

The shock of her sudden appearance hit Jake like a wave, almost knocking him over. He pressed the phone to his ear and said the first thing he could think of to explain why he was crouched on the sidewalk near a little girl he didn't know, "Yeah. I can hear you now. Can you hear me?"

"He's funny, Mama."

The mother gave Jake an irritated look, and he responded with a gesture that was meant to communicate how ridiculous it was that he had to crouch on the sidewalk to get better reception. The woman pulled on her daughter's arm and dragged her back into the nearby store, scolding her as she went.

Jake got to his feet and flipped his phone closed. That encounter could have been uglier, he thought, but not much. If he wanted to retain a shred of self respect, he would have to change his tactics. He needed someone, someone who couldn't see the children to tell him if they were real or not. If only he could have brought Dan, Jake could have spotted the children, and Dan could have confirmed them. That would be better than him looking like a stalker—or worse.

He left the intersection and walked around the block in the direction of his apartment building. The Schoolhouse, as it was called, was in downtown Sunbury across from the old federal building not far from the center of town. If he couldn't find any prospects on the streets, or in the park, maybe he could find the little girl he'd met in front of his building this morning.

Along the way he saw two suspicious children, but in both cases they were unapproachable, and neither showed any interest in him. He walked through the park, up the grass hill at the far end, and across the parking lot to The Schoolhouse.

The front of the building had three sets of granite steps which led up to a small courtyard surrounded by a low cement wall. Two trees offered shade for the courtyard, one on each side of the middle set of stairs.

Jake climbed the stairs and came to a stop when he noticed his new neighbor's daughter sitting on a finely molded cement bench under one of the trees. Her face was in her drawing tablet, so she didn't notice him approaching.

"Hi there," he said, as he passed by.

She looked up with her pretty blue eyes and dragged her straight brown bangs to the side. "Hello."

"Aiyana? Right?"

"Yup," she replied.

"What are you drawing now?"

"Same thing," she said. Her hand rubbed across the thick pad in her lap.

"I can't wait to see it when it's done," he said, looking back over his shoulder.

Jenna was coming down the sidewalk from the parking lot, and when she saw Jake, she began to jog. "Jake!" He met her at the bottom of the stairs. "Have you heard anything? Is Gabe okay?"

He pulled away gently. "No. We haven't heard anything."

Being highly attuned to emotion made Jenna an excellent actress, but didn't benefit her much in daily living. He could already see the tears encasing her eyes as her emotional meter tapped into the low end of the scale. For Jenna there was a narrow margin between the highs and the lows. Outside of that place of perfect harmony, she was usually crying. "Are you okay?" she asked, her voice quivering.

"Yes," he said evenly, "I'm fine."

"You must be so worried."

He attempted to stabilize her by downplaying his own fears of losing Gabe. "They'll find him. The FBI are good at what they do. Until then, it doesn't help to worry."

Realizing her compassion would have no outlet with him, she leaped to a new target. "How's Holly?" she asked, her tears breaching her lower eyelids. She tilted her head slightly to the side and smeared the wetness across one cheek.

"She's good. Dan's with her."

"Oh," she said, choking back even more emotion. "Dan's with her? He's such a nice guy."

He grabbed her by the hand, "Come on. Let's go upstairs and see if anyone has left a message on the machine." It was a thinly veiled attempt to avoid an emotional scene in front of their apartment building, but Jenna was too overwhelmed to notice. He led her upstairs to their cozy couch with its big soft pillows, and grabbed her a cold glass of grape juice—and a box of tissues, just in case.

Like a professional race car driver, he steered the conversation toward the facts of the situation, avoiding any discussion of how anyone was feeling about the horrific events that were unfolding. He had learned early in their relationship to identify emotional triggers and steer clear of them at all cost. Piece by piece he laid out the facts of the case and what they were doing to help the FBI, including the big reveal that Holly's roommate was dating a man who had been present at one of the crime sites. Jake was careful to bring it up in an empirical manner, citing it as evidence the FBI could use to close the case, and avoiding the obvious feeling of betrayal Holly and her roommate were feeling. His careful handling of the report did not go unnoticed by Jenna. Instead of gratitude for sparing her wave after wave of emotional trauma, he was rewarded with contempt.

"I don't know how you do it," she said.

"Do what?"

"Stay so calm about all of this."

Calm was an interesting word. He was hardly calm. It was more of a detachment. When he thought about what could possibly happen to Gabe at the hands of this murderer, it ripped at his heart. He had to choose to look at it forensically, examine it as a doctor would a gaping chest wound. There was no profit in compassion if it came at the expense of swift action. "It's a simple matter of necessity. Gabe needs me to be strong and keep my head clear."

"Aren't you worried about him?"

"Of course I am."

"How can you just blather on about facts and evidence as if you're talking about a frog you're dissecting?"

"Because I don't want you to do that thing you do, get all emotional when there's nothing I can do to help. I can't deal with anyone else I love hurting right now. I don't have anything left."

A tear trickled down the side of her nose. She turned her head away and pressed her lips to her knuckles.

"See. That's what I'm talking about. I can't do this right now."

"I'm not trying to add to your stress." She sniffed.

"Then let me grieve when I'm ready. For now I need to stay focused on doing what I can to help Holly —and I can't do that if I'm having an emotional breakdown." He released his stress in a long exhale. "Look. I'm going for a walk. I'll be back."

Jenna's response was silence. It was the best she could muster when her emotions began to peak into the red. He was grateful it wasn't hysteria. That was the next stage, which usually ended with Jenna in a fit of crying, unable to talk or breathe.

CHAPTER 1º

Holly scanned page after page, devouring everything she could about the Cape murderer, hoping some pattern might emerge. Agent Grant was correct in her assessment of him, there weren't many similarities between the cases. His calling card was the children's blocks, and after the first case, he'd started connecting with the mothers through video. The first video was a recorded message, but that developed into the live streaming presentation she had witnessed. There were no videos on the website; Holly was thankful for that. She would not have been able to resist watching them, yet she was sure they would have driven her to the shattering point. The way her emotions were rocketing from one extreme to the next, there was no doubt she was pressing the tolerance of her ability to cope. Her only relief was to continue to search for answers. The searching offered her hope, and kept her mind busy.

Her head swam. The three Tylenol tablets had barely touched the incessant pounding which made it difficult to process the facts. She squeezed her eyes shut, then focused on the screen. Four children, all between the ages of two and six, taken from mothers on state assistance who had sought counseling for their pregnancies as teenagers. The author of the website also made a connection between the mothers and drug abuse, but the evidence was mostly circumstantial.

Each case was more elaborate than the last, yet each death less gruesome. The first mother found children's blocks on her doorstep: four numbers that represented a time, the time the killer intended to shoot her son dead in cold blood. When the clock struck 14:15, military time, a bullet broke through the glass of her living room and killed her son while he sat watching cartoons. That was it. It was over.

Victim number two was a little girl. She was taken and executed on a recorded video. No ransom was requested. The only evidence tying the case to the Cape murderer was the stack of blocks in the back yard that spelled out the location of the box where a pre-recorded video could be found.

By this time the Cape murderer had developed a style. He began looking for ways to communicate with the mothers of his victims, apparently as some form of self therapy, always making references to how difficult it was to live life as the child of a degenerate mom.

Victim three was a beautiful little chubby blond girl. Police had found her in a dumpster wrapped in plastic. The cause of death: suffocation. Victim four was a little boy, age five. Cause of death: sleeping pills. In the last two cases the Cape murderer sent several messages, first with children's blocks, but later by other elaborate means. His notes all had the same accusatory tone and all were a reminder that he was not responsible for the death of the children, because he wasn't the one who chose to have them.

Dan poked his head into the kitchen. "Hey, Holly. Want me to pop out and get us some sandwiches or pizza or something?"

She pulled her hair back and glanced up at him. "Do you think the police will let you back in?"

"I can ask."

"I don't think I can keep much down, but a slice of pizza might make my belly ache less."

His face beamed. "I'll run down the street and be back in a few minutes. Here," he said. He came into the kitchen, leaned cautiously over her, and brought up a sticky note on his computer. "This is my cell phone. If you hear anything, call me, and I'll come back immediately."

She avoided eye contact. "Thanks."

He backed away. "Are you sure you're okay with this?"

She was almost amused by the fact that she would dread his departure. He wasn't much company, but the apartment felt safer with someone in it.

"Yes. I'm fine."

"Okay. Call me. I'll just be down the street." He left the room, then, in classic Dan fashion, sprung back into the kitchen. "What do you want on your pizza?"

"Anything is fine. I probably won't eat much anyway."

"Okay." He smiled again, then was gone.

She turned her attention back to the website and continued to dig. With each post the composite sketch of the killer solidified in her mind. This was a man filled with hatred. He was angry about his difficult childhood and looking for someone to accuse, probably because the one who had caused him so much pain, his own mother, had passed away.

He had mentioned Holly being one hypodermic needle away from leaving Gabe alone in the apartment, wondering when his mom would come home. Was that the killer's own experience?

She brought up the picture of Gary and stared at it. Had he ever mentioned losing his mother, or dealing with trauma as a child? Had he ever shown a bitterness toward teen moms? She couldn't remember, but she didn't think so. It seemed like all the times she could remember him coming over she was high on something. Remnants of conversations swam around in her drug-impaired memory.

She pushed away from the computer; she was irritated, but not entirely out of frustration for her inability to remember her conversations with Gary— there was a low beeping noise she could not ignore any longer. It was probably the furnace or some appliance she'd left on. It was barely audible, but was enough to bother her.

She left the kitchen, searched the bathroom, the hall, and then her bedroom, turning her ears to find the sound. It was definitely in the bedroom, but seemed to be coming from everywhere. It repeated in a loop, three short beeps then five seconds of silence. What did she own that made three short beeps? The only thing she owned that beeped was the phone in the living room. It beeped when the battery was dying, but it didn't sound like this.

She checked the closet and the dresser drawers, then looked behind the bean bag in the corner, and under the bed. The noise was stronger under the bed. She circled and found it to be strongest on the right side, but there was nothing on the floor and nothing attached to the bottom of the box spring. She placed her ear to the mattress. There could be no doubt, the noise was coming from inside the bed itself. She ripped the covers up onto the bed. On the side of the mattress, a hole had been stitched. She dug at it with her fingers, but the stitches held. The thread was thick and black so it would be noticed easily, no doubt, the work of the killer.

She got to her feet and ran to the kitchen. Her fingers fumbled for a steak knife and she pulled it to her chest. She had no idea what she was doing; each action was commanded by impulse; she had to know what was in that bed. There was no thought of the danger, though her heart beat rapidly in her chest. If she had thought of the danger, she would have stopped herself. She ran into the bedroom and slid across the wood floor to where the black stitches marred the side of her mattress. She drove the knife into it, cutting at string and mattress with desperation.

Once a hole was formed, she plunged her hand in and groped for the source of the sound. Her fingers touched something. It was hard with round edges, and could only be pulled out with index finger and thumb. She slid it back and forth until the device pulled free. It was a two-way radio, but not like anything she had ever seen at a store.

A tiny red light blinked on the top. Next to the light was the word "Page." She watched the light blink on and off as if it were the only thing that existed in her universe. Here was her connection to the cold-blooded killer she had read so much about. She knew his methods. This was how he planned to torture her before finally killing her son. There was no doubt in her mind. Yet still, she pressed the button and forced herself to speak.

"I'm here."

CHAPTER 19

Jake slammed the door behind him, startling Aiyana. She was once again sitting on a cardboard box in the hallway, her tablet still in her lap.

"I'm sorry," he said, "I didn't know you were there."

She scanned him with her blue eyes. Her eyebrows rose in the center and scrunched. "Did you have a fight?"

"Ah, no, not a fight," he said, downplaying his embarrassment. "It's just boy girl stuff."

"Oh," she said, making a face.

"What's that look supposed to mean?" he said, forcing a smile.

"Don't worry," she said, "you'll grow out of it."

He stared at her. "Out of what?"

"This phase of your relationship."

He rolled her words around in his mind. What eight- or nine-year-old says phase of your relationship? Could this girl be one of them? As soon as it came into his mind, he was beating himself up for thinking it. She was the next-door neighbor's child. He saw them moving in this morning. He laughed inwardly at himself. Get a grip, Jake. You're starting to see ghost-children everywhere.

"Yes," he said. "This phase of our relationship will pass. It's astute of you to know this. Is your mom or dad a marriage counselor or something?"

"No." She looked puzzled.

"Then how do you know so much about relationships?"

She thought about it. "I don't know anything about them. I just know that there is a season for everything under heaven." She shrugged. "A time to laugh and a time to mourn, a time to build and a time to tear down. This season you're going through won't last forever. You'll move past it into something else."

Again Jake stared at her. A season for everything under heaven...? What child talks like that? "You're smart for a little girl. Do you read a lot of books?"

"Not yet, but I hope to."

"You hope to what? Read?"

"Yes. I love using my imagination, like making up adventures with heroes and villains and dragons."

"So you want to be a writer, too?"

"No. I might do that a little, but not much."

"So, you're going to focus on being an artist."

"I love the feel of the paper and the way shapes play with each other in the grey mists." She blinked, and her eyes sparkled. "It's like a song only I know how to sing, and I sing it with my finger tips."

Jake marveled. "What are the grey mists?"

She held her hand up, revealing the pencil lead coating her palm and fingers. "When I look at the white of the page, I see a land filled with brilliant white light, and as I slide my hand across," she made the motion with her dainty fingers, "the grey mists appear."

"Oh. I see."

139

"And in the mists the shapes play with each other." She rubbed the face of the drawing tablet. "Then I give them life."

Jake was mesmerized by the little girl. There was no doubt she was different from every other child he had ever known. But it seemed likely she was just some sort of artistic savant. Her grasp of abstract concepts far exceeded Jake's own knowledge of the subject. A ghost wouldn't have an understanding of such things. Would they?

He thought back to the first little girl. She'd had a similar air about her, as though she were aware of concepts only an adult would be aware of. But the boy at his work and the chubby girl who terrorized him at Holly's were definitely childlike in their behavior. Maybe they were all different—and maybe Aiyana was one of them.

He could solve the problem quickly enough by knocking on the neighbor's door and asking where their daughter was. If she was real, they would be quick to say she was right behind him. But if she wasn't real, and they didn't have a daughter, they would wonder why he was asking—then what would he give for an answer?

Perhaps he could welcome them to the building and see if they happened to talk to Aiyana during the conversation. Jake strolled toward their door; doing something was better than doing nothing. All he had to do was keep cool and only speak to Aiyana if they spoke to her first. The last thing he needed was for his new neighbors to think he had lost his marbles.

He raised his hand to knock, but just then a door opened and closed down the hall. Maybe he didn't have to bother his new neighbors. He headed toward the elevator to see who it was. At the intersection he ran into the red-haired woman with her green-eyed daughter, Abby.

The woman stumbled slightly when she turned, and Jake noted a slight wobble in her walk. There was a definite sluggishness about her as well.

"Hi again," said Jake.

Her face lit up. "Hi! You're the guy from the elevator! I mean, you don't live on the elevator, you know what I mean."

He could smell alcohol on her breath as she neared.

"Yeah. I live up the hall."

Her eyelids were heavy. She took in a breath and looked up the hall. "Oh? Are you moving in?" she slurred.

"No, actually, these boxes belong to the people across the hall."

"Oh," she said.

"Can I ask you something?"

"Shhure," she said with a subtle bob of her head.

He stood with his back to Aiyana, and lowered his voice. "What do you see at the end of the hall?"

Her brows lifted. "At the end of the hall?" She swayed to the side. "Boxes, windows—coupla doors."

He turned and looked. Aiyana had not moved from her perch.

"Boxes and windows and doors? Are you sure you don't see anything else?"

She looked again, this time with a squint. "Is this a game? Like where's Waldo?" Her hand came up and gripped his tricep. Her eyes opened wide. "I see a boat."

"A boat?"

"Yeah," she slurred. "In the shadows on the floor. See the two masts and the sails and the hull right there?"

The way the shadows fell on the floor did create the vague shape of a boat, if one were to really stretch their imagination. Jake was happy to use it as an excuse to end his game; he had what he needed.

"You found it!" he said.

She beamed and put the weight of her warm body against him.

"Well," he said, uncoiling himself from her, "I just wanted to see if I was crazy, but, sure enough, there's a boat there."

She took his nonverbal hint and backed off. Her fingers went to fixing her hair as she tried to hide a look of dejection. "So," she said, trying to comprehend the situation with her groggy senses, "you're all set then?"

"Yup. I just needed a second opinion. Thanks."

"She pressed a fingernail into the elevator button, and the doors immediately opened. "Call me anytime, hun," she slurred and got on the elevator. Her daughter weaved her way on behind her.

Jake looked at Abby as she spun forward. Her eyes had the same heaviness as her mother's, and there was a distinct sluggishness in her head and neck. Was she drunk, too? Jake struggled with the words to say, but before he could get anything out, the elevator doors had closed and his opportunity to confront her had passed.

What kind of a mother would get her little girl drunk? His mother, even with her infinite flaws, had never sunk that low!

His mother had unwittingly exposed him to everything as a child. By three he knew what beer tasted like, and at nine he had already tried pot. The reprobates she invited over to the trailer were liberal with their vices, or negligent to leave things lying around where children could reach them. But she never knowingly allowed him or Holly to get stoned or drunk in her house. That was another whole echelon of bad parenting.

Jake shook it off. There was no time to dwell on other people's problems; his plate was filled with his own. But he had hope now. His delinquent neighbor had managed to do one good thing this evening. She had confirmed Jake's suspicions.

Aiyana was one of the ghost-children.

CHAPTER 20

Holly held the radio in her numb fingers and waited for the response.

The radio crackled. "Are you alone?" It was the same digitally altered voice she had heard on the video.

"Yes," she squeaked, "I'm alone."

"Are you listening closely?"

"Yes."

"It is important that you understand what I am about to tell you."

She hung on his every word.

"I do not intend to kill your son."

Her body seized up, and her gut rolled. Could she possibly believe him? This was a cold-blooded killer. But in all that she had read, he had never promised anyone their child would be saved. Never. His communications were always centered on punishing the mothers for the evil they had done by not providing a safe home for their child to grow up in.

"Did you hear me, Holly?"

She swallowed hard. "Yes," she said. "I heard you."

"It is important for you to understand this point. Yours is the last child I'm going to take. He is not like the rest. The others led up to this important event. The media is ready to hear what I have to say, and you are going to tell my story."

The radio went silent for several seconds, and a panic arose inside Holly. She ground the radio button with her thumb. "I'll tell your story. I- I'll do anything you say! Please don't hurt my son! He's all I have!" She released the button and stared at the radio in her shaking hands.

"There is one rule," the voice returned. "If you reveal to anyone that I am speaking to you, your son will be like the rest, and I will wait another year to finish what I have started. Do you understand?"

"Yes! I won't tell anyone. I promise. I'll do everything you say."

"I will kill your son, and I will make him suffer, if you fail." His words touched a vulnerable spot deep in her gut.

"I won't fail."

He spoke again, as if he knew her deepest fear. "You can't go running back to the Oxys. They won't just kill you, they'll kill your son."

Hearing him speak the name of her vice drove home the horror that this killer knew her intimately.

"Reach into the mattress again and feel around." She set the radio down and did as he instructed.

"There is a box deep inside."

She couldn't feel it.

"Pull it out of the mattress."

It wasn't there. Her fingers dug deep into the cotton with desperation, but there was no box.

"Do you have it?"

She grabbed the radio. "I don't feel the box. I can't feel it. I'm looking."

"Find the box, Holly."

She jammed her hand further into the mess of stuffing, and something scratched the side of her arm. She slid her arm out and groped that area. The object was hard with rounded edges. It was the box! She was sure of it. Her fingers gripped it fiercely and pulled it free from its socket.

"I have it! I have the box!"

"Open the box, Holly."

The plastic box opened on a spring loaded hinge. Inside, on top, was a linen cloth, and beneath this were two items: a small, sealed, hard plastic cylinder, and a device with a key holder on top. Holly didn't recognize the symbol, but she was sure it was a car brand.

"The cylindrical item in the box is a bomb. If you open it, it will go off."

Her hand snapped back.

"The other device is a digital key. If the key is within a foot of the lock it is programmed for, it will disengage that lock, allowing the door to be opened. Do you understand the items that are in the box?"

"Yes."

"Good. I have made an appointment for you," said the digital voice evenly, "at the Doris Boardman Woman's Health Center tomorrow at 9:00 a.m."

Holly's mind reeled. He *was* connected to the clinic!

"This is what you will do. You will be escorted past the bullet-proof glass where the receptionists sit, and they will put you in one of two examination rooms. Make sure it is examination room B. It must be examination room B. Do you understand?"

She pressed the radio button. "Yes. I understand, examination room B."

"When you are left to get undressed, I want you to go to the office directly across the hall. The device in the box opens the door to that office. If the device is in your pocket the door lock will turn green. Do you understand?"

"Yes."

"Inside the office are two filing cabinets. Place the bomb in the right file cabinet to the rear of the bottom drawer. Repeat this back to me."

"Right file cabinet, rear of the bottom drawer."

"You will need to do this quickly and get back to the exam room before the doctor's assistant returns. Do you understand?"

"Yes."

"I will page this radio again tomorrow at twelve noon. Make sure you are in your bedroom, alone, when I call."

She trembled. "I will. I'll be here. Alone."

"Listen carefully, Holly. You can save your son. Repeat after me, I can save my son, Gabe."

"I can save my son, Gabe." Her throat constricted as she said his name.

"He is not like the rest. Repeat it."

"He is not like the rest."

"My son will live."

"My son will live."

"Good. Now put the radio back and hide the box. I will contact you tomorrow."

The radio lay lifeless in her hands, and panic seized her. She squeezed the button on the radio. "Can I talk to him? Can I talk to my son?"

There was no response.

"I want to know he's alive."

Still silence.

She stared at it. Waiting. Not willing to believe the killer was gone. But the longer she sat there staring, the more strength left her body—until she was lying on the floor next to the box and the radio, lifeless as a corpse.

She had no idea how long she had been lying there, but a knock on the front door brought her back to reality. Her heart surged as she rolled to a kneeling position and stuffed the items back into the mattress.

The knock came again. She flipped the blanket down over the hole, snatched the knife, ran down the hall past the kitchen to the door, and swung it open.

Dan looked at the knife and the panic in Holly's eyes. "Woah! Don't shiv me. I bring a peace offering of pizza."

She looked at the knife and half hid it as she moved to let him into the apartment.

"Man," he said, "I leave you alone for thirty minutes and you go all Rambo on me."

She followed him into the kitchen and set the knife in the sink.

"Do you have any paper plates?" he said, slapping the pizza down on the kitchen table.

It took her a second to shift gears. Adrenaline spikes were still making her ribcage tremble.

"Yes. Under the counter." She moved to get them.

"Anything exciting happen while I was gone?"

She forced a casual tone. "No. Same as it's been. Here," she said, handing him the plates.

"Thanks." He flipped the cover up on the box. "So what's next?"

Holly got quiet. What was there to say? She didn't need Dan's computer anymore, and according to the killer, Gabe was safe as long as she did what she was told. Having Dan in the apartment was a liability. She couldn't take the chance of him hearing the radio in her room or asking questions about the box.

"I think it would be best if you went home," she said, sticking her fingers into the tiny pockets of her skirt.

He turned and faced her. "Don't you want me to stay awhile? You know?" He gestured toward the box. "Pizza?"

"I think I need to be alone right now."

Alone was the last thing she needed to be, but it was too risky having him around. She couldn't afford a mistake.

Dan took a step toward her. "Okay. If you want me to go—I'll go."

She didn't have the strength to look him in the eye, for fear he might see how vulnerable she was. What would she do once he was gone? Would she run to the package of Oxys under the sink? Would she run to the store and grab a cheap bottle of wine? Would she do what she always did and soak her fears in a pool of numbness? It was an inevitable reality.

Her eyes ran from Dan's thick hand up his hairy forearm to his bicep. Even under his shirt she could tell he was strong, and she needed that strength. She needed someone to be strong for her, because she felt so ashamedly weak.

Then she did something that surprised her even more than it surprised Dan. She put her arms around his waist and buried her cheek in his muscular chest. His body was like a rock in her grasp. She clung to the rock with desperation, a deep part of her pleading for him to rescue her—from herself.

Dan's arms went up in the air at first, but then slowly came to rest on her back.

"So," he said, "is this just you thanking me for the pizza?"

CHAPTER 21

Angela Grant emptied her gut in the McDonald's toilet at exactly 8:00 p.m. She had tried all day to use Saltines and soda water to ward off her daily bout with morning sickness—though why people called it that she had no idea It came every evening at 8:00 p.m. With merciless regularity. She splashed water on her face and stuffed a piece of gum in her mouth before heading back out to Perez.

He was sitting in the car with papers scattered across his lap and an Ipad on the dash. He moved a stack from her seat. "Did you get your daily fry fix?"

She didn't give him the satisfaction of a response.

He slid the Ipad off the dashboard. "I just got confirmation that Gary Carter was in Texas during the time of the third murder. That puts him on the ground at two separate crime scenes."

"That's enough to get a warrant."

"We're already working on it. Oh. And get this. Our mild-mannered person of interest works at the local women's clinic."

That turned Angela's head. "You're kidding."

"He's an administrator, and not just for the Sunbury site, he travels around the country to other clinics which means..."

"He has access to records at other clinics."

"Exactly."

"Where is he right now?"

"MIA. We have an unmarked car sitting in front of his apartment building, but he hasn't been home. You think we should search the residence?"

"No. Not yet. If he does come home, we don't want to spook him. We'll wait."

"So what's the play?"

"Put another team on surveillance at the clinic. In the meantime, let's keep digging on this guy. I want to know who his friends are, where he hangs out, and what his favorite ice cream flavor is. When he does pop his head up, I want to be ready to take him down and keep him down, for a very long time."

CHAPTER 22

Jake stood in the middle of the hallway of his apartment building, unable to take his eyes off the mysterious child named Aiyana. She scratched her invisible tablet with her invisible pencil and rubbed at it with her invisible fingers, intently working on a drawing no one would ever see. No one—except Jake.

Where did she come from? And why was he the only one who could see her? Was she a ghost? Had she walked these very halls in years past? Perhaps she'd been the victim of a fatal accident and was now forced to roam about her old schoolhouse with her drawing tablet—a stark reminder of the art career she would have had if her life had not been tragically cut short. If that were the case, wouldn't she be wearing clothes from that era? Jake studied her. Blue sweater, pink plaid vest, wrinkled blue pants—and blue flowered canvas top sneakers. Hardly the style of a child from the past. Besides, this used to be a high school, and she was too young for that. So, if she wasn't a ghost haunting the old school house, then—what was she?

There was only one way to find out.

Jake approached cautiously, knowing now that Aiyana was not simply a little girl with a drawing pad, but something beyond his understanding, and possibly even dangerous.

At five feet he came to a stop.

She noticed him. "Why are you looking at me like that?"

"You don't know?" he said.

A puzzled expression creased her forehead and tightened her brows. "Why would I know?"

"Because you're one of them."

"One of who?"

"The ghost-children."

"What's a ghost-children?"

He studied her, looking for any sign of deception. There didn't appear to be any. "You really don't know what I'm talking about, do you?"

She shook her head.

"Where are you from?" he said.

"I don't know, I can't remember."

"Where do you live?"

"Here," she said, "at least, I think so. It is all kind of fuzzy."

"Do you have a message for me—something you're supposed to tell me? Something about Gabe?"

"No." She frowned. "Not that I can remember. Who's Gabe?" She noticed the frustrated look on Jake's face. "I'm sorry I'm not more helpful."

"If you're not here to help me, then why are you here? And why am I the only one who can see you?"

"You're the only one who can see me?" she blurted.

"You don't know that?"

"Oh, wait. I do know—now." She cocked her head as if listening, or considering an idea. "Oh, that makes sense."

"What makes sense?"

"Why no one can see me but you."

"And that would be because..."

"I'm not really here."

Her words were like a javelin in his chest. He had feared the possibility that these hallucinations where all in his head, but to hear her confirm it with her own lips sent currents of anxiety through him.

"You're—not here."

"No. I'm in your head."

The neighbor's doorknob rattled, and Jake could hear talking on the other side. He looked around frantically, twisted, and started walking toward the elevator as though that was what he'd been doing all along. He didn't want to go to his door with the possibility of having to open it and alert Jenna to the fact that he was in the hall talking to a figment of his imagination. And he didn't want to have to explain to his neighbors why he enjoyed standing alone in the hall talking to himself.

As his new neighbors entered the hallway behind him, he took a quick right toward the east wing and glanced back as they reached the elevator. The man was back to, but his pregnant wife stood sideways, facing the elevator. Their son, who appeared to be around four, was keeping himself busy with two action figures in his hands.

When the elevator dinged, Jake's mind flashed back to the pregnant woman he had seen earlier at the elevator in the east wing, to his coworker Debbie at Data Tech, and to the one he'd seen checking her mail that morning. He couldn't remember seeing a pregnant woman at all in the past year—except Debbie once or twice—but now in one day he had seen four. That was strange, to say the least—but completely on par for the bizarre day he was having.

His neighbors got on the elevator, and the door closed. Jake headed back up the hall, half expecting Aiyana to be gone. But she wasn't. Part of him was terribly unrelieved to see her.

She looked at him with innocent eyes. "Are you okay?"

"No," he said, walking toward her. "I'm not okay with seeing hallucinations of children and having to hide from the world that I have completely lost my mind. I have a nephew in real danger, and I need answers. What's happening to me?!"

"I don't know," she said meekly.

"But you know something. You have to know something. You can't just not know anything." He stared at her. "You know your name. How do you know your name?"

"I don't know. I just do."

"How do you know there are seasons for everything under heaven?"

"Because there are."

"But who told you?!" His voice filled the hallway.

"Oh," she said, "that I can't tell you."

"See! You do know things!" His eyes tilted downward to the tablet in her lap, and adrenaline surged in his chest. On the page was the most incredible image he had ever seen. In startlingly detail she had drawn an angel bursting through a barrier of half liquid and half fire. In his arms was a baby.

What made Jake pause in awe wasn't that she had drawn an angel, it was what the angel looked like. It was not comparable to any angel image he had ever seen. The only similarity was that her angel had wings —and even those had an otherworldly quality. Jake pointed and, for a moment, he couldn't speak. "Wh-what is that?"

"It's my drawing."

"I thought you were drawing a bird," he said.

She looked surprised. "No. It's an angel. I've never seen a bird."

Never seen a bird? But she'd seen an angel? Jake's brain spun in his head. What on earth...?

But before he could formulate another question, the door to his apartment opened, and Jenna stood in the doorway. Her eyes bounced from him to the elevator down the hall and back. "Why are you screaming in our hallway, Jake?"

He swallowed. "Was I screaming?"

"Yeah. I could hear you all the way in the bedroom."

Aiyana gripped her tablet to her chest. "I'm sorry. I didn't mean to get you in trouble."

He could feel the nervous breakdown looming over him like the grim reaper, its dark suffocating presence sliding over him like the creeping shadow of a setting sun. He had no answer to give her. Reality was shattering and hope was retreating. His plan of rescuing his nephew had evaporated with his sanity, and now he was expected to explain the unfathomable reason why he was standing in his hallway screaming at thin air.

Emotion began to surge from deep within, and his eyes began to sting. He fought it back with anger. There was no time for a pity party, no time to explore his fears of the unknown or his feelings of helplessness.

Jenna came to him, her eyes searching. "Are you okay?"

"No," he said. "I'm not okay."

She slid her arms under his and hugged him. "I'm here, Jake. You're not alone in this."

He gripped her and let her warmth fill him. The fragrance of her hair and the perfect fit of her body reminded him that they were made for each other, like two pieces in a puzzle. He wasn't alone in this crazy mess. There was so much comfort in her embrace that he felt sure she would stand by him even if she did find out he was crazy as a loon—but he wasn't ready to test that theory.

"Let's go inside," she said, pulling free and taking his hand.

He looked at Aiyana's innocent eyes silently watching them. They seemed to be pleading with him to keep her secret. Not for her sake, but for his. He could see the intense apology on her sweet face. She didn't want to see him hurt any more.

"Come on," said Jenna, tugging on his wrist. "Let's go sit on the couch. We don't have to talk. I'll just sit with you while you work out whatever's going on in your head."

He let her guide him through the door, watching for one last glimpse of Aiyana. The apartment door sealed like the door to a vault—a vault containing all the secrets of the universe, if only he could get Aiyana to remember them.

CHAPTER 23

Jenna led Jake to the couch and he sank into it. She turned on some soft music. "Do you want some tea, you know, to calm your nerves?"

"I don't think there is any way of that happening, but sure, if you're going to make some anyway."

He sat with his thoughts while Jenna worked in the kitchen. He wanted to find an excuse to get back out into the hallway to talk to Aiyana, but he couldn't think of anything reasonable. There was a limit to how much strange behavior he was going to get away with for one day. So instead, he sat stoically, running down an imaginary list of the day's events. There had to be a connection.

After a few minutes, Jenna returned with the tea and sat across from him on the couch.

"I'm sorry if I've been emotional, I mean, even more emotional than normal lately," she said, sipping her tea.

They shared a smile.

Her intense emotional fragility was sometimes frustrating to deal with, but most of the time it was something they both found humor in. Like the time he had bought her a kitten, and she couldn't even go near the cardboard box for over an hour. She had wanted a kitten her whole life, but her mother was allergic to them.

When she realized what was in the box all she could do was lay on the couch and cry. They both knew why she was crying, but he had happily prodded her to give a reason. He asked her if she was sad that he had brought a iddy bitty kitty home, and her response had more in common with a squeak than a word. He loved how her voice rose up when she said no, and how through the tears he could see a look of apology on her face. She realized how silly she looked, but she couldn't help it. She was a woman of deep connection to all things. It was one of the qualities he loved most about her.

Jake had a hard time caring about anything. He had suffered too many broken relationships growing up. Even his love for Gabe was dull compared to Jenna's love for that kitten. She had the unique ability to give herself entirely to love, with no fear of the consequence. To Jenna, loving deeply was worth the chance of hurting deeply, and, in a way, Jake envied her.

"More people should care about things as fully as you do, Jen."

She squeezed her bare toes down on his leg. It was her non-verbal way of saying thank you. "Well," she said, "in the spirit of caring about others, how are you holding up? Do you want to talk about it?"

He rolled the question around in his head. Did he want to talk about it? If by it she meant the psychotic hallucinations he was having, the answer to that was most assuredly, NO. He wasn't interested in convincing his girlfriend that he belonged in a rubber room with padded furniture. If she meant the situation with Gabe and the gnawing helplessness he felt leaving the investigation in the hands of the FBI, then that was a solid no as well. He didn't want to explore his feelings on the matter. It would only churn up a cloud of self-condemnation that was best left ignored.

He rubbed her foot. "I don't know what to say about all this. I just can't believe it's happening."

"It's scary, isn't it?"

"This kind of thing just doesn't happen in Sunbury."

"I know." She paused. "And there's nothing we can do?"

"I'm just waiting to see if anything develops. The FBI knows what they're doing."

"So we just hold tight?

"What else can we do?"

She laid her head back on the arm of the couch. "I guess all we can do is wait." She knew there was more going on inside him, but for the sake of harmony, she left it in his court and sat quietly beside him, allowing him time to process his thoughts and giving him ample opportunity to voice those thoughts.

But there was only one thing on his mind: the little ghost-girl outside their apartment door—and he had no intention of talking to Jenna about that! He was going to have to wait until she went to bed to work out any solutions to that problem.

CHAPTER 24

It was late when Jenna finally went to bed.

He pulled his phone out and gave Dan a quick call to check up on Holly.

"Heylo," said Dan. He sounded groggy.

"Hey, it's Jake."

"Hey, bud, what's going on?"

"Not much, how was Holly when you left her place? Is she stable?"

"Yeah," he said elongating the sound of the word. "Here's the thing. I'm kinda still at Holly's place."

"Really? She's letting you stay all night? I never would have called that one."

"Me either, man. I thought for sure I was getting the boot earlier, but then the next thing I know she's making a bed for me on the couch."

"She's probably scared to be alone."

"Yeah. She's battling with something, but there's no way she's telling me what it is. She's like Fort Knox."

"Have you seen her taking any pills?"

"No. She's definitely not taking anything, well, except Tylenol. She's about as strung out as I've ever seen anyone."

"She's gotta be hurting for them—and it wouldn't be hard for her to convince herself that half a pill would just take the edge off. I saw my mother do it a hundred times. It was always just one little one, then

I'd find her lying half comatose on the living room couch."

"Well, at the moment, she is anything but comatose. I think she's been to the bathroom ten times."

"I appreciate you being there, Dan."

"What are friends that are being hooked up with other friend's sisters for? Right?"

He had to laugh at the unexpectedness of Dan's humor. "Just keep an eye on her. I'm not looking to marry you off."

"On a creepy note," Dan spoke low into the phone, "did you find any ghost-kids?"

Jake knew the question would come, but he still wasn't prepared for it. "Yes," he said, "but not the one I was looking for."

"Really? Another one?"

"Yeah. She's right outside my door. Well, at least she was. I checked a little while ago, but she was gone."

"Were you able to get any info?"

"I learned some things, but not what I was hoping for. She doesn't know anything about Gabe."

"Sorry to hear that, man. You must be bummed."

"Yeah. I'm back to square one."

"So, what did she say? Did you figure out what these apparitions are?"

What could he share with Dan? Could he tell him the truth, that these ghost-children might only be in his head? No. Not yet. He needed Dan to trust him. He couldn't afford to alienate him now.

"It was hard to get anything out of her. She seems to have some kind of selective amnesia, but I wasn't able to find out how selective because we were interrupted."

"Do you believe her?"

"I don't know what to believe. She seemed truthful."

"And what are you going to do now?"

"I don't know what to do, except look for her tomorrow and try to get some answers."

"But she said she doesn't know about Gabe?"

"She may not know about Gabe, but she knows something. It can't just be a coincidence that my nephew is taken by a serial killer and I start seeing ghosts the same day."

"Good point."

"Are you going to stay with Holly through tomorrow?"

"Well, I'm not working, so I'll stay—until she throws me out on my ear, which might be sooner than later if I have to get between her and her pills."

"She may get to a point where she thinks she has nothing to offer. I'm almost there myself. But don't let her dive into those pills because then she'll really have nothing to offer."

"I'll do what I can."

"Good. Thanks again, Dan. I'll let you get back to sleep."

Dan was quiet a moment. "What? Are you still talking? I must have dozed off."

"Night, Dan."

CHAPTER 25

Jake awoke to the sound of multiple car doors slamming, and he rolled over to see Jenna standing by the window in her nightgown. He rubbed his eyes. "What's going on?"

"I don't know, but it's something big. The street's filled with police."

Jake bolted out of bed and joined her at the window. Sure enough, four unmarked cars and three cruisers sat in the middle of the street with lights flashing. "What are they doing?"

"I don't know. Maybe it has something to do with the kidnapping?"

"Nah. Why would they be here?"

"I hope they're not coming for you."

He glared. "That's not even funny."

"Look," she pointed. "They're heading around to the east side."

Jake pulled on some shorts. "I'm gonna go check it out."

"Are you crazy? You could get shot."

"I'll be careful."

"Jake, don't be stupid. They'll have it on the news later."

"If this is about Gabe, I want to know what's going on." He pulled a tee-shirt over his head and slid his feet into his sneakers.

"What can you do that the police can't?"

"I don't know," he called, weaving through the living room.

"Jake!"

But it was too late. He was out the door.

Aiyana was there. She got to her feet when he came flying out of the apartment. "What's happening?"

Jake nearly jumped out of his skin. "You scared me!"

"What's happening? Is someone in trouble?"

He started down the hall. "I don't have time to talk about it."

"Can I come?"

"No! It's too danger..." He stopped himself. "What am I talking about, you're not even real."

"I'm real," she said indignantly.

"Look," he said, turning and walking backwards toward the elevator. "I don't think I can handle having any—hallucinations around while I'm talking to the police. Could you just stay here? Please?"

"I won't say anything. I'll be very quiet."

"You'd just be a distraction. Just stay here. Okay?" He turned the corner and ran toward the door to the east side—with Aiyana in hot pursuit.

"Please, Aiyana! Go back."

"I won't say anything. You won't even know I'm here."

He opened the stairwell door and closed it, but she passed through as though it wasn't there.

"Please! You're freaking me out! If this has anything to do with Gabe, I need to find out about it, I can't be distracted."

"But maybe I can help," she said brightly.

"Help? By making me look like a spastic nut job? I won't be able to put two sentences together with you around."

"I'll hang back. You won't even know I'm here," she repeated.

"I find that hard to believe." He turned and leaped down the stairs three at a time. Reaching the bottom he looked out the thin rectangular window in the door. Four FBI officers lined the wall, and some had already broken into an apartment down the hallway.

Jake creaked the door open—and came face to face with an FBI agent in a flak vest. The intensity of his gesture to stay back made Jake leap backwards.

Aiyana watched from five stairs up—staying back as she'd promised. Jake peeked through the window again. Two more agents entered the apartment, leaving two in the hall. The agent who had motioned him back now stood in the center of the hall between him and the doorway.

Jake pushed against the wall in frustration. What am I doing? There was no way these officers were going to let him onto a crime scene. Had he lost his mind? Did he have any mind left to lose? He wanted desperately to feel like he was contributing something to the rescue of his nephew. He wanted to do something, anything. Waiting around would eat him alive. He pushed the door open a crack.

The agent shot him a severe look.

His hands went up and he let the door close. Then he started pacing, as Aiyana observed him from a crouched position on the stairs. "This is hopeless! How can I find out if this is even about Gabe?! They won't even let me..." His head snapped up to look at Aiyana. His eyes lit up. "Aiyana! You can pass through walls, right?"

"Um. Not exactly."

"You're a ghost. You can walk down that corridor, unseen, and go right into that room and find out what's going on, right? I've seen you do it!"

"It doesn't work that way."

Jake shook his head in frustration. "What do you mean? What doesn't work that way?"

"This," she said, referring to herself.

"Well then how *does* this work, because I just saw you walk through a door, and I really need you to walk through this door right here and go down the hallway and tell me what's happening in that apartment!"

"I can't see it if you don't see it."

"Are you kidding me?"

She cowered slightly.

"I'm sorry," he said, attempting to reign in his temper. "I'm just trying to figure out why you're here. The only thing you kids seem to be useful for is making me crazy. And who knows, maybe I am crazy."

The door behind him bumped him in the back, and Jake came unglued. His arms shot out at weird angles and he let out a yelp.

169

"Jake Paris? Is that you?" It was the voice of Agent Grant.

"Yes, ma'am," he said, straightening up.

"What are you doing in the stairway?"

"I saw the cars out front and wanted to see if it had something to do with my nephew."

"You do realize how suspicious it looks to have the victim's uncle lurking about, don't you?"

"I'm not lurking. I live here."

She pushed the door open farther, and Jake tried desperately to mask his shock. Standing in the hallway, peeking through the door, was the little Cabbage Patch girl, her stuffed rabbit hanging from her grip. He ripped his eyes off her and focused on Agent Grant.

"Jake. I'll be straight with you. We followed up on that lead you gave us regarding Amber's boyfriend Gary. It led us here."

Jake tried to even out his breathing and lock into what the agent was saying. She was doing him a favor sharing information about the case. He couldn't ruin it by fixating on the Cabbage Patch girl.

"Gary lives here? How come I've never seen him before?"

"From what we've gathered, he's somewhat of a recluse."

Jake tried to digest this new information. "Well— is he in there? Did you get him?"

"No. He's still unaccounted for."

"Have you learned anything about Gabe?"

"No. Not yet, but as soon as we do we'll contact you and your sister. Now get out of here before you draw unneeded suspicion upon yourself."

"Yeah, okay," he said, backing up. "I will. Thanks."

She gave him a pressed smile.

"Bye bye, Jake," said the little blond girl in her high gravely voice. She waved her pudgy hand enthusiastically.

Jake almost waved, but quickly turned to see Aiyana still sitting on the stairs. She was looking in the direction of the other girl, smiling.

He looked over his shoulder at the blond girl, then back at Aiyana with surprise.

Aiyana must have read his expression.

"Yes," she said, "I can see her, too."

CHAPTER 26

Holly heard her bedroom door creak open, and footsteps entering quietly. Her eyes snapped open, and her hand gripped the sheet tightly. Though she knew it had to be Dan, that didn't stop the terror from coiling around her, choking off her air. She was unable to resist the feeling that her room had been breached by the author of her nightmares. All she had to do was turn and see, but the fear held her locked in its unbreakable grip.

She listened as the footsteps approached the bed, her breaths growing more shallow with each footfall. Why would Dan enter her room unannounced? As she built the courage to turn and confront the intruder, a voice broke the silence.

"Holly? Are you awake?"

The fear retreated as quickly as it had advanced. Holly rolled over to see the slender form of her roommate standing over her bed. Amber's straight brown hair was slightly electrified by the dryness of the room, and her brown eyes seemed richer on her recently tanned face. Holly had never been so happy to see anyone her life.

"Oh, thank God it's you."

"Who did you think it was?" Her countenance dropped. "I'm sorry. What am I saying..."

"It's okay, Amber. I'm—a little jumpy, to say the least, but you don't have to walk around on egg shells."

Amber came around and sat on the edge of the bed. "You look terrible," she said bluntly.

Holly slithered a forearm across her sweaty cheek. The room felt like a furnace, and all her joints ached.

"I'll be fine," she said.

"You must be exhausted."

Holly detected the pity in Amber's voice; she gritted her teeth. Though she'd been strong the night before and had resisted the urge to run to the pills, she could not escape that look. It always came from the people in her life who claimed to love her the most. Poor pitiful Holly can't get out of her own slop. How tragic her life is. How pathetic she looks.

She fought the headache and the nausea and slid to a sitting position. "It looks worse than it is," she said. "I just need some water."

"Did I say something wrong?"

"No. I'm just an emotional wreck. I'm sorry. Thanks for coming back."

"What are friends for?"

"I completely forgot about you coming home."

"I meant to come back last night, but my grandmother's condition is getting worse, and she needed me."

"If you need to go..."

"No. She's okay at the moment. I'm here to help in any way I can."

Holly looked at the clock; it was almost eight. "I need to get ready!" she said, kicking her legs off the bed. "I have an appointment at the woman's health center at nine."

Amber moved out of the way so Holly could get up. "Now?"

Holly turned and looked at Amber sitting on top of the spot where the killer had hidden the box, and the room began to shrink. Near Amber's leg, part of the black thread could be seen poking out from the sheet.

"It's an important check up," she said, forcing herself to look away from the marred spot on the mattress.

"But—why do you have to go today?" Amber's freckly cheeks dropped and her eyes grew round. "Are you really sick?"

"No. I- I don't know. The doctors say it may not be anything, but I need to find out as soon as possible, if they have to treat it."

"Do they think it's cancer?"

"They don't know." She quickly plucked random clothes from her dresser. "I'm going to take a shower. I'll be out in a second, okay?" She exited the room and scooted toward the bathroom at the far end of the hall.

Amber followed. "Do you want me to make you some breakfast or something?"

"I doubt I can keep anything down, but I'll try, okay?"

"Well—whatever you don't eat I can give to that cute guy sleeping on your couch."

Holly turned to look past Amber at Dan standing in the living room in his jeans with no shirt. He must have heard Amber's comment, because he reached out and snatched his shirt from the back of the couch. Under other circumstances Holly might have noticed his muscular build and zero percent body fat, but her head felt like she had been hit with a sledgehammer, and all she could think about was sneaking back into her bedroom to cover the hole back up.

She stepped into the bathroom and closed the door, then fell to her knees before the keyhole. Amber hovered for a moment, then looked back into the bedroom. Holly's heart started to thud in her ears at the thought of Amber going back in to make the bed, or tidy up. She couldn't let that happen. She couldn't allow Amber to find the tear in the side of her mattress. There could be no mistakes; her son's life depended on it.

Amber started into the room, and Holly's hand shot to the doorknob. Was she going in? The angle of her body made it appear as if she might only be reaching in for something. Holly watched with intensity. Slowly Amber came back into view, and the bedroom door made a click. Holly released a long hot breath and pulled away from the keyhole. There was no time to work through her emotions; she had to get ready for the hard task ahead.

The heat of the shower did nothing to sooth her spirits. She made quick work of it, got dressed, and went back to her room, unnoticed by Amber and Dan in the kitchen. She carefully dug the box out of the mattress, opened it, and placed the two items into her purse. It was real now. She was going to go through with this mission and hope that what the killer said was true, that he didn't intend to kill her son. She had no reason to doubt what he had told her. He had said this case would be different from all the others.

Holly clung to that statement, praying desperately for it to be true.

CHAPTER 27

Jake walked down the second floor east hallway toward the door to the west wing, venting the entire way. "That's it, I'm mad. I am completely mad. I've *lost* my mind! It was only a matter of time, given my childhood. Losing my job must have been the last crack in my armor. Now what? I lose my girlfriend, I lose my friends. Oh!" he exclaimed sarcastically. "Maybe I can have one of those rubber rooms at a government facility. That's a pretty cool gig—three square meals plus pills. And I never have to work again! I can just lounge around in the television room hobnobbing with other crazy people, people even crazier than me, with bike helmets and drool issues. Maybe I can even introduce them to the phantom children THAT CAUSED MY BREAKDOWN!" He slammed through the double doors that led to his section of the building, with Aiyana still on his heels.

"I don't imagine you'll tell me why you chose me. I don't imagine you're going to explain why I'm chasing ghosts in my head instead of helping my sister find this serial murderer." He turned on her. "You know what? How about this? If you're not going to help, why don't you just go away."

She came to a stop.

And he watched in horror as his words sunk deep into her heart. Her shoulders sank and her sweet innocent face began to quiver. "I'm sorry I don't know why I'm here," she said. "I'm sorry I'm just in the way. And I'm sorry you don't want me around!" She slipped past him and ran up the hall, crying.

He followed her around the corner and almost knocked Jenna to the ground. His hands shot out to stabilize her.

"I'm sorry," he said. "I didn't see you."

She looked around. "I thought I heard your voice when I came out of the apartment. Were you talking to someone?"

"No. I was just venting. They tracked Amber's boyfriend, Gary, to our building, of all places, but they won't let me anywhere near his apartment."

"Amber's boyfriend?" Jenna's eyes grew wide. "So—he's the guy? Are they sure?"

"I don't know, but judging by the number of agents, he's probably the guy."

"Did they get him?"

"No, they can't find him."

Jenna's mouth hung open. "I can't believe it. The killer we've been hearing about for years lives here in Sunbury? In our building? What does this mean?"

"Well, at the very least, it means he's had the opportunity to stalk my sister for more than a year."

Jenna looked at her watch. "Oh, Jake, I really need to go." She looked up, frustrated. "I want to talk more about this, but... Listen, if you need me, I'll drop everything and come back, okay? It's just that this is really important."

"I understand. Go ahead. There's nothing you can do anyway."

She turned and looked at the elevator. "Can you walk me down?"

Jake frowned. "Why?"

"There's an FBI investigation going on, and Gary could be lurking anywhere. It's kinda creepy."

"I doubt he's anywhere near here now, with all those agents crawling around."

"Please, just walk me to the front door." Her baby-blues pleaded with him.

"All right."

"Thanks," she said, giving his arm a squeeze.

They went down together, and he walked her to the front door. The hallway and the front courtyard were empty, except for a couple of police officers and the janitor, who was notorious for being a talker. Jake saw him stop Jenna on the front steps and turned quickly back toward the elevator.

It had gone back to the second floor, so he poked the button and waited for it to slowly creep back down. When the bell sounded and the doors opened, Jake was startled to see his neighbor and her green-eyed daughter inside. Judging by the redhead's face, she remembered their last encounter and was embarrassed. He graciously moved aside to let them pass; they did so without a word.

But when he stepped into the elevator and turned, the little girl was standing in the hallway looking at him. "Can you do something for me?" she asked, her eyes sad, and her expression weary.

Jake blinked. "Um, I can try."

"Please tell my mommy I forgive her."

Jake remembered the child standing drunk with her mother in the elevator the night before, and his heart broke. What was this poor little girl going through that would cause her to say such a thing? And why couldn't she tell her mother herself?

The doors began to close.

"Please, promise you will," she said, earnestly.

"Now?" he said.

"No. When I'm gone."

He let the doors shut and put his palm against the cold metal. What was that supposed to mean?

He rested his head against the door. How was this his problem? He immediately felt disappointed in himself for the thought, but that didn't stop it from blossoming in his mind. It saddened him to think of the little girl and her troubles, but if he allowed himself to be stretched any thinner, he would reach his breaking point—if he hadn't already passed it. Abby didn't appear to be in any immediate danger, at least, nothing irreparable, so Jake tabled it, to be addressed at a later date, and turned his attention to the more immediate problem of fixing his relationship with his inner demon.

Aiyana sat crying on the wide windowsill at the end of the hall, her knees tucked up to her chest. How odd she seemed to him now, transformed by the realization that these children were capable of such emotion. It did make sense though. He remembered the anger the Cabbage Patch child had displayed when she thought he was ignoring her. They were the emotions of a real little girl who was incapable of masking frustration.

Jake leaned slightly to get Aiyana's attention.

But she stared out the window with sullen disinterest.

"I'm sorry I yelled at you."

She offered a deaf ear.

"Do you know what it's like to love someone? Well—I love Gabe, and right now my heart is breaking because I want him home safe, and I don't know what to do."

She sniffed.

"When Gabe was born, my sister brought him home in the blankets the hospital had given her. She put the blankets in a drawer in her dresser and laid him in the drawer, because we didn't have money for a crib. That boy cried and cried until my sister couldn't bear it any more. She made a place for him on her bed, but he cried there, too. He wouldn't stop crying. She tried feeding him. She tried changing him. She tried rocking him to sleep."

Aiyana seemed to tilt her head to listen.

"Finally my sister stomped out of her bedroom and shoved Gabe at me. She said she couldn't take it anymore, and went outside to smoke a cigarette. I held him in my arms for the first time, and you know what happened? He stopped crying. For as long as I had him in my arms, he never made a peep. That little guy loved me from the first moment he met me. How could I possibly not love him in return?"

A tear streaked down Aiyana's cheek, but he imagined is was a different kind of tear, similar to the one now trickling down the side of his own face.

"So you see, I want him back so badly it hurts. That's why I got angry with you. I thought maybe you'd been sent to me so that I could find him."

She sniffed again and looked up at him with pleading eyes. "I wish it was true. I wish I could help you. I wish it with my whole heart."

The neighbor's door opened, and Jake turned away from it to wipe the tears from his face. God only knew how much the neighbor had already seen through the peephole.

"Oh," said a female voice, "hello there." There was an inflection of surprise in her voice. Was it possible she hadn't seen or heard him talking to himself in the hallway? Jake dared to hope. He turned to see his pregnant neighbor in the doorway with her little boy holding onto her leg.

He offered a pathetic smile. "Hi. I live across the hall. I'm Jake."

She noticed his watery eyes, but didn't draw attention to them. "I'm Pamela Thomas." She looked down. "And this is my son, Alan." As she spoke, she rubbed her pregnant belly with her hands.

Jake tried not to stare, but how could he not? In a whole year he had not seen as many pregnant women as he had in the last twenty-four hours. Was there a baby boom going on that he was unaware of? Before he could stop himself the words were out of his mouth. "You're pregnant."

She looked puzzled, and responded with a "Yes..." that was elongated, and had a distinct question in it.

"I mean, obviously you're pregnant. H- how long before you have the baby?"

"Actually, I'm a week overdue. The doctor says we should induce labor, so we were just about to mosey on over to the hospital to meet my husband." She started down the hall. "Sorry I can't chat, but it was very nice to meet you, Jake."

The little boy turned back and waved. "Bye!"

Jake thought it would have been appropriate to respond with her name to possibly minimize the damage his first impression had caused, but in the excitement, he had forgotten part of it—the most important part. He remembered her last name, Thomas. But if he called her Mrs. Thomas, she would know he'd forgotten her first name. He decided it was best to just be obligatory and cut his losses. "It was nice meeting you, too," he called after her. "Hope everything comes out okay."

Pamela laughed. "Thank you for that wonderful sentiment. I hope everything comes out okay, too."

He wished he could retract the statement, but she and her son had gone far enough away that it would just make things even more awkward than they already were. And that was saying something.

183

CHAPTER 29

Angela Grant stood in the living room of Carter's apartment, talking to the agents from the SBI, the Maine State Bureau of Investigations. This was a federal case, but with Gary Carter being a Maine resident and prime suspect, it was partly their jurisdiction.

As it turned out, Gary Carter was squeaky clean. He had no criminal record of any kind, not even a parking ticket. The only suspicious evidence a thorough search of his apartment had turned up was four images on his computer, screen grabs from news sites on the web. For whatever reason, he was saving digital clippings of the Cape murderer's exploits. Researching a murderer, however, was not a crime. They would have to keep digging.

Perez tapped her on the arm. "Sorry to interrupt, but we spoke with the suspect's sister, and she says her brother's been acting weird lately. She doesn't think he's capable of murder, but she's worried he might be mixed up in something."

"Does she have any evidence?"

"No. She said he used to visit their mother every weekend, but about two years ago he stopped going. She says he's always agitated, and always watching the news."

"Well that doesn't sound like the behavior of a serial killer, more like a man being terrorized. I wonder what happened two years ago that made him go into hiding."

"We're speaking to the rest of his immediate family. Maybe something will turn up."

"Yes, he's all we have at the moment. Turn over every rock you can find."

"When do you want to stop by the clinic and check his office?"

"We'll go when we're done here."

CHAPTER 29

The Doris Boardman Woman's Health Center was part of a well manicured commercial complex. The buildings looked more like houses than business offices. It was tucked away in a small pine forest on the edge of Sunbury where specialty doctors held their practices. Beautiful stone paths lead up from the main sidewalk to each business door, with inviting rows of potted plants between.

Holly parked her '96 Sunbird in a parking space out front and turned to Dan with a threatening finger. "Okay. I let you come, but you're staying in the car. Don't come in no matter what."

"I'm here for moral support."

She looked at the time on her phone, and nervousness twisted in her gut. She wanted to go get this over with, but she also wanted to stay in the safety of the car as long as possible. She looked at the building. "This place just freaks me out."

"Well, I'm not going to add to your stress. I'll be right here in the car, waiting. I won't go anywhere, even if I have to go to the bathroom. I can always clean these pants later when I get home."

Her face soured. "Ew..."

"I'm kidding." He deflected a smack. "I'm kidding. Unless you take a really really long time, then I'm not kidding at all."

She swung at him again.

"I'm kidding!"

"Why'd I let you come?"

"Hey, you can't be serious all your life."

"How can you joke about everything? Life isn't a joke."

"Life is only serious when you let it be."

"This is serious. Right now it's serious, Dan!"

"Okay. I get it. I'll put on my serious face." His face went blank and he stared at her with the most unusual expression. There was an intensity to it, yet it was devoid of any recognizable emotion, almost as if he was applying an excruciating effort to not be happy or sad. The absurdity of it brought a bubble of laugher to the surface, but she immediately stifled it. This was not a time to laugh, and Dan was a moron for not realizing that fact.

She pushed him again.

"What? I'm being serious."

"You're like a child who never grew up."

"Growing up is for grown-ups and people who are afraid to get bubble gum in their nose hairs."

She rolled her eyes. "Just stay here." She exited the vehicle and nervously approached the front door, her fist tightly squeezing the strap of her purse. It would be over soon. All she had to do was drop the package, and get out without being seen.

A horrible thought entered her mind. What if there were more jobs like this one? What would he ask her to do? And would she be willing to do them? She pushed the thought away like a diseased thing. There was no time to consider what came next. She needed to stay in the moment and hold it together.

The entrance room was small but cozy. Maine themed paintings of lobster men, pine trees, and moose hung on two of the walls, and to the right was a metal door. Beside the door was a microphone with a red push button, and above the microphone, a long thin surveillance camera dangled from the ceiling.

Holly pressed a nervous finger to the button.

"State your name," said the impersonal voice on the speaker.

She leaned into the microphone. "Holly Paris."

"Reason for your visit?"

She fought a shiver in her belly. He hadn't given her a reason. What was she supposed to say? If she didn't give a reason for the visit, this whole thing would be over before it started. He'd said exam room B. Was this an appointment for a health exam? A pregnancy test? Something else?

She leaned in and said simply, "Exam." The door lock buzzed, and she pulled it open. Beyond the metal door was a large waiting room off to the left. Straight ahead was an open doorway to a tiny room. The plaque to the side of the doorway said reception. Holly shuffled into that room.

On the left wall and part of the wall across from her was a thick glass, bullet proof, the kidnapper had said. There were two receptionists. One was speaking on the phone; the other waved her in to a seat in front of her reception station.

188

Holly spoke into the microphone that rose out of the counter like a metal snake. "I'm Holly."

The receptionist looked at her screen. "We have you set for a nine o'clock gynecological exam."

Holly held back a look of shock. There was no way that was ever going to happen! She would make sure her task was complete before the nurse or doctor came in, then she'd come up with an excuse to leave quickly.

"Have a seat in the waiting room. The nurse will be with you shortly."

Though it was difficult to stand, her legs felt like jello and she thought she was going to be sick, Holly managed to get up and go into the lobby.

The waiting room was as plush and inviting as the initial entry room. Padded seats lined the walls, and in one of them sat a red-haired woman Holly thought she recognized.

"Hi." Holly took a seat across from her.

The young woman looked up sheepishly, as if the last thing she expected in this place was to have someone talk to her.

"Hey," she said.

Holly looked at the coffee table covered with magazines and informational trifolds, then peeked back up at the woman across from her. "I'm sorry," she said sitting back. "Don't I know you?"

The woman looked up, slightly embarrassed. "I- I don't think so."

"Did you go to Sunbury High?"

"No. Foxcroft Academy."

"Oh," said Holly, "I know some guys from up that way."

She pressed a polite smile, but her eyes said, leave me alone. Holly took the hint. It was evident from the woman's posture and the tightness in her brow that she was not here for a routine exam. It was probably something much more troubling. The Doris Boardman Center was the only clinic in central Maine where a woman could get an abortion, and Holly couldn't help but wonder if that was what this pretty redhead had come here to do. It would explain her discomfort. After all, this visit was supposed to be quick and discreet—and running into someone who recognized her was hardly discreet.

There was a buzz, and a nurse came out of the reception room. She looked at Holly, then at the redhead. "Elizabeth?"

The woman stood and followed the nurse through the reception room and the door beyond.

CHAPTER 30

Jake jumped up and sat on the window ledge by Aiyana's feet. She was still upset, but at least the tears had stopped.

"Do you think maybe we can start over?"

It relieved him to see her nod.

"Do you have any idea what you are or where you come from? Maybe if we can figure that out, we can figure out if you were sent to help rescue Gabe."

She shrugged.

"Do you remember anything before being here in the hallway?"

She shook her head slowly. "Just a little, but I'm not allowed to talk about that."

"Why?"

"It's unlawful."

"Unlawful—you mean, against the law? Whose law?"

She thought for a second, then said, "God's law."

He hadn't considered God in the equation. How odd to think he could be the one sending these children. "It's against God's law to tell me where you're from?"

"No. It's unlawful for me to tell you what I've seen in heavenly places."

His eyebrows rose. "Okay..."

She thought again, harder this time, then said, "Can we talk about something else? I don't want to get in trouble."

Jake nodded. "All right, so there are some things you can't remember, and other things you're not allowed to talk about. Is that right?"

"Well, I can remember a lot more now, but not everything."

"But you still don't know why you're here."

She shook her head.

"Do you know what you are?"

"Of course I do. I'm a girl."

"I know, but are you a ghost?"

"No. I'm in your head, and..." she thought again, "and also in my mother's belly."

Jake's mouth dropped open. His mind raced to go over each of his strange encounters with the "ghost" children. Were they the spirits of unborn babies? In the craziest possible way, it actually made sense. It would certainly explain all the pregnant women he'd been seeing. He studied Aiyana; was she the baby his new neighbor was expecting?

"Why are you looking at me that way?"

He gave his head a little shake. "Aren't you a little old to be a baby?"

She thought a moment. "I look as old as I want to look." Suddenly her eyes grew wide. "Oh no."

"What? Did you say something wrong? Did I get you in trouble?"

"No. My mommy's getting too far away. You won't be able to hear my thoughts anymore."

Hear her thoughts? Was that the secret behind all of this? There was no time to process this new information. He pushed off the ledge. "You think we can catch her?"

"I don't know."

Jake lifted her by the armpits and set her on the floor. "Come on, let's try to catch her!"

They ran down the hallway and Jake stabbed the elevator button. A light yellow number three glowed above the doors. It was on the third floor! "Come on," he said, "we'll take the stairs." He jogged down the hallway, keeping pace so Aiyana could keep up. If the pregnant lady next-door was Aiyana's mother, she would be close to the parking lot by now. Would they be able to catch her before she drove away?

He pushed into the stairwell and held the door for Aiyana. Her slight body lost its balance as she came through the opening, but she recovered without falling. It was amazing to see her push off the wall as if she were actually, physically with him. There was even the subtle lack of motor coordination he would expect from a child her age. How could she only be a thought in his mind? She was so real!

They raced to the first floor and down the hallway to the right. There was a door that led to the parking lot, but it was only for emergencies. Jake didn't care. He desperately wanted more time to talk to Aiyana. He pushed through the door.

No alarm sounded.

He spoke over his shoulder. "If you can think of anything we can tell your mother that would make her believe I'm not crazy, and that might keep her here till we can..." He glanced back, and slowed to a stop. The hallway was empty.

Aiyana was gone.

CHAPTER 31

Holly scratched her wrist nervously as she waited for the nurse to haul her off into her lair. It was a morbid thought, but she couldn't help it. There were so many odd qualities to this government-funded health center with its bullet-proof glass, reinforced steel doors, and surveillance cameras. She felt like she was in the novel, 1984, by George Orwell, like her every move was being carefully monitored.

How odd it seemed that a health clinic, built to help women, should be so fortified and guarded. Every effort had been made to make the room feel plush and inviting, but fear floated in the air. The chum was in the water, and the sharks were circling.

Holly had seen it first hand. The sweet middle-aged woman who had done her interview when she was pregnant with Gabe had never once suggested that she keep her baby. In her defense, she'd never said she should abort it either, but there was an understanding between them. The center wanted to help her make her troubles go away, and her troubles were all connected to the baby she wasn't ready to have.

It could have been her overactive imagination, but Holly never felt comfortable here. Though everything about the clinic was created to make women feel welcome, she always got the sense something was a little off.

"Holly?"

She looked up. A thin nurse who looked Holly's age stood in the doorway to the reception area. She wore an official white lab coat and carried a clipboard. "We're ready for you," she said.

Not sure if her legs would work, Holly stood. This was it. There was no turning back. Whatever agenda the kidnapper had, she was now a cog in the machinery. She didn't know where it would all lead, but if the first step was setting fire to this place, she was okay with that.

She followed the nurse into the reception area where they were buzzed through the door. The corridor beyond was thin, long, and mostly white. They went halfway down, took a left, and went halfway down the next hallway to a room marked examination room A.

"A?" Holly stammered.

The nurse turned around. "I'm sorry?"

"Examination room A?"

"Yes? Do you have a problem with that?"

Holly had to think fast. What problem did she have with that? Why hadn't she come up with a pre-made excuse? Events were moving too quickly; her brain felt like it was wrapped in cellophane.

"My, ah, sister had a really bad experience in room A," she lied, "and I'm already so nervous, would it be okay to use another?"

"I'm sorry to hear about your sister. We have another room down the hall if you'd prefer."

"I would appreciate that so much. I'm sorry to be a pain."

"Oh, you're no pain," she said. "Follow me. We'll take you down to exam room B."

Holly didn't have to fake her emotions; she was relieved to be going to the right room, and relieved that the nurse was so eager to please. They continued down the hall and to the right, then halfway down the next.

"Here we are," said the nurse. She went right into the exam room. Holly studied the foreboding door across the hall—the door she had been tasked to infiltrate. In its center was a black nameplate with white letters. The name on the plate made her heart squeeze in her chest. Gary Carter. Her eyes widened. *Was* he the killer? If he was, then why would he send a bomb to his own office? And if he wasn't... If he wasn't, then he was at least connected to him in some way? Her throat constricted. Was this a trap? Had she been lured here for something else?

Without realizing it, Holly stepped too near the office door and the device in her purse made the lock beep. Holly leaped back toward the opposite wall. She stood motionless. Did the nurse hear the beep? Holly saw a vision of the nurse dragging her across the hall to make the door beep again, but she forced it from her mind and stepped into the doorway of examination room B.

The nurse stood with her back to Holly. "Come in and have a seat." She flipped through the papers on her clipboard. Either the noise of the papers had covered the sound of the beep, or the nurse was so used to hearing it, she'd tuned it out. Whatever the reason, Holly was relieved.

She sat down on the sterile exam bed, and her body took on a rigidity as the tactile feel and sound of the paper brought the haunting memory of her last visit to the surface. It was the single most traumatic moment of her life. She remembered sitting there like a wounded animal, frightened and alone—hoping for someone to remove from her body the object of her suffering, yet feeling strangely protective of it.

"All right, Holly," the nurse said in a friendly voice. "What is your full name and date of birth?"

Holly cleared her throat. "Holly Anne Paris. June 27, 1992."

"Very good, very good." She flipped a page. "Our records say you've been here before."

"Yes," she said, "about six years ago." Her voice quivered.

"There is nothing to be nervous about. This is just a routine checkup."

"Okay," she said, gripping her purse harder than she should have.

"Do you want me to take that and put it somewhere safe till you're done?" she said, cheerfully, holding out her hand.

"No thanks..." Holly gripped it harder, and didn't offer a reason, because she didn't have one to give.

The nurse let her hand hover for a moment, then withdrew it and swiveled back to her paperwork. "Everything looks good."

Holly could hardly breathe, and her ribs had started a periodic shiver which was getting harder to conceal.

The office chair squeaked. "Here," said the nurse holding out a johnny. "Put this on and when you're ready, open the door, okay?"

Holly took the folded cloth and set it on her lap.

The nurse gave a friendly smile. "See you in a few minutes."

Holly sat shaking. It wasn't too late to call it off. She could just get up and walk out. And there was no way she would submit herself to a doctor's exam. She hated those exams under normal circumstances. But to allow herself to be probed by a doctor in such a vulnerable manner at the request of this freak was unimaginable. It would be like the killer himself was the examiner.

Her anger had a dampening effect on her fear, and she squeezed out every bit of it she could. She took the plastic medical gloves from her purse and slid them over her trembling fingers, then placed the johnny on the papered bed and peeked out the door. There were people talking, but the sound was distant and muffled. She peeked out further. No one was up the hall. No one was down the hall. This was it. All she had to do was hurl herself to the door and push her way through.

She felt like a diver standing on a high cliff, contemplating whether to obey her fear or rise to the challenge. She closed her eyes and pushed everything away. Sometimes rising to the occasion was a simple matter of disregarding the consequences, and sadly, that was a skill Holly had almost perfected.

She launched herself across the hall, listened for the beep, and pushed through into the dark office beyond.

CHAPTER 32

Jake sat on the front steps of The Schoolhouse with his head in his hands and his fingers clutching chunks of his curly brown hair. The stress of the last twenty-four hours had finally caught up with him, and had struck with a vengeance. Every time he felt he was making progress, the solution would dance away, mocking him as it went. If these children had some kind of connection to God and angels, then why were they taunting him with mysteries? Why not come out and say what they'd been sent to tell him? Why not show him what he was supposed to do? Was he doing something wrong? Was he chasing the wrong child?

No. She was the right one, somehow he felt sure of it. Clearly Aiyana wasn't the one with the answers, but maybe she could lead him to the answers? Her mother said she was going to the hospital...

Jake looked up.

What better place to find these supernatural children than at the maternity ward? He stood. If these children had a connection to something beyond this world, and if this ability to see and talk to them had been given to him to save Gabe, then that was where he needed to be.

But first he needed to check in with Dan to make sure he hadn't missed anything. He pulled his phone out and pressed Dan's number onto the pad.

"Heylo?" said Dan.

"Hey, Dan. Any news on Gabe?"

"Not yet, bud. I'm sorry."

"How's Holly doing?"

"Honestly, Jake, I don't know. She's acting even weirder today. Maybe it's lack of sleep. I don't know."

"What do you mean weirder?"

"Well, yesterday all she could think about was finding information on the serial killer and figuring out which one of her friends could be involved. She was an emotional wreck. Then it was like a switch went off and she just stopped. I thought maybe she was just exhausted, you know, from the stress of it all, but today was the same. She hasn't mentioned looking for Gabe at all."

"Maybe she's burnt out."

"If my kid was missing, I'd be knocking down every door in the city."

"Well there's only so much she can do without a solid lead. That's where I'm at with this whole thing. I can't do a better job than the FBI, so I'm doing the only thing I can by trying to find out if these ghosts are here to help. It's absolutely crazy, but I feel like they're my only chance to make a difference. Holly doesn't have any weird ghost-children to chase, so maybe she's just shutting down because she doesn't have anything to occupy her mind. The stress is probably getting to her."

"Yeah, that makes sense."

"So, what is she doing now? Resting?"

"No. She had an appointment and she brought me along. That was kinda why I mentioned the whole thing about her not thinking about Gabe. I think it's weird that she would go to an appointment, you know, while all this is going on. But I guess it makes sense. She said it was important, and maybe she's trying to keep her mind off Gabe by staying busy."

"What kind of appointment is it?"

"Apparently some kind of screening. She says her doctor thinks it's probably nothing, but he wanted to check her for something. She didn't say what."

"Okay, well, let me know if you need me and I'll come right over."

"Where are you now? Have you figured out who these kids are yet?"

"I'm at my place. The little girl, Aiyana, revealed some interesting things. Whatever they are, they have some kind of contact with angels and other supernatural stuff. I'm hoping that means they can find things out, like, where the killer is holding Gabe."

"That rocks, man. I wonder if you're the first person in history to be a ghost whisperer?"

"I don't know, but I can't wait till whatever this thing is passes and I can go back to being normal again."

"I'd book myself on the talk show circuit and make a million dollars."

He let out a wry laugh. "I'd give a million dollars to have my sanity back."

"Is it that bad?"

"Worse."

"Okay," Dan's tone changed. "So what are you doing now?"

"I'm going to look for more children to see if I can get my last few questions answered. Until Holly finds something I can help with, or the FBI discovers something new, it's all I can think of."

"See if you can get next week's lottery numbers."

Jake groaned. "Yeah, I'll put that right up on the top of my list, Dan."

"Sorry."

"Call me if anything develops."

"I will, man."

"All right. Keep an eye on Holly, don't let her do anything suicidal."

"We-ll, Jake. If she's going to kill anyone, I'm pretty sure it will be me."

CHAPTER 33

Angela Grant followed the agents from the SBI over to the Doris Boardman Clinic. They'd offered to take care of it themselves, but she wanted to keep her standing as point on this case, so she respectfully declined. Interagency cooperation and matters of jurisdiction were her least favorite part of the job, especially since she was a woman. She constantly had to work harder and fiercer in order to earn the respect of the agents around her. There was no room for mistakes.

She got out of the car with Perez and met the two men from the surveillance team and the SBI officers on the sidewalk. "What's the situation?"

Agent Blake, from the surveillance team, fielded the question. "There's been no sign of the suspect and no suspicious activity in the parking lot."

She gave a reserved nod and started up the path toward the clinic.

"There is one thing I think you'll find interesting, though," he added.

She paused. "Yes?" There was a twinge of irritation in her voice. "And what would that be, Agent Blake?" She wasn't a fan of surprises. If there was information to be relayed, she preferred a direct laundry list.

"Holly Paris showed up just before nine. She is currently on the premises."

First Jake Paris showed up at Carter's home, now his sister was at Carter's work. Was there a connection? "Do we know why Miss Paris is at the clinic?"

Blake stepped up to her and leaned in. "The women's center played the client confidentiality card, but you might want to ask the young man in the rust bucket what he knows." He looked in the direction of the vehicle. "He showed up with her; he's been in the car waiting."

Angela looked toward the rusted white Sunbird, but there was no one visible inside the car. Her eyes rose up to meet Blake's. He stood a foot taller than her, but she equalized the size difference by giving him a look of boredom to communicate her lack of interest in playing his game.

Agent Blake lifted his chin. "Oh, he's in there."

Angela strolled over to the car and looked down into the passenger's seat. Its occupant was curled down over the stick shift with his back to her, but she recognized his clothing. It was the young man who'd come to Holly's apartment with Jake Paris. Angela rapped on the side of the car.

Dan flew up to a sitting position. "Oh, hey. I didn't see you there. I was looking for change, you know, for the poor."

"You're Jake's friend, right?"

He looked up sheepishly. "Yes?"

"Did you come with Holly Paris?"

"Yeah. She has an appointment."

"And you're just innocently waiting for her, doubled over in the front seat, hiding from the authorities?"

"Well when you put it like THAT it sounds suspicious."

"It is suspicious." She groped her memory for his name. "Dan, is it?"

"Yeah."

"Did Holly tell you why she's here, Dan?"

"I told you."

"Did she have a weapon on her?"

"No, not that I know of. Why would she?"

"How was she acting? Was she in an agitated state?"

"That's the only state she's ever in. Truth be told, I think she is the governor of that state."

Angela maintained a neutral expression. "Did she leave you any instructions?"

"Yeah, wait in the car and don't say anything that would indict her with the federal government. I said I'm all over that first one, but you might be in trouble if they start sliding bamboo shoots under my fingernails. I'm delicate."

"You do realize it's a crime to mislead a federal officer?"

"I'm being straight with you. I don't know anything. She's here for an appointment, and I'm waiting for her. When I saw you guys, I don't know—I guess I got weirded out."

"And why is that? Would it have anything to do with the fact that her appointment is at the workplace of a suspected serial killer—a man she may believe is holding her son with the intention of killing him?"

Dan's jaw dropped. It was obvious he was unaware of the connection. "Is it—Amber's boyfriend? He works here? Are you kidding me?"

"You were not aware of this?"

"No," he said, in utter shock.

"Did Holly know?"

"If she did, she didn't tell me about it."

"Was she acting suspicious?"

"She always acts suspicious."

"Did she tell you her reasons for coming to this appointment during this crisis with her son?"

"She hinted at it being a checkup for, I don't know, something serious like cancer or something. I figured that made sense."

Health centers did do checks for ovarian cancer —and that would certainly be a valid, though unlikely, reason for her to come to the clinic while her son was still being held by a known murderer... But the pieces didn't quite slide together. There was something else going on, something Dan was probably oblivious to. He didn't strike her as the type who could hide anything.

"All right, Dan. Thank you. We will be speaking to Miss Paris so she may be awhile."

"Can I come in?" He gripped the door handle.

"No. Stay put. If I see you anywhere near that building, I'll arrest you for obstruction. Do you understand?"

His fingers slid off the handle. "I'll just wait here then."

She left Dan and joined the other officers on the sidewalk. Perez had stood close enough to hear the conversation, but she brought the others up to speed with one sentence. "Holly Paris claims to be here for some kind of screening. Her friend Dan believes she is unaware of the connection between Gary Carter and the clinic."

They all acknowledge her assessment.

"Let's go find out what's really going on."

CHAPTER 34

Gary Carter's office looked official with its L-shaped chestnut desk, black leather office chair, and cushioned visitor chairs. Potted plants adorned chestnut cabinets in each rear corner, and the walls were sparsely decorated with more of the same kind of paintings found in the rest of the building. This surprised Holly. Why would he choose the same style of painting for his office? They had the same outdoor Maine theme with the same heavy brush strokes, the same gold-spec frames. Was Gary responsible for choosing the décor of the clinic? Did he run it?

If he was the killer, this would make sense. He had pursued a career that allowed him to be a gatekeeper of life, deciding which mothers were fit to have children, and which should be pressured to abort. But running an abortion clinic wasn't enough for him; he had taken his ideology to the furthest extreme. He wasn't content to spare unborn children a life of hardship and pain; he was driven to randomly select living children to rescue from a life of despair, the life he himself was forced to live. But the children were not random. She had come here six years ago and rejected this clinic's advice to abort her baby. Gary Carter must not have been content with that. Too many mothers must have slipped through his fingers. Too many babies had lived to suffer at the hands of their unfit mothers. It must have eaten at his insides. If his whole identity was locked into saving babies from a long life of pain, it had to kill him when they slipped through his fingers.

So what was his role at this clinic, Holly wondered, doctor or administrator? Was he directly responsible for executing the procedure that cut the babies from their mother's womb, or did he just facilitate it? Her time was terribly short, but she couldn't leave without knowing.

Frantically she searched the wall behind his desk and found his medical diploma. There it was. Gary Earl Carter, M.D. Graduate of Tames School of Medicine. How nice. He burned his way through some backwoods medical school and found a place to nest here in Sunbury where he could prey on young women in crisis, all on the government's coin. Her stomach turned at the thought of how many unsuspecting young girls had put themselves in his hands, believing he was helping them out of a sense of compassion, when secretly he hated them.

She looked at the file cabinets on the right wall. What was in those cabinets? And why did he want to torch them? Did they contain evidence of malpractice? Would she be helping him escape prosecution for the crimes he had committed?

Was she willing to sacrifice the well-being of other children to save her own? She wished she had just mindlessly done the deed. At least then she would have been oblivious to her crime. But was it too late? She could slide the drawer open and drop the bomb in without looking. She didn't have to carry the guilt of knowing what or whom she had sacrificed to save her child.

She took the bomb out of her purse, dropped to her knees in front of the bottom right drawer, and clasped the handle. But she couldn't bring herself to open it. A war raged in her heart. If she did not do this horrible thing, he had promised to kill her son. Her son's life was sitting on a pile of explosives, and her finger was on the button. But she couldn't do it without knowing.

She yanked the drawer open and rifled through the paperwork. The folders inside contained financial records for the clinic. There were no documents for patients. She opened the next drawer. It was filled with official looking government paperwork. Again, nothing to do with patients. The top drawer had more of the same. Did he want to destroy the financial history of the clinic? Maybe this wasn't about the children at all. She pushed the top two drawers closed and pulled all the folders in the bottom drawer to the front.

The bomb was small, and the cabinet was made of metal. It was a trade, financial records for the life of her son. She could live with that. She placed the bomb near the rear wall of the drawer, pushed the folders back into place, and shut the cabinet.

CHAPTER 35

Angela Grant moved briskly down the hall with the receptionist in hot pursuit.

"Is this the one?" she said, pointing to the approaching doorway of examination room A.

"No, she's in the next one."

Angela turned the corner. "Down here?" she said.

"Yes, ma'am. Halfway down on the right."

Angela stepped into the examination room and looked around. "This is the room?"

"Yes," said the receptionist pushing in behind her. "The nurse said she left her in room B."

"Well." She shot the woman an accusing look. "She's not here now. I want the building shut down. No one leaves without my authorization."

"I'll have to get Dr. Page to approve this."

"You call whoever you want, but I have a warrant to search these premises and detain any individuals I believe are suspect in this investigation. If you allow Miss Paris to leave this property, I will hold you personally responsible. Got it?"

The woman looked as if she might pass out. "O-okay." she stammered. "I'll see what I can do." She started to exit the room—then screamed.

There was another scream from the hallway. Angela pushed past the receptionist and unstrapped the revolver on her belt.

Holly stood in the hallway squeezing her purse to her chest. Her irises floated in a sea of white.

Angela released her grip on the revolver. "Miss Paris, what are you doing in the hall?"

"I had to pee," she squeaked. "I didn't want to have an exam with a full bladder, so I went to look for the bathroom. Why is everyone freaking out?"

The receptionist was clutching her chest, so Angela put a hand on her shoulder. "Why don't you go sit down, and tell Agent Perez we found Miss Paris."

The woman walked away, looking like she had just stepped off a fair ride.

Holly looked rattled as well. Her brow and top lip were noticeably moist and her body quaked with subtle tremors.

"Are you all right, Miss Paris?"

"Y- yes." she said. "Why?"

"You're sweating and trembling."

"She scared me half to death!"

"Being startled doesn't make a person sweat."

"Yeah—well—I- I'm so nervous about the exam. I don't think I can go through with it."

Agent Grant watched her closely. Either Holly was telling the truth, or she was an excellent actress. Her neck muscles and eyebrows tightened when she said the word exam which meant the emotion attached to that word was real. She was not happy about having this exam, but was that the only reason for her heightened emotional state?

"Come in and have a seat, Holly." Angela moved to the side and let Holly go in and sit down on a chair in the exam room.

"Why are you here?" Holly asked.

This was Angela's opportunity to check for motive. If Holly knew Gary's office was in the clinic, she would have no choice but to lie. Admitting that she knew this, but had still come, would be highly suspicious. She had to know that. If she was truly unaware of the connection between Gary and the clinic, her first and uncontrollable response would be shock.

Angela chose her words carefully. "We believe Gabe's kidnapper works in this clinic. We are here to search his office."

There was no shock, not even feigned shock. Holly just looked puzzled.

"Holly?"

Her eyes flitted up. "Yes?"

"Your lack of response tells me you had foreknowledge that the suspect in your son's kidnapping works at this facility. What do you have to say about that?"

"No I didn't," she said.

"Just now, when I told you we were here to search his office, you showed no signs of surprise or shock."

"I wasn't shocked," she said.

"And why is that?"

"I saw his name on the door across the hall." She pointed.

215

It was true. There it was, Gary Carter, written on a plaque in the middle of the door. How had she missed that? "Was that why you were nervous in the hallway?"

Holly hesitated. "I don't know. Yeah. I guess."

"Why the hesitation?"

"I don't know! Why are you grilling me like I'm a suspect? I didn't know Gary worked here, and even if I did, what could I possibly do that you can't do?"

"Revenge," Agent Grant said, holding her eyes steady on Holly's.

"What? Kill him? He's holding my son!"

She had a point. It made no sense for her to come here for revenge. She couldn't kill him, not while her son was still being held somewhere.

"Then tell me why you're here, across the hall from the man who is holding your son."

"I have an appointment! It was made before any of this started. Ask the clinic."

"Before this all started?"

"Yes," she gasped.

"And you didn't know Mr. Carter worked here until you came here today?"

"That's what I'm trying to tell you. Can I go, please?"

"Go?"

"Yes. I think I'm going to be sick."

"What about your exam?"

"I barely wanted to do it in the first place. Please! Can I go?"

If she made the appointment before the kidnapping took place, that removed the motive. There was no reason to detain her. "Yes. You're free to go."

Holly burst from the chair and pushed by. Angela watched her walk briskly down the hall and take the corner. Had she misread the whole situation? Was it only a coincidence? If so, she could understand Holly's fear. This would be the last place Holly would want to be.

Angela made a quick call to Perez. "Holly is on her way out. Let her go."

There was a hint of confusion in the way he said, "Okay."

"Make sure you find out from the office staff when Holly made the appointment at the clinic. If it was before yesterday, she has no motive."

"I'm on it."

"And tell our SBI friends to join us in Mr. Carter's office. I want to tear the room apart."

CHAPTER **36**

The friendly hospital receptionist looked up and over her glasses. "May I help you?"

Jake attempted to relax. "Yes," he said, "I'm looking for a patient—last name Thomas."

"When was she admitted?"

"Today," he said.

She clicked some buttons and scanned her screen. "Pamela Thomas?"

"Yes. Yes, that's it."

"Are you a relative?"

"I'm her brother." He immediately regretted the response. It was probably a bad idea to lie to a woman with the resources of a computer in front of her. He had no idea what kind of information they kept on those things. It would have been safer to say no and have to search the maternity ward than give a suspicious answer and have security escort him off the premises.

"She's in room 814. Take the elevators to the eighth floor and follow the hallway to the nurses' station. You can check in there."

"Right. Eighth floor. Thank you." He hid his relief, and crossed over the hall to the elevators. It felt as if every eye in the entire lobby was glued on him. It wasn't true of course, but inward guilt has a way of toying with one's perceptions.

The elevator doors opened, and he herded onto it with other visitors and squeezed toward the back. It was a short trip, and by the time he reached the eighth floor, the elevator was empty.

Ding. The doors slid open, and he stepped out into the corridor. Everything was quiet. To his right was the waiting room where he noted an old couple, a young man by himself, and a father with his two children. There were no pregnant women, so Jake took a left down the hall. Immediately he saw a set of double doors with a Restricted Area sign on it.

Standing in front of the doors was a three-year-old in blond pigtails with a mixture of shock and excitement on her face. She turned and ran through the doors—without opening them.

Jake made a quick check to see if anyone was looking, then walked briskly to the doors. He peeked through the window to see that the corridor beyond was empty, then pushed through and walked down to where the hall turned right. He could hear giggling coming from the next hallway, so he slowed and carefully peered around the bend.

Four children stood staring at him.

"See! Is him!" squealed the girl in pigtails. "Heah in da hossible!"

An olive-skinned two-year-old boy standing next to her smiled a crooked smile, while a pair of twin girls behind them hopped and clapped.

Jake took a step back to avoid being seen; the children came around the corner. He crouched down. "You guys know me?"

"Yah," said the pigtailed-girl. "We know you. Yaw Inas dod."

Jake cocked his head. "I'm what?"

The olive-skinned boy put his hand on Jake's arm. "Yaw wam."

The twins came around and touched his skin, too. He felt like the subject of a lab experiment with their little fingers rubbing and poking.

"Do any of you have a message for me? Something you're supposed to tell me?"

The girl in pigtails said, "I don' ting day memmer yet. Day happy cos day nevaw tauch stuff."

"But do you remember?" he asked.

She nodded enthusiastically.

"How do you know me?"

"Some ov us know eesh ovor befaw."

"Before what?"

"Befaw we lef."

"Left where?" He looked at her intently. "You were somewhere before you came here?"

"Yah, but nawt wong."

"Do you know what that place was?"

"No. I don' know it."

"But—you remember it."

"Yup."

"Are you here to help me?"

"No, I don' ting so."

"Then why are you here?"

She appeared confused by the question. "Cos you c'n see me."

220

"But why? Why can I see you? And not anyone else?"

"I don' know."

"Think hard. Try to remember."

A black woman in baby blue scrubs came around the corner. The children all backed up. Jake blinked up at her, innocently.

"Can I help you, sir?"

How was he going to explain crouching and talking to himself in a restricted area of the maternity ward? This was it, they'd kick him out for sure.

"I'm sorry, I felt sick," he said, slowly getting to his feet.

"Mmm-hmmm," she said, with a curl of her lip. Her arms came up and folded across her chest. "And who are you here with?"

Out of sheer desperation, he said, "Pamela Thomas."

She gave a suspicious squint. "You're Mr. Thomas?"

"Yeah."

"Your wife's not even in here yet."

That was good news, and bad. Bad because it didn't explain why he was acting squeamish in the hall, but good that she wasn't in a nearby room in labor. He could only imagine the look on his neighbor's face if the nurse had dragged him into the room while she was giving birth.

"Where is she?" he asked, hoping she would avoid addressing the elephant in the room.

Suddenly one of the twins let out a piercing screech that sent Jake's soul bouncing off the wall. His eyes opened wide as he stood rigid before the nurse. Somewhere around the corner another scream filled the air.

The girl screeched again and her eyes got big. "I think I'm comin' OUT!"

The nurse took a step back.

"I AM! I'm comin' out! Push, Momma! Puuuuuuuush!" cried the little girl. Her sister started hopping and clapping.

There was another scream and a loud groan from down the hall.

"Your wife is in her room, Mr. Thomas." The nurse pointed back toward the double doors. "But you're going to have to go around. I don't want to see you in this hall again, unless you're with your wife, understand?"

Jake started backing up. "Yes, ma'am. Thanks."

The twins ran down the hall, followed by the other children. Jake could hear the little girl continue her excited screams. "Push, Momma! You c'n do it! I'm comin' out! I'm comin' *OUT!*"

Jake left the restricted area. His options were dwindling. These children didn't have any answers for him, they were just as confused as he was about the whole situation. He could see them, and they could experience things while he was around, but to them it was just a weird experience. They weren't supernatural messengers. They had no connection to some ethereal world where information could be acquired by some extrasensory ability. They were simply children waiting to be born, and somehow, when he was near, they could experience a taste of the world around them. Aiyana had mentioned not being able to see anything he couldn't see. Why then had all the children run down the hallway to watch the birth? How would they see it, if Jake wasn't seeing it?

There was only one way to get more answers, and that was to travel deeper into the bowels of the maternity ward and find Aiyana. She was older than the other children and much more articulate. His chances of getting meaningful answers lay with her.

CHAPTER 37

Holly got into the driver's side of her car and slammed the door. Her body quaked as she gripped the steering wheel and tried to pull herself together. She needed something to numb the pain. She couldn't do this anymore. It was too much. She had to ditch Dan and her roommate and get to her pills.

Dan studied her. "You all right?"

"No. I'm not all right." She clutched the keys and started the car with force. "I'm about as not all right as I've ever been in my life!"

The tires spun on the dirt as she pulled out.

"Woah. Slow down speed racer. Those are police officers over there. You want me to drive?"

"No. I've got it," she snapped.

"Do you—wanna talk about it?"

She glared at him. "What do you think, Dan?"

"I think you're upset and you need someone to lean on."

What she needed was something to numb her into oblivion, and for Dan to shut his big mouth. She stamped on the accelerator.

"Uh oh!" said Dan, looking into his side mirror.

"What?" her eyes checked the rear-view mirror.

"Quick! Pull over!" he said.

What was he doing? There was nothing behind them.

"You have to trust me. Pull over!"

She kicked the brake and pulled the car to the side of the road.

"What? The police? What do you see?"

He reached over and twisted the keys out of the ignition. "I see a crazy person, that's what I see."

"GIVE ME THOSE!"

He dodged her angry hands and got out of the car.

"DAN! Give me my keys or I swear..." She opened her door and stumbled out.

"No," he said. "You're going to get both of us killed, and that's not going to help anyone."

She slammed the door with all her strength. "I don't want to help anyone! Give me my keys! Or I'll claw your eyes out!"

He backed away from the road as she came around the car. "Holly. Look at you. You're not this person. You're not angry. You're hurt, and that's completely understandable."

"You don't know anything about me!"

"I know you love your son more than life itself, and that you would do anything to get him back."

His words drove into her ribs like an arrow, but she forced through it and took a swing toward his head. "Give me my keys!"

He squeezed them in his thick hand and held her back with the other. "I know you have doubts and fears, I know you don't think you're strong enough to get through this, but you don't have to be."

"SHUT UP!"

"You don't have to do this alone."

Again his words were like a weapon cutting into her flesh. She wanted to believe him, but she didn't know how. Her anger flared again. She hated herself for needing help, and she hated him for reminding her.

She leaped at him, struggling to get the keys from his hand. His body was like iron, but his grip was gentle. Though she dug into his flesh with her nails, he didn't fight back. He simply held his ground, allowing her to rail against him over and over with all her strength.

"Give me my keys, Dan!"

"You're not angry, Holly. You're wounded."

She gripped his bicep and tried to pull his hand with the keys toward her, but his arm was solid and unyielding. She dug at it with her nails.

"Let me in, Holly. I can help."

"I don't need your help!" She tried to pull on his arm again, but her strength was failing. She pushed off his chest, slipped on the muddy grass, and went crashing to the ground. Pain shot into her shoulder.

He reached down to help her.

"GET AWAY FROM ME!" She swung her hand out and caught him across the cheek as she crumbled back to the ground.

She braced herself for a retaliation, but none came. Why would it come? Dan wasn't like that. He wasn't vindictive and petty like she was, or like the string of men she had shacked up with. He was different... stronger... kinder. He was reaching out to her still, even though she had bitten him like a frightened animal. How did he do it? She gave him nothing but hatred and contempt, yet he offered only mercy in return.

Something inside her broke, and the anger released like mist into the air, leaving only sadness and despair. She dug her nails into the ground and started to cry. She cried from the deepest part of her gut, unable to hide even the tiniest fraction of her sorrow and regret. Her son was gone. And this wasn't who she wanted to be, but she wasn't strong enough to be the woman she wanted to be. She was so terribly weak, and from the depths of her being she cried out for someone to show her how to be strong, for someone to show her how to rescue her son.

Dan said nothing, but sat next to her on the grass like a statue. No. Like a guardian angel keeping watch over her, protecting her while she lay bleeding her heart into the cold moist ground.

CHAPTER 39

Jake walked down the hallway to the nurses' station and as he rounded the corner, stopped in his tracks. The large room was crawling with children. One boy was climbing a medical rack beside the nurses' station. Another was racing cars along the floor. On the counter in front of him was a large boy pretending to sword fight. One fist waved through the air, the other was on his hip. "Haaaaaa!" he said, thrusting forward. "You are no match for my blade!"

On a bench to Jake's right was another child, a little Chinese girl, holding a baby doll in her arms. She rocked her baby and sang a sweet song. He listened. It was hauntingly familiar—someone had once sang that song to him. But who? His mother had never sang to him. Jake stood and listened a moment longer.

Finally he turned and looked at the room numbers, then followed them down to 814. The two nurses behind the desk paid no attention to him. Other visitors were milling around inside and outside of the hospital rooms, so Jake must have blended in.

The door to 814 was closed, and Aiyana was not sitting out front as he had hoped, so he sat down on a cushioned chair in the hallway, tucked behind a large metal push cart. He pulled out his phone. If he had to wait, he figured it would be good to check in with Jenna.

The phone rang a couple times before she picked up. "Hello?"

"Hey, Jenna. How are things going at the theater house?"

"Good..." Her voice had a subtle vibrato.

"Are you okay?"

"Yes. I'm great actually."

"You don't sound great."

"The job is mine," she said. Her voice cracked on the last word.

"You got signed? That's incredible!"

He could hear her quietly regrouping on the other end of the phone.

"This is great news, Jen!"

"I haven't exactly taken it though. They offered it, but I'm just not sure."

"Wh- what? What do you mean? Don't worry about how this is going to affect me. This is your big chance. Take it, take the job."

"It's complicated."

"No it's not, it's easy. You've been given a once-in-a-lifetime opportunity, and I'm behind you a hundred percent. Why would you want to throw that away?"

Jenna was quiet.

"Jenna?"

"Don't you ever think about the future, or having a family?"

The question opened a wound he hadn't had time to emotionally cauterize. What kind of family could they have with him unemployed? Jenna taking this job was his chance to have some breathing room. From what Jenna had told him, these production companies offered a considerable signing bonus, and paid all moving expenses.

"Jenna," he said gently, "you are my family. The rest can wait."

"Don't you think about kids?"

"More than you could possibly know," he said, looking over at one of the children sitting cross-legged beneath the nurses' station removing his finger from his nose and placing it in his mouth. Really?! He turned his head in disgust.

"More than I can possibly know? What's that supposed to mean?"

Her tone pulled him back to reality. "I don't know what it means. I guess with all that's happening with Gabe, I've been thinking a lot about what it means to be a father." It was a half-truth, and for him a half-truth was easier to pull off than a whole lie.

"Do you think about marriage?"

There it was, the mother of all bombs. Jenna knew his feelings on marriage. His childhood had been destroyed by divorce, and he didn't want that destruction in his life anymore. She knew marriage was a sacred institution to him, and when he decided he was ready, it would be forever. But he wasn't ready.

This pending job change was obviously rattling her cage for her to bring up the topic of marriage. She knew it was a touchy subject for him, a conversation that never ended well. What she wanted to know was, would he leave if things got tough? So he addressed her insecurities.

"Jenna. You're the only one for me. If you need me to pick up and move, I'll move. If you need me to stay and wait, I'll wait. You don't have to worry about me."

There was silence on the other end of the phone.

"I don't know what you want me to tell you."

"I don't want you to tell me anything. Look," she said, "I have to go. I'll take the job."

"Okay then," he said, happy to move on.

She took in a breath and let it out. "We have forever to talk about the future, right?"

"That's right, and that's how long we're going to be together, okay? Forever."

"Okay," she said, "I'll talk to you tonight and tell you how it goes."

"Okay."

"Bye, Jake."

"Bye."

He wasn't sure, but he was fairly confident that the conversation couldn't have gone much worse. Why was she bombarding him with questions about marriage and children? She was sitting on an opportunity she had been dreaming about for years. Everything she wanted from life was now within her reach. Did she want to be a wife and mother more than pursuing her dream job? Had her priorities changed? If so, the bigger question was, what did that mean for him? He was hardly in the position to support a family.

He got up and started walking back toward the nurses' area. Most of the children had taken to running down the hall and back up again, screaming and laughing as they went. The noise bouncing off the confined walls of the hospital corridor hurt his ears, but what could he do? He couldn't exactly scream at them and tell them to be quiet.

"Jake?" He looked down at a messy-haired girl who had reached up and clasped his pinky. Her tiny lips puckered, and her round innocent eyes gazes up at him. "You don' have to be awfwaid, evwy-fing wiwl be awight."

Jake walked her back away from the nurses' station and crouched down. "What will be all right? Gabe?"

"He's awight," she said, over enunciating her words.

"How do you know?"

"I'm naw supoze to tewl. Is agenz da wah."

"Okay. But where is he?"

She shrugged.

"How do you know he's all right if you don't know where he is?"

"Oh! Wook!" she said, pointing to a man walking down the corridor toward the nurses' station.

He stopped and leaned over the counter. "Hi, I'm looking for my wife. She's in 814."

"Yup," said the nurse, "right over there."

"Thanks," said the man. He turned and headed in Jake's direction.

232

Jake stood and took a step toward him. "You just moved into The Schoolhouse Apartments, right?"

The man slowed. "Yes. Yesterday. Have we met?"

"I'm Jake Paris," he said, offering his hand. "I saw you coming off the elevator with a box. I'm your neighbor across the hall."

"Oh, yes, Jake Paris. I saw your name on the buzzer board. What brings you to the maternity ward?"

"I—ah, have a sister who is pregnant."

He smiled. "Cool. My wife's expecting. What a small world."

"So, is she having the baby today?"

"No, tomorrow. They're inducing her today, and she's going to stay the night in the hospital." He made a subtle shift toward the room.

"Well, I won't keep you."

"It was nice to meet you, Jake. I'm sure we'll run into each other again."

"Oh," said Jake. "Have you decided what you're going to call her?"

The question surprised him. "I'm sorry?"

"The baby. Have you decided what you're going to call her?"

"Oh!" he said. "It's not a girl. It's a boy. We're going to call him Alan."

Jake could scarcely take a breath. He remembered the little boy clinging to his mother's leg. She had looked down and rubbed her belly when she'd introduced him. Her son wasn't next to her, he was in her belly! That left one vastly disturbing question.

If their son was Alan, then, whose child was Aiyana?

CHAPTER 39

The files on Gary Carter's computer, his schedule, and his e-mail, showed no indication of any suspicious activity. It was cleaner, even, than his home computer. Angela ran a root kit and scanned for recently deleted files. There were some interesting searches that had recently been deleted from the browser's cache, but nothing incriminating. Carter had browsed websites for information on serial killers here at his work, just like he'd done at home. So if he wasn't the killer, he was certainly curious about him.

Perez pulled the last group of folders out of the filing cabinet and looked up at her. "You might want to take a look at this," he said, reaching for the light on his belt. He stabbed the end of the flashlight with his thumb and a beam lit up the back of the cabinet drawer. Resting there was a small, sealed, hard plastic cylinder.

"What do you make of that?" said Perez.

"Whatever it is, I don't think it was meant to be found." She slid her hands into a pair of rubber gloves and reached into the cabinet.

Perez stopped her. "Are you sure about this?"

"What?" she said. "You think it's a bomb?"

"I think it's a suspicious item with no markings. Maybe we should get forensics to check it out."

"By the time we get that to happen, this kid could be dead," she said, twisting her arm gently from his grip. "If you're worried, you can always go wait in the hallway and suck your thumb."

His face drooped. "You're going to get me killed one of these days, and my wife is going to hunt you down and beat you like a pinata." The word pinata sounded funny in his Mexican accent.

She smiled. "There are few things that scare me in this life, and your wife is one of them."

"You and me both," he said. His face took on the air of a child that just got caught stealing from the cookie jar.

She reached into the cabinet again, pulled the cylinder from its resting place, and brought it over to the desk. There were no words on the shiny, black surface to indicate what was inside. She gripped the lid and pulled it free.

The container held four small plastic Ziploc bags. She turned the container and let the plastic bags slide out onto the desk. Inside the bags were samples of hair —four samples of hair, two brown and two blond.

She looked up at Perez. "You're kidding me, right?"

"He kept a chunk of each of the kids' hair in the back of his filing cabinet at work?"

She read his expression. "I know. This is too easy. Why would a serial killer who has eluded authorities for four years leave DNA evidence in such an obvious place?"

"Maybe he wanted it in a place he could grab it quickly."

"This is all wrong. I can't put my finger on it but —I don't think he's the guy."

"But you're holding evidence that says he is."

"It doesn't add up. This guy isn't a premeditated murderer. He's a man on the run. As soon as all this started, he disappeared, but left his trophies behind? Trophies that just happen to be hard DNA evidence? I don't think so. And look at his search habits on the internet. He wasn't looking up how to wire listening devices, or how to set up an untraceable IP address. He was searching for information about the Cape murderer. I think he knew something, or stumbled onto something, that brought this killer to Sunbury. I don't think Gary Carter is the guy, but I think he knows who is."

CHAPTER 40

Holly opened her apartment door and was immediately greeted by Amber. She noticed the dirt and grass stains on Holly's shorts, gave her a concerned look, and draped an arm around her.

"You poor thing. Let's get you into some new clothes."

Dan came in behind them, and she heard her car keys clank on the coffee table. He was probably glad to be rid of the diseased things. They were, after all, the source of his torment for the last thirty minutes.

Amber took Holly past the kitchen, past the place where her pills were hidden, and into the bedroom where her nightmare waited. There was a part of her that wanted to go back for Dan, but the best she could do was take comfort that he was near. The clock was approaching twelve noon when the kidnapper would be calling, and no one could know about the call, not Dan, not Amber, no one.

"I appreciate the help, Amber, but I need to be alone for a bit."

"Do you want me to run a bath for you?"

"No," she said, "I'll just rinse off and get changed."

"Is there anything I can do?"

Amber meant well, but Holly resented her motherly attention. She was only five years older than Holly, but she acted much older. Holly usually appreciated Amber's confident girl-power attitude and secretly hoped it would rub off. But in times of self-loathing, feelings of envy and resentment always managed to boil to the surface. However, it wasn't Amber's fault—as always, the blame rested with Holly. "I just need to be alone right now, okay?"

Amber accepted her answer, though Holly did notice the almost imperceptible slide of Amber's gaze, making one more quick scan of the room, as though she had the ability to detect drugs with the brush of her eyes. "If you need anything, I'll be in the kitchen."

Amber closed the door behind her, and Holly threw herself onto the bed. She wanted to scream into her pillow. She wanted to thrash and kick. Her head was splitting and there was nothing to deaden the pain —nothing to kill the anxiety and numb the hopelessness.

Why? Why was she like this? Was she just a miserable person? What made the contentment, that others seemed to have, so unattainable for her? Was she broken inside beyond repair? Was she truly incapable of crawling out of her own filth?

She coiled on the bed in torment. The killer was about to call her, and all she could think about was dropping an Oxy. The relief they offered was temporary and fleeting, yet she longed for it. Her body was being destroyed by them, but she didn't care. Somewhere deep inside there was a desire to be dead, forever separated from the pain of her life.

She ripped herself from the bed. It wasn't just *her* life anymore. She was responsible for another, one far more precious than her own. He didn't deserve to watch his mother waste away. She owed him more than simply bringing him into this world. If there was one thing the killer had right, it was that she had a responsibility to give her son a home, a good home, and that was going to start today!

She went into the kitchen, opened the cabinet under the sink, and tore the pill package from where it was taped behind the sink drum. Dan stood in the doorway, but said nothing.

She pulled herself to her feet, stomped down the hall past Amber, who had opened the door to her bedroom to find out who was making the noise, and poured the contents of the bag into the toilet. Her hand began slapping the handle on the flush, but the slap turned into a pound, and the pound grew fiercer and fiercer. She beat at it until the bottom of her hand was bloody and the handle shattered. Dan snatched her fist as it rose up to strike the jagged plastic left on the broken handle.

She began screaming and kicking, but he gripped her tighter. "I hate them! I hate them! I hate them!" she screamed over and over until finally her body went limp, and her voice dropped to a whisper. "I hate them..."

Dan's voice cut through the dead space around her. "You got this, Holly. You can kick this thing."

She looked up at him as if for the first time. Who was this guy holding her with his strong arms? No one had ever believed she could do anything. But he did, and it wasn't an act. It wasn't a show of pity. He believed in her. She touched the bloody scars on his arm where she had dug him earlier, and began to cry. "I hurt you, Dan. I'm so sorry." She ran her hand down his forearm, surveying the wounds he had taken.

"It's okay," he said with a weak smile. "It only hurts a lot."

She smeared the tears down her cheek with the back of her hand and let out a half-laugh. How was he able to find humor even in this? She studied his face. This wasn't a joke to him. There was real concern in his eyes, not pity or condemnation, but a genuine concern for her safety. And something else—a vulnerability that made her feel as though they were both wounded animals, helping each other survive. His honesty melted her defenses, and her muscles loosened.

"I'm a mess aren't I?" She pushed the curls to the side.

"You're the messiest," he said.

She hit his chest with her hand and flinched as pain shot up her wrist.

Worry flashed on his face as he cradled her hand. "Easy. Easy."

She sniffed again and let out a short quiet breath. "I'll be okay. It probably looks worse than it is."

"Do you want to wash it off?"

"Yeah," she said. "I can get it. Do you mind?" She gestured toward the door.

"Not at all." He turned and took a step away.

She gripped his arm. "Dan?"

He looked back. "Yes?"

"Why are you so nice to me?"

His face took on a serious expression and he nodded to himself, as if it was time he confessed a deep inner secret he had been holding back. "Truth be told," he said, "I'm hoping you'll validate my parking."

She pushed him out of the bathroom. "I should have known better than to ask you a serious question."

"You're right," he said, "I'm way better with unserious questions. Quick, ask me an unserious question." The door clicked shut.

She heard him stand for a moment, then walk back to the kitchen. She wanted to revel in the momentary relief Dan had given her—but it was almost noon and the killer would be calling. She washed her hand, wrapped it with gauze from the First Aid Kit, and slipped back into her bedroom.

The clock above her bed gave her three minutes. She folded the covers up and pulled the radio from the hole. Her throat tightened. What if Dan and Amber heard him? She slid the lock on her bedroom door, then climbed into the back of her closet on the other side of the room. There was a volume knob on the top of the radio, and, based on the markings, she had it turned almost completely off. She gripped it nervously with her thumb and index finger, focusing on the tactile feel of it—while the darkness pressed in on her.

The page light flickered and the beep sounded. She held it close to her mouth. "I'm here."

Static whispered from the device. She turned the volume up to hear his response. "You are not alone," he said in the familiar digital base.

"I'm in the closet. No one can hear." Her heart started racing.

Silence filled the tiny space. Then... "Did you drop the package?"

"Yes," she said. "But the FBI was there."

"Good. I want them to know who I am. It's all part of telling my story."

She squeezed the radio. "Are you Gary?"

The response was almost immediate. "I'm tired, that's who I am, tired of this world, tired of this burden. You're going to tell the world my story and then you're going to save your son's life. That's what you need to know. Do you understand?"

"Yes..."

"Are you listening?"

"Yes."

"This is what I want you to do. I want you to call every news station in the telephone directory and tell them who you are and that something big is going to happen on the 395 overpass at exactly 2:00 p.m. today." He waited for her response.

"I'll call them and tell them."

"You will tell them who you are," he enunciated clearly, "and that something big is going to happen on the 395 overpass at exactly 2:00 p.m. today. Repeat it."

She fumbled with the radio and repeated his request word for word.

"There is a compartment in the bottom of this radio. Inside you will find two ear pieces. At exactly 1:30 you will put them in your ears and put the radio in your pocketbook. From there I will give you

243

instructions on where to go and what to say. Do you understand?"

"Yes."

"I want you to go into Gabe's room and write 395 overpass 2:00 p.m. in blocks on the floor. Tell them I wrote it. Do you understand?"

"Yes."

"If you do everything I have explained to you, every eye in the world will be on you, and my story will be heard. That is what I want. Your son does not need to die. You can save him. Repeat it. I can save my son."

"I can save my son." She choked on the words.

"Do you believe it, Holly?"

"Yes."

"Tell my story, and save your son."

The radio went dead. She quickly ran through the instructions in her head. Write the note in blocks. Make the phone calls. Put the earbuds in at 1:30. All she had to do was tell his story, and her son would live. She could do that. She had to. She had to save her son.

CHAPTER 41

Jake Paris headed down Main Street, through Sunbury Center, and up toward the Sunbury Theater House where Jenna was working. He circled once and found a parking space down the street. There was an entrance in the back of the theater. He took it and walked down through creaky back corridors, behind the stage, and down the old concrete stairs that led to the room on stage right. He met a man coming up.

"I'm looking for Jenna. Have you seen her?"

"Yeah, man. She was with Mina near the dressing rooms."

"Is that down here?"

"No. That way," he said, pointing.

Jake headed up the stairs and down the other hallway in the direction the man had pointed. It brought him to a large room filled with costumed people, stage hands, and props. To the left were several doors with name plates on them. He walked down until he got to the door with Jenna's name on it.

"Can I help you?" said a round man in an untucked dress shirt and cargo shorts. He shoved his thick glasses up the bridge of his nose.

"I'm Jenna's boyfriend. I need to talk to her."

"I'm sorry, you can't be back here. I'll tell her you're here."

"It will only take a second," Jake said, standing his ground.

The man pointed to a set of stairs. "You can wait in the lobby. There are refreshments you can enjoy while you wait."

"You don't understand..."

He gripped his clipboard. "Please don't make this awkward for both of us. She is under a tight schedule and..."

Jake pounded his fist on the door. "Jenna! It's Jake! Open up!"

The round man flagged another man whose neck was as big as his head. He looked Polish—and angry.

Jake pounded harder. "Jenna! I need to talk to you! Please!"

Most of the eyes in the room were now on Jake, and on his impending removal from the theater.

The big man approached, and Jake threw his hands up. "Okay, big guy. No one needs to get hurt."

The man towered over Jake, his muscles practically ripping his tank top. "I'm going to ask you once, nicely," he said, "then there will be a lot of pain."

The door to the dressing room flew open, and Mina stood there quickly fastening her robe. "Jake!" she said, in her Mediterranean accent. "What are you doing here?"

"I need to talk to Jenna," he called past her. "Jenna!"

"Come on!" said the meaty Polish man, gripping Jake by the back of the shirt.

Mina held her hand up. "Stop! I'll handle thees. I know you're jus' trying to help, but I think he should know."

246

"She's not gonna like this, Mina," the round man stammered. "You tell him, she'll kill you."

Jake's eyes flashed from him to Mina. "What is he talking about, Mina?"

"Thees man has gone through enough in the las' couple of days, and he has a right to know."

"Know what?" said Jake.

She pulled him into the room and shut the door.

"Seet," she said. She hopped over to the counter. The cast on her right foot peeked out from the bottom of her satin robe.

"I'm freaking out here. What's going on?"

"Well you're here, so you must suspect something." Her accent caused her to enunciate the consonants. "What ees it you suspect?"

"I- I don't know. She just didn't sound right on the phone. Mina, tell me. Please."

"I think you know."

Did he know? There was something nagging at him, but he hadn't fully worked it out in his mind. So he was surprised to hear the words fall from his tongue. "Is Jenna pregnant?"

Mina's eyes watered; she gave an almost imperceptible nod.

Jake's eyes grew big. Was Aiyana *his* child? His mind raced. Now that he thought about it, she did resemble Jenna.

"You know how much you love Jenna?"

He looked at her, confused by the question. "Ah, yeah, of course." He blinked, still trying to digest the fact that he was going to be a father.

"I love her dat much. Maybe moor. And by telling you thees, I may ruin our friendship forever. Do you see how dis hurts my heart?"

He nodded.

"She is so scared, Jake. She doesn't wan to lose you, and yet she feels you slipping away."

"Why would she think that?"

"Because she wans you to commit to her forever and you don! She wans you to prove you will always love her, but you don."

"How? Marriage? We have an understanding. It doesn't have anything to do with her. I'm just not ready."

"She things you are jus' not certain she wheel be the one—and she is afraid."

"Well if she's pregnant, that certainly changes everything. I don't have a choice."

"That ees the problem," she said.

Jake blinked, then squinted at her. "Sorry, I'm lost."

"She does not wan you to choose her because you have to, she wans you to choose her because she is the one you wan to spend the rest of your life with."

"So—she would rather hide the baby from me and—what?" His voice grew intense. "Is she planning to leave me?"

Her chin quivered and a tear crawled down her cheek. "She loves you too much to leave you."

Jake's pulse quickened. What was Mina saying? Jenna would rather kill the baby? He launched to his feet. "Mina, you need to square up with me. Is she planning something stupid?"

She licked her lip nervously. "She planned dis a week ago, but couldn't go through with it."

He gripped his head. "That's why she's been prodding me about our future and having children. I'm so *stupid!*"

"She was going to tell you, but then everything changed yesterday. I hurt my foot and she found out you lost your job and..."

"She knows about that?"

"Yes. Your boss called the apartment and left a message for you. She figured it out."

"Where is she now?"

Mina shook her head.

"Mina! Where is Jenna now?!"

"She asked to take the rest of the day off to go to an appointment. She wans to get this done before it turns into more than just a blob of tissue."

Jake's mouth hung open. He felt like he was coming apart at the seams. "She's a child, Mina. Our child. She's beautiful, and she's talented like her mom." He choked back the emotion. "And she notices things, things other people miss. She's quiet and gentle..."

He looked at Mina who was trying to understand what he was saying, and a realization washed over him. Jenna didn't understand either. She didn't know what she was doing. She hadn't seen what he had seen. She had no idea the beauty she would be destroying. All she was thinking was that her future was going to be destroyed by a baby she wasn't ready to have, and she wanted to stop it before it was more than just a blob of tissue!

Jake grabbed Mina by the shoulders. "Where is her appointment, Mina?"

Mina pulled back, wide eyed. "She's probably not there yet."

"Then where is she?"

"She said she was going home first."

He started for the door.

"Please," she said, "if there is any way, don' tell her I told you. Tell her you figured it out on your own. I can' bear to lose her as a friend."

"No matter what happens, Mina," he yelled over his shoulder, "you did the right thing!"

CHAPTER 42

Angela Grant's belly grumbled as she clicked through the clinic records. The bureau in Washington was given a new angle to check, and they were crunching the numbers while she searched locally. If Gary Carter was running scared, as she suspected, then the real killer had to have contacted him in the last three years. There had to be a phone record, an email, something. It could be someone from one of the branch clinics he visited on trips, or someone working at the clinic in Sunbury. Whoever it was, he had revealed himself to Carter, and Carter refused to be a part of it. That was her guess.

She had spent years studying the behavior of serial killers. If Carter was the Cape murderer, he wouldn't have left evidence from his victims in his place of work, or made searches for serial killers on his computer. There would have been no connection at all to his secret life. At work, he would have been a different person, not even allowing thoughts of his secret sin to enter into his mind. It would be as if he were two people, living two separate lives. Whatever role Carter played in all of this, he wasn't the Cape murderer, that much she was sure of.

But was Carter a victim? Did the killer prey upon him for some resource only he could provide? A name of a victim? Miss Paris' name? The clinic records indicated that Holly Paris had visited the clinic when she was fourteen. Was there a connection between that visit and her selection as a target? If so, that brought up another question. Why was Gary Carter dating Holly's roommate? Perhaps the killer had convinced Carter to help at first, but Carter got cold feet?

Perez tapped Angela on the shoulder and sat on the desk next to her. "We got a hit."

Angela swiveled in her chair.

"Carter's sister owns a camp on a lake just south of Sunbury. According to a neighbor, the camp's supposed to be empty, but there was a mysterious pin point of light in the basement window last night. We went by there yesterday and left a card, so they called us. Local law enforcement checked it out this morning. The window is covered with cardboard, and someone has been there recently. There are tracks on the path up to the door that would have been washed away by last weekend's rain."

"That's sounds promising. Have they set up a perimeter?"

"Yeah. They have local police, SBI, and forest rangers on site. They're waiting for the go ahead."

"How far is it from here?"

"Thirty minutes."

"Tell them to hold tight. I want to be the first to question him if he's there."

"There's more." His face scrunched. "Holly Paris is making calls to local news agencies claiming that something big is going to happen at 2:00 on the 395 overpass."

She sat back in the office chair with a squeak. "Hmmm."

"Two officers have been dispatched to question her."

"Do you think the killer is in contact with her?"

He shrugged.

"I want you to go over and check it out personally while I head up to the camp. If what Holly says is true—we're running out of time."

CHAPTER 43

Jake ran up the stairs toward the lobby of the theater, digging out his phone as he climbed. He punched Jenna's number in and put it to his ear. It rang four times then dumped him to voicemail. "Jenna I know what you're doing, and I understand why you think you have to do this, but please, call me. I really need to talk to you." He ended the call as he crested the stairs.

Downtown was congested with lunch-hour traffic, and Jake's temper was hot. After several near-misses and a number of angry honks, he tore into the parking lot of The Schoolhouse and ran inside.

"Hold the elevator!" His arm snagged on the metal post between the double doors at the entrance of the building, drawing blood. He wobbled to regain his balance and ran toward the closing doors of the elevator. "Hold the elevator!"

A hand appeared in the crack and the doors started to open back up. Jake got in and turned to see his red-haired neighbor standing toward the front corner.

"Thanks," he said, gulping for air, and wiping the sweat from his face. He looked around for her daughter, but she was conspicuously missing. "Where's your daughter?" he said, hoping to make light conversation and take the attention off his obvious emergency.

She turned to him, stunned, then her face took on an air of disgust. "What's that supposed to mean?"

The doors of the elevator sealed them in together, and immediately Jake wished he had taken the stairs.

"Is this some kind of sick joke? Do you think this is funny?" Her posture became threatening.

Jake took a step back and threw his hands up. "I-didn't mean anything. I was just curious where she was."

"Oh, just curious where *she* was? What are you, some kind of an activist? Have you been following me?"

"No! Why would I follow you?"

The elevator dinged, and the door began to open.

"Look, moron," she said, driving a finger toward him. "Stay out of my business!" She stomped off the elevator and down the hall to the left.

He had no idea what he had just stepped in, but clearly there was something going on with his neighbor and her daughter. Probably an ugly custody battle. That would explain what the little girl had said to him earlier. She knew her mother was giving her up, and she wanted him to let her know that she forgave her. Jake had clearly messed up the chances of that happening. There was no way that fiery redhead was going to let him get anywhere near her now.

The door slammed, but it sounded a mile away. Jake had already given up worrying about his neighbor's plight and was in a full run down the hallway to his own apartment.

255

"Jenna!" he screamed as he entered. "Jenna!" He ran through the living room and brushed past the recliner. The door to the bathroom was open, he could see that it was empty. The bedroom was also empty— and some of Jenna's drawers had been left open. He cursed and flew back down the hallway. At the threshold of the living room, Jake came to an abrupt stop. In its center stood Aiyana, quietly gripping her sketch pad.

"She's not here," she said with a mouse of a voice.

"Can we catch her? Did she just leave?"

"We are in the car together. At the lights."

"Where?"

"I don't know. I'm sorry." The corners of her mouth squeezed down, and her chin tightened.

"No, don't cry. It's okay. We'll catch her." He snatched her up in his arms and started for the door. "You said you're in the car with her?"

"Yes."

He pushed through the door without closing it behind him. "You can be with her and me at the same time?"

"Yes."

"Good. Can you see outside the car?" He ran to the elevator and pushed the button.

"There's a sign with flowers."

"Is there a big yellow flower?"

"Yes, and little purple ones."

"You're there right now?"

"Yes."

"That's good. That's just up the hill."

"We're moving again," she squeaked. "I'm scared."

He pounded the panel on the elevator. "Come on!"

Ding. The doors took forever to open.

Aiyana clutched his shirt with her small hand. "I don't want to leave. Please don't make me leave."

Was she talking to him—or Jenna?

"I've got you," he said reflexively. "Everything is going to be okay."

Jake pushed on the doors to force them open, then started running for the side exit. He slammed through the door and raced down the concrete steps that lead to the parking lot.

"Don't make me go!" she squealed.

Suddenly he passed through her as though she were mist. He skidded to a stop. He spun and looked for her as though she had been taken by physical means. The shock of losing her played tricks on his mind. There was no attacker. There was no escape route. It was him, alone on the stairs. Get a grip, Jake! He thought.

She wasn't dead. She was still alive with her mother in the car! He just had to catch up with them. He vaulted over the railing, slid down the grass to the parking lot, and ran to his car. He ripped his phone out of his pocket and punched Holly's number into it. It was busy. He called Dan instead.

"Yellow?" said Dan.

"Oh, thank God, Dan. Are you with Holly?"

"She's kinda busy."

"I need her, Dan."

"She's on the phone, man."

Jake peeled out of the parking lot and headed up the hill toward the florist. "I know she's on the phone, that's why I called you!"

"One second." He heard him talking to her.

The phone rumbled, then Holly spoke. "This is a bad time, Jake."

"Holly I need your help."

"Like I've needed your help? Where've you been?"

"I'm caught up in something—I've been checking in. Ask Dan. If anything new came up with Gabe, I would have been there. Something is going on with Jenna, and I need you!"

Holly was quiet, but he could hear her frustrated breathing. "What do you need?"

"I found out that I'm going to be a father, Holly. But Jenna's going to the clinic to abort her."

"What?"

"I don't know where it is, and I'm trying to catch her. I'm at the florist on Center Street. Do you know where that is?"

"Yeah. Across from the pizza place, right?"

"Yes. I'm there now. How do I get to the clinic from here?"

"Do you know how to get to Pine Street?"

"Yes."

"Follow that all the way to the intersection at Mall Road and keep on going about a hundred feet past the intersection. Their driveway is on the right across from the optometrist's office. There's a sign as you drive in, it will have the number on it. Look for Doris Boardman."

"Okay. Doris Boardman."

"I'm sorry, Jake, but I have to go. God, I hope you catch her."

"Wait. If I don't catch her, how do I get into the clinic?"

"You can't. They have bullet proof glass and reenforced metal doors. If you don't catch her, it's over."

Jake gripped the steering wheel and let his frustration channel into it. "Can I call them? Will they let me in if I explain the situation?"

"I don't think they will. You know, patient confidentiality... They can't even tell you if she's in there."

"You're kidding me!" He raced through a yellow light. "Then I'll just have to catch her."

"Wait a second! There is something you can do." Her voice lowered. "But you have to promise you won't tell anyone I told you this."

"I promise, Holly."

"I mean bring it to your grave."

"Holly. You know me. I won't tell anyone."

"There is an office on the side of the building." She spoke low. "It has a large window. You can't immediately see it because it's on the side of the complex facing the forest. Follow the mulch down the side of the building to just past halfway. Inside, you'll

259

see an L shaped chestnut desk. The window is unlocked."

"Got it."

"And if you find anything buried in the dirt outside the window..."

"What?"

"Never mind, forget I said anything."

"O-kay..." Jake looked in his rear-view mirror. "No! No! You've got to be kidding me!"

"What? What is it?"

He clenched his jaw. "I'm being pulled over."

CHAPTER 44

Holly sat across from Agent Perez at the kitchen table. He was an intimidating hulk of a man, six feet tall and mostly muscle—except for his gut—with a face that looked like the sheer side of a mountain. But when he spoke, his deep raspy voice had a calming effect on her. "We're on your side, Holly. If the perpetrator is communicating with you, we can help, but you gotta let us in."

Did she dare let them in? She believed he wanted to help, but he was just like the rest. His hands were bound in red tape, his every course of action guided by some rule or regulation. She couldn't afford to be betrayed by a force beyond his control. "I've already told you, I acted on my own."

"You found blocks in your son's room and decided to call the news instead of the authorities who are working to rescue your child?"

His reasoning shut her down.

"I know you're scared, Holly, but this doesn't have to go down this way. You don't have to play his game."

"I told..."

He slammed the table with his hand.

She flinched.

"You told us lies, and lies won't save your son!"

Dan spoke up from the corner of the kitchen. "Hey, ease up, man."

Perez turned on him. "If you interrupt again, I'll have you removed from the premises."

Dan started pacing like a wild horse.

"There's something you're not telling us, Holly, and we're going to find out what it is."

Her neck tightened. "You're wasting your time grilling me when you should be searching that bridge."

"We have a unit dispatched." He studied her a moment. "What I can't figure out is, why aren't you upset?"

"About what?"

"Something big is going to happen at 2:00 on the overpass? Have you even thought about this? Your son has been taken by a known killer, Holly. Have you thought about what this might mean?"

He was right. Why wasn't she upset? In Perez' mind, the killer had left the location of her son's dead body, and she wasn't upset. She wasn't acting like a worried mother, she was acting like an accomplice. He had every reason to think she had been contacted by the killer—and she had no way to convince him otherwise.

"I don't know what it means."

His eyes disengaged. "You know what it means. You're not that naïve."

"If you're implying that my son is dead, you don't know that."

"That's how this guy operates. He takes a child. He kills the child. Then he leaves his calling card."

His words had a ring of truth to them, and a part of her was able to respond with the correct emotion.

There was a very real possibility that the killer was merely toying with her. Her son could be dead on the overpass, the promise of letting him live could be a lie.

Tears filled her eyes. "My son is alive. He has to be. As soon as I stop believing that, I have nothing."

His eyes narrowed. "Why are you protecting this guy?"

She turned her head from his judgmental stare.

Agent Perez creaked in his chair and leaned forward. "He told you your son would live, didn't he?"

She willed herself to not respond to the jolt of shock. He was right. It was obvious. There was no other reason for her to deny the meaning of the blocks. There was no other reason for her to call news agencies and have them circle around her dead son like buzzards.

"What is he planning, Holly?"

She looked through the sweaty curls hanging like vines across her face.

"Take me to the bridge, and I'll show you."

CHAPTER 45

Angela Grant pulled her gun from its socket. She could smell the cologne of the agent in front of her and hear the footsteps of the agents behind her crunching leaves under foot as they moved into a line. The water on Phillips Lake was still and barren of boating activity. It would have been a nice day to go for a swim or go fishing in the cool breeze and warm sunshine—with the piney mountain and blue sky painted in the distance.

Instead she was heading into the den of a cornered animal. The earbud in her left ear buzzed.

"Alpha Team in position."

"Copy. Bravo Team has eyes."

"Charlie in position."

"Go, go, go!"

She placed a hand on the Kevlar vest of the agent in front of her, and the line began to move. There was a pop, and the front door splinted, leaving a hole where the handle had been. The first three agents disappeared inside.

The earbud said, "Rear and kitchen clear."

She followed her choreographed path through the living room to the left of the basement door. "Living room clear."

The basement door was locked. An agent slapped a charge on it. "Basement door has the charge."

She and the other six agents moved back. There was a flash and a bang. The agents pushed down into the basement.

The earbud went crazy. "We have contact! We have contact!"

She heard shouting as she descended the steep stairs.

"Get down! Hands where we can see them! Down! Down on the floor!"

The basement was filled with shelves of food, a cot in the corner, a table, and a television next to it. In the center of the room, a thin man in jeans and dress shirt lay on the floor with a shotgun next to him. Agents were working to handcuff him and read him his rights.

Angela said, "Basement secure. Suspect is in custody."

"This is Bravo, perimeter is secure. There is no activity."

"This is Charlie. Attic is secure."

She pulled the earbud out of her ear, coiled the cord, and shoved it in her pocket. The middle-aged man with neatly trimmed beard and mustache was lifted and put into an old rusted kitchen chair.

Angela cocked her head. "Dr. Carter?"

He looked up with fierce eyes.

"You're a hard man to reach. Are you on vacation?" She kept her tone light and indifferent.

His eyes brushed the floor and probed the dark corners of the room.

"Do you care to tell us why you are hiding in the basement of your sister's camp?"

"I'm not hiding," he said.

She surveyed the room. "It looks like you planned on staying here a while." She indicated the evidence. "Shelves of food, cot, television. Does your sister know?"

His chest heaved up and he blew a breath through his nose.

"We have evidence connecting you to the murder of four children..."

Shock flashed across his face. "What?! What evidence?!"

"We found hair samples in your file drawer at work. That, and photographic evidence showing you at two of the four crime scenes, gives us enough to put you away for a very long time."

Sudden rapid-eye-movement, just as Angela expected. This was not the behavior of a serial killer. Carter was processing what he had just learned, searching for a way out of the trap that had been set for him.

"You're not the killer, are you?" she said, watching for the appropriate response. At first there was surprise. Then a hint of relief, followed by introspection. What was he thinking about? Had he been coerced? Threatened?

"Did the killer threaten you or your family?"

His eyes darted up and locked onto hers. He looked scared.

"Okay. I get it. You're worried about your family. You don't want to tell me anything because you're afraid of what the killer will do to them."

"I didn't say..." He looked around at all the agents in the room, and shut down.

She looked at Agent Blake from the SBI standing beside her. "Clear the room."

He turned his back to Carter. "You know we can't leave you alone with the suspect."

"I'm aware of the policy," she snapped. "Leave a man at the bottom of the stairs to observe, but otherwise, clear the room."

He nodded silent agreement. The agents made one last sweep of the basement and filed out until it was just Angela, Agent Blake, and Carter.

"Does this work for you, Dr. Carter?"

He assessed the distance between him and Agent Blake at the foot of the stairs, and dropped his voice. "I'm being framed. I didn't do this. I couldn't possibly..."

"That's what we suspected. But you need to tell us who *is* doing this."

He hung his head and stared at the floor. "Promise me." His voice faltered. "Promise me you won't hurt her."

The hair rose on the back of Angela's neck. She hadn't even considered the possibility of the killer being a woman.

"She doesn't know what she's doing. It- it's like there are two of her."

"How long have you known the identity of this killer?"

"Only five months for sure, but I suspected it for over a year."

"You do realize this makes you an accomplice? Why didn't you go to the authorities?"

The light from the lantern flickered in the whites of his eyes as he looked up. The shadows danced across his hard features. "Because I love her. That's why."

CHAPTER 46

Agent Perez and the agent with him in the front seat of the car hadn't spoken a word since they left Holly's apartment. Dan was also surprisingly quiet. The tension in the car was a living creature, watching for movement, waiting to devour the first to speak—and none of the occupants were willing to be its first victim.

Traffic was backed up long before they reached the overpass to 395. Random horns could be heard in the distance, and the car periodically jolted to a stop.

Holly looked in the rear-view mirror at Agent Perez whose eyes were fixed on the traffic in front of them. She leaned toward her door and casually pressed in on the earbud seated in her left ear, fearful that it would slide from its place and expose her secret companion.

The earbud buzzed. "When you come to a stop, go to the right edge behind the channel 8 news van and wait for instructions."

She looked at the agent's eyes in the mirror reflexively, half expecting him to be looking back with suspicion. He was not. His eyes were still on the car in front of them.

Holly digested the instructions and meekly turned her eyes toward Dan. He was so quiet; it felt wrong somehow. She would not have been adverse to one of his ill-timed jokes, and it might have brought her some

semblance of comfort to have him banter mercilessly
with the agents in the front seat. Anything to not feel
smothered in silence. But Dan had taken Agent Perez
seriously when he threatened to have him removed; he
hadn't said a word since. Holly wouldn't have believed
that Dan had the self-control to not blabber on and on,
but once again he'd surprised her. There was more to
Dan Clark than she had ever expected.

What might have happened if she had responded
to that note in the eighth grade? What would her life
have been like with someone safe like Dan by her
side? But—then there would have been no Gabe. That
much she did not regret about the road she had taken.
She would gladly face all the pain again if it meant
having him. She'd made so many bad choices out of
weakness, but he was her one victory. Her precious
baby was the prize for not taking the easy road—for
once in her life.

She had used so many men for the drugs that
would kill her sorrow, and they had used her. But
looking at Dan sitting next to her, so brave and quiet,
she had a glimmer of hope that things could be
different. With him she might actually be happy. She
slid her hand on top of his and was grateful that he
didn't move it away. His skin was warm to the touch;
she soaked it in.

He pulled his eyes from the window and looked
down at her hand on top of his, then spread his fingers
to allow her to grip them. They didn't smile, they didn't
speak. It was enough to simply be connected.

On the 395 overpass was the most organized media circus Holly had ever seen. News trucks, news cars and miscellaneous vehicles lined the breakdown lane from where the bridge started all the way to the peak where a small group spoke with police officers. The right lane was blocked off by squad cars with lights flashing, and an officer was directing traffic to move past. Agent Perez flashed his badge. The officer waved him straight ahead behind the orange cones running up the center of the bridge.

Near the center the car came to a stop. Agent Perez looked over his shoulder. "Here we are. Now what are you going to show me?"

"We have to go to the side of the bridge. It's over there."

"What's over there?" he said.

"What I want you to see." She pulled on the handle to her door, but it was locked. Her brows tightened as she peered at him in the rear-view mirror. "Am I under arrest?"

"You're not leaving until you tell me what we're going to look at."

She snarled. "If I'm not under arrest, you better open this door right now."

Their eyes stayed locked for an excruciating five seconds, until Dan said, softly, "...Awkward..."

"Fine," said Perez. "I'll let you out, but if you're deceiving me, I will cuff you, and you will be under arrest."

The door lock clicked, and Holly got out, followed quickly by the others. She walked around the back of the car, grabbed Dan by the crook of the arm, and dragged him between the parked cars to the side of the bridge.

A woman from one of the local television stations locked onto Holly and pushed through the group and between the cars. "Miss Paris, may I have a word with you?!"

Dan stepped between them. "She's not talking to anyone right now."

"Miss Paris, what do you believe the killer intends to do?"

More reporters began moving in their direction.

The agents flashed their badges. "Step back or you will be charged with obstruction of justice." They pushed the group back between the cars, and Holly pulled Dan toward the peak of the bridge.

The earbud came to life again. "Climb up onto the cement rail and shout, 'I'm going to jump!' Make it sound convincing!"

Holly pulled away from Dan and looked around frantically. Was the killer near? Was he watching from one of the vehicles on the side of the bridge? She looked at the cement edge and cringed. The drop was at least a hundred feet.

"Do it now, Holly, or your son dies!"

Dan was watching her with concern. There was no way he would let her climb onto the cement wall. Once again she was taken by surprise at the turn of events and was unprepared to do what she was being directed to do. She looked at the confusion around her as the agents and police kept the media at bay.

The earbud buzzed again. "This is your last warning."

She swung her arm around and pointed. "HE HAS A BOMB!" The crowd turned and some ducked for cover. Dan pivoted to see what she was pointing at and made an attempt to shield her.

She seized the few brief seconds to clamor up onto the cement edge. The lip was two feet wide, but it felt like inches. The dizzying height caused her balance to falter as she stared down at the rushing rapids below. The dam upriver had a cycle of opening and closing which caused a high and low tide in the river. It was currently at low tide. Water bubbled and churned around large rocks below. There had been discussion by the local municipalities about putting up a chain link fence on the bridge, but the lack of suicides had kept the wheels of progress from moving forward.

Holly forced herself to turn her back to the dangerous scene below, and one by one every eye turned back to her, including Dan's. With clenched fists she took a deep breath and shouted.

"I'm GOING TO JUMP!"

CHAPTER 47

Dr. Carter slumped forward. "Have you ever been in love?"

Angela crouched down. "Yes."

"Have you ever been so in love you were willing to do anything to protect that person?"

"Yes."

"Before I realized what was going on, I had fallen deeply in love with her. I still am. But she is broken. The pain of her childhood has split her in two. I wanted to fix her and make her whole again, but as we got closer to her birthday, to the day when her other-half takes complete control, I realized it was going to happen again. And I knew I had to do something. I thought the two halves of her were separate, and I tried to convince her to stay with me in a locked room till the day passed. But she turned during the conversation, and her other half tried to convince me to help. She said we were the same. In some sick way she sees herself as helping children. She thinks she is helping them avoid the torment she faced as a child—assuming it is better for them to go into oblivion than live this tortured life."

He looked down at his hands and heaved a sigh. "I asked her, what about the women? What about the pain she is causing them? And that's when I saw the evil inside her. She hates the mothers of these children. She wants them to suffer for their crimes. That's how she sees it. She can't understand why a thief is locked in prison for stealing a television, while negligent mothers roam free on our streets."

Angela interrupted. "I appreciate your testimony, but time is of the essence. She's threatened to do something at 2:00 today and we need to stop her. It's 1:50. We need a name, and we need it now."

"But she'll kill them," he said, hanging his head.

"Who?"

"My friends and family." He looked up. "She doesn't want to hurt the innocent, but she said I would be the one hurting them. She said her anger toward me for making her hurt them would make their suffering all the more violent. That's why I went underground. I was afraid you would interrogate me and I wouldn't be able to stay quiet. It is all for them." His eyes pleaded. "Promise me you'll handle this with discretion."

"You have my word. I will only do what is necessary to stop this from happening."

He looked at agent Blake then back at Angela. "I'll whisper it to you, and only you. But you didn't hear it from me."

She fastened the strap on her hand gun, and leaned in. "I'm listening."

His voice was dry in her ear, but there was no mistaking what he said:

"It's Amber Flynn."

Holly wobbled in the wind as the crowd pushed in toward the edge, and traffic came to a complete stop. Every eye was on her teetering form on the cement barrier.

Dan reached up, but she screamed, "Don't!"

He froze. The look on his face was a mixture of horror and confusion. "Holly—what are you doing?"

"Don't touch me!"

He looked over the edge and back up at her. "Holly, come on." He fought to keep his voice level. "Come on, Holly. Get down."

Agent Perez edged in. "Listen to me, Holly, whatever he told you to do, you can't trust him. He's using you. He's..."

"STAY BACK!" she screeched.

The earbud buzzed. "Tell them you have a demand."

"I have a demand!"

"Tell them you want a microphone."

"I want a microphone!"

Dan crept forward.

She turned on him with ferocity. "BACK OFF!" Her head snapped up. "I want a microphone!"

Every news agency scrambled to be the first to give her one.

The earbud buzzed again. "Tell them you want everyone to hear."

"I want everyone to hear! Make sure everyone can hear!"

Dan pleaded with her. "I don't understand. Why are you doing this, Holly?"

She shot him a venomous look.

"We can work this out. Come on, just come down. Holly—please."

She spoke so only he could hear her over the wind and the noise of the media frenzy. "You have to trust me."

The intensity of his eyes felt like an electrical current passing through her. "I trust you," he said, "I have faith in you."

No one had ever had faith in her before. How odd it should come at the worst possible moment of her life, when she was least deserving of that trust.

A man came pushing toward her through the crowd. She edged backwards. "Here," he said, "this is connected to the truck, and everyone is plugging into that so we'll all have a signal." He held out a green box with a lapel mic and black cord coiled on top.

She pointed at Dan. "Give it to him."

Dan held his hand out; the man put the unit into his palm and backed away. Dan held it out, and Holly plucked it from him like a mouse going for the cheese. He didn't attempt to grab her, but took the opportunity to move an inch closer.

She attached the mic to her shirt and clipped the box to the pocket on her shorts.

"Good," said the killer. "Now you will tell my story, pretending to be me."

The words slowly sunk in. Pretend to *be* him? And have everyone believe she was the murderer?! Was public humiliation the penalty for her crime? She wanted to protest—but how could she? The communication was only one way; all she could do was listen, and obey.

"Repeat everything I say."

She did as he requested, without hesitation, as though his voice and hers had melted into one. "I killed those children," she said. "I did it out of mercy, the mercy I was not given by my own mother. My mother was an alcoholic and a drug addict. She sold her body for drug money and did her business in the ratty one-room apartment we lived in. I was beaten by men who didn't know me, forced to gratify them in ways too painful to mention, and victimized by school bullies. To avoid torture I sought refuge in a local gang and was forced to hurt others to be accepted. By the age of nine, I had killed another human being. By the age of twelve, I had prostituted myself to protect my mother. Then at sixteen I stabbed her to death while she slept.

"What kind of life was I given? What right did my so-called mother have to bring me into her filthy world? Are you a mother, watching me right now? I am speaking to you. You have no right to make another human being suffer in the swill hole of your bad judgment! Do you hear me, mothers? Do you women hear me? You have a responsibility to make a home for your child. Something must be done. Someone must stand up and rid this world of unfit mothers! This torture can not be allowed to go on.

"Today you will see the consequence of your evil deeds. Today you will see the hopelessness of an unwanted child. Watch and remember what pain your weakness has birthed into this world!"

The earbud went quiet.

Holly teetered on the cement lip, like a hollow husk, emptied of every ounce of strength, and horrified by the words she had just shared. There was no movement in the crowd. All eyes were glued on her. Some stared in shock, some in disgust, others in pity. It was the pity she hated most.

"Do not repeat this. Just listen," said the earbud at last. "This is the part where you save your son's life, Holly. Are you listening to me? Are you ready?"

She scanned the crowd, looking for him. Where was he? He had to be here, watching. She looked into the window of every truck and every car parked on the bridge. Whole families watched out their windows in horror. There was hardly a movement on the bridge, as if time had come to a stop.

Her eyes came to rest on a blue car with its hood up in the breakdown lane on the other side of the bridge. At first her mind rejected the face in the window. After all, why would she be here? She'd said she was going to stay at the apartment. But as Holly kept her eyes locked on the window, there became no doubt it was who she thought it was.

The voice spoke in her ear again, and Holly watched in horror as Amber's lips moved just out of sync. "There is a bomb strapped to your son..."

Holly's mind reeled as she tried to comprehend. Amber?! She looked around erratically. The killer was right there, in plain sight. How could no one see her?

"...If you move from where you are standing, Holly, I will end his life with the press of a button. You know I will."

She was there in plain sight, but all eyes were on Holly! In some bizarre way, they had traded places—but for what purpose?

"I know you can see me, Holly," said the voice in her ear. "Don't be confused. Your little brain is going to think I am your sweet roommate, but you need to fight that feeling. I am a killer. What you will decide is, who have I come to kill? This is your chance to do the right thing for once in your miserable, sorry life. It is time for you to save your son. It is a trade, your life for Gabe's."

Holly's knees weakened, and Dan reached for her.

"STAY BACK!" she screeched.

He recoiled.

Amber spoke again in her deep black tone. "It's simple really. I've been killing the wrong ones. Gabe is a victim. You are the problem. He doesn't deserve to have his life cut short. He deserves a better life, a life without you."

The words sliced deep into Holly's gut.

"I love your son, Holly. If you make this one sacrifice, be assured, I will let him live. It all rests on you. Whose life is worth more?"

Amber was right. What was her life worth compared to his? When this all blew over she would go back to the Oxys and the wine. She would destroy whatever had kindled between her and Dan. It was a fairytale to believe he could actually love her. He was better off without the misery she would bring into his life. The whole world was better off without her in it. What had she ever done of value? She was a user, and so tired of feeling pathetic. At least her death would have meaning. With one act she could redeem herself —and at the same time end her pain.

She looked skyward and made her decision. All her fear and shame released into the heavens, leaving only a complete and perfect peace she had never known before. Her last thought went out to Gabe. This is for you, my love. Live a good life and make me proud. Your mom loves you.

She closed her eyes.

Opened her arms.

And fell backwards.

CHAPTER 49

Jenna's car was parked in front of the large residential-looking building that held the Doris Boardman Clinic. Part of Jake couldn't believe she was actually here. He'd held out hope that Mina was wrong, or, at the very least, that Jenna had gotten cold feet. But she hadn't. She was here. And he was too late.

He got out of the car and ran discreetly to the left corner of the building. There was no activity in the parking lot and no movement in the woods, so he ran along the mulch bed between the cover of pine trees and the left wall of the clinic until he found the window Holly had told him about. He inched along the wall, carefully peered inside, and saw the L-shaped chestnut desk she had described. He got to his knees and tested the window. As he pressed his knee down into the mulch, something hard dug into it. He brushed the top layer aside and pulled up a black key chain with a Mazda emblem in raised silver. Odd. What was Holly doing burying a key chain outside a window of the clinic? And where was the key?

There was no time to ponder the implications; he needed to get into the cover of the office. Whatever her reason, he doubted he would pursue it anyway. She had apparently taken great personal risk in exposing this secret to him in order that he might rescue his daughter. So he intended to honor her trust.

He put it into his pocket and tried the window. It was unlocked just as Holly had promised. The thick glass made it a heavy slide, but he managed to brace it with his back and worm his way inside.

The room was lightly shaded by the half-drawn blinds and the coverage of the pines outside. He closed the window gently and crept toward the door.

The light on the handle turned green and let off a beep.

Jake scrambled for cover; someone was coming in! He crawled under the desk and huddled, silently controlling his breathing. His pulse throbbed in his neck and sweat had already begun to push through the pores in his forehead.

He squeezed his eyes shut and pressed his hot ear to the cold metal under the desk. Listening. There was no sound. Why? He was sure the door lock had been activated.

He remained motionless for a couple of minutes, then slowly climbed out and peeked over the desk. The door lock was red again. Whoever had activated it had apparently changed their mind and moved on.

Finally he had caught a break.

He got up and crept toward the door again; the light turned green and beeped! Jake's heart jumped as he withdrew to the desk, but when he looked back the light was red again.

Was he somehow activating the lock? He inched forward, and the door beeped and turned green again. He was! But how? His hand patted his pocket—and it clicked in his mind. Someone had programmed the key chain to trigger the locks inside the building. But Holly didn't have that ability; it had to have been someone else. Did the key chain belong to her, or did she just know about the key chain buried under the mulch?

He forced the mystery from his mind; Jenna was in the clinic and Aiyana's life was in danger. He didn't know how long it took to get a patient through this procedure, so he assumed the worst and moved quickly. The key chain mystery would have to wait, but, for the time being, he would choose to be grateful for the access the device provided.

He turned the handle, opened the door a crack, and listened. There was no sound of footsteps or conversation, so he crept the door open and looked out. The hall was empty. Across the way was a lit examination room. He sneaked to it, peeked in, and retreated back to the office. All was clear for him to head down the hall, but which way? Going right would bring him towards the front of the building, so he decided to go left.

"Daddy?"

He jumped out of his skin and twisted around, clutching his chest. Aiyana was standing in the middle of the office; she ran and immediately threw herself onto his neck. His arms went around her and clutched her to him.

He breathed her name into her soft brown hair and tiny shoulder. "Aiyana. Are you okay?"

"I'm scared," she cried.

"I'm here, honey. I'm not going to let anything happen to you."

She gripped him tighter.

"We need to find your mom so I can talk to her, okay?"

She nodded.

"There isn't much time; I need you to help me find her."

She pulled back, still gripping his shirt.

"Can you see where she is right now?"

"Yes, she's in a white room."

"Is she alone?"

"It's just us. She's on a high bed. It has paper on it."

"Does she have one of those medical gowns on?"

Aiyana looked puzzled. "No, she's wearing her clothes."

Jake exhaled. "Good. Can you see outside the door? Is it open?"

She nodded. "It's a hallway."

"Can you walk down the hallway and look around the corner and tell me what you see?"

Her mouth bowed into a frown. "I can only go back the way we came in."

"Why is that?"

Aiyana shrugged.

"Well, can you tell me how close you are to the reception area? Do you know what that is?"

"Is it the place where the two ladies sit?"

"That's it. Walk back that way and tell me what you see."

Her eyes glossed over. "I'm leaving the room. There's a hall and another hall that goes all ways. I'm going back the way we came. There is a big door and another open door where the two ladies were, but I can't see them now."

"Okay—so your mom is back toward the entrance."

Aiyana's eyes focused on him again.

"That's good, honey. Now I know which way to go." He let go of her, took her by the hand, and opened the door. The hallway was still empty. "Come on," he whispered.

They walked quickly toward the turn. At the corner was a camera pointing up the next hall. Did they have cameras everywhere? He snapped a look back at the other corner. There was no camera back there.

He slowly peeked around the corner. A woman in blue scrubs was walking his way, but her eyes were on the clipboard in her hand. He jerked back and hid, listening for her approach, poised to run back to the office. But the sound of her footsteps quickly faded. She must have entered a room down the hall. He ventured another peek. The hall was vacant, but he could hear muffled voices.

Aiyana gripped his arm. "Someone is with us now."

He looked down at her, trembling on his arm. "Is it a woman?"

"Yes, in sky-colored clothes."

This was it. Jenna was in the room down the hall. But now what? He couldn't just go strolling into the exam room and start asking questions; he'd be thrown out for sure. He had to catch Jenna alone.

"Aiyana. Can you tell me what they're saying?"

She nodded, slightly dazed. "The woman is asking if we want to go to the other room and wait for the doctor or wait here."

"Can you communicate with your mom?"

"No. I can only talk to you. Now she's saying it doesn't matter."

"Why can you only talk to me?"

She shrugged. "We're leaving now."

"Are you coming this way," he whispered, "or back the way you came?"

"Back the way we came."

He peeked around and caught a glimpse of Jenna walking down the hall behind the nurse. He wanted to call out to her. He wanted to tell her to stop. But it wasn't time. They turned left and disappeared.

He gripped Aiyana by the elbows. "Describe where you're going so I can find you."

She tilted her head. "We're going straight to the end and we're turning."

"Which way, right or left?"

Her eyebrows scrunched. "I don't know what that means."

"Are you going farther away, or coming back this way?"

"I think farther away. We're going into another white room now. There are big lights on the ceiling, and no windows."

"Is anyone in there?"

"Just the same woman. She's telling us to sit on the bed."

Jake snatched her hand up. "Come on."

He guided her down the hall to the bend and peeked around. A large man in a white medical robe was standing five feet away with his back to them. At the far end of the hallway, the nurse appeared briefly and disappeared into another room across the hall.

The man in the white robe opened the door next to him and stepped inside. When the door clicked, Jake moved briskly down the hall. There was a camera on the ceiling at the intersection, but there was no way to avoid it. If he didn't strike while the iron was hot, there would be no second chance. He crossed over the hall and ran toward the operating room.

"Hey!" a male voice shouted behind him. "Stop!" The big man had come back out of the room and was heading their way.

Aiyana poked her head through a door." Daddy! This one!"

The lock turned green and let off a beep. He scooted into the room, closed the door, and turned the lock on the knob with one fluid motion.

"Jake?" He didn't turn to respond to Jenna, but started sliding equipment and furniture in front of the door. "What are you doing?"

"We have to talk, Jenna."

"What are you doing here?"

The doctor's shadowy form appeared in the sliver of frosted window in the door. He started pounding. "Open up!"

Jake backed away. "We don't have much time; you need to hear me out." He turned to face Jenna.

She'd been getting undressed, and was now frantically pulling her jeans back on. "Are you insane?!"

"Why didn't you tell me you were pregnant?"

She glared at him. "What? Why... It- it's complicated!"

"This isn't just your decision to make."

"It's my body!"

"But it's our child!"

"It's not a child! It's a mistake! I'm not supposed to be pregnant; I'm on the pill! How was I going to tell you, Jake? You would have thought I was playing some kind of game with you, trying to force you to marry me. I couldn't live with that!"

"But you didn't even give me a chance."

There was more pounding on the door. A hollow voice yelled, "The police are on the way!"

"Jake!" She pleaded with her eyes. "Let them in."

"Not until you promise me you won't go through with this."

"I have to! I can't wait another day. I can't let it grow inside me and become something I'll regret removing."

"She already is something, Jenna."

Jenna looked aghast. "She?"

"We're going to have a girl." He looked at Aiyana cowering in the corner. "If only you could see her, Jenna. She's beautiful and talented like you, and quietly observant like me, and when she smiles it makes my heart melt. She isn't a blob of tissue, she's a frightened little girl. She's our daughter."

The denial on Jenna's face turned to outrage. "What are you trying to pull, Jake?" She spat out his name. "Do you think this is easy for me? I'm doing this for you! I'm doing this because you lost your job, and I have a chance to help us get through this without losing everything."

"Jenna, I know you..."

"I'm doing this because I don't want you to feel trapped into marrying me."

"I know, Jenna..."

"And you come in here with this bull crap story about how this is a little *girl* inside me? How dare you? HOW DARE YOU!"

The objects in front of the door slid easily as the door pushed open. A uniformed officer pointed a pistol at Jake. "Hands where I can see 'em! Down on the floor!"

Jake could feel the weapon pointed at him; his hands flew up reflexively.

"Down on the floor!" The officer pushed past the threshold. "Down!"

Jake crumbled to the ground.

"Don't hurt him!" cried Jenna. "He's my boyfriend, and he's not armed!"

The officer gripped one wrist firmly and cuffed it. Jake's face pressed into the cold tile floor. The officer grabbed the other wrist and clamped the cuff around it. Then two sets of hands lifted him off the floor.

"Jenna! Don't do this!" Jake's voice cracked. "She's real, Jenna! Our daughter is real!"

Jenna stood like a zombie in front of the bed, with Aiyana crouched down beside her, knuckles pressed to her lips, fear glistening in her innocent eyes.

Jake began to thrash. "You have to believe me, Jenna! Don't do this! Don't! She's real! She's real!"

The police dragged him from the room.

CHAPTER 50

For Dan Clark it was like looking at high-motion film. Hundreds of frames flashed before his eyes as Holly's body fell backwards over the edge of the bridge. His eyes locked onto her ankle, and every muscle in his body launched him forward with one singular objective: snatch it! Adrenaline-heightened senses calculated the angle of her rising toes as his hands found their mark just above the foot. Her body swung down and hit hard against the side of the bridge.

"No! Let go! *Let me go!*" she screamed.

He gripped her with every ounce of his strength as her body flailed over the rapids far below. Her skin burned in his grip, and the cement bit into his triceps.

She screamed into the wind, writhing and kicking, "You're killing my son! You're killing him!"

Her words solidified what he already knew. Holly wasn't the killer. It was all just a twisted game straight out of the mind of a lunatic. Somehow he'd crawled into her head and convinced her that the only way to save her son was to take her own life, and Holly had swallowed it, hook, line, and sinker.

As she'd stood on the lip of the bridge giving her horrible confession, he knew the words were not hers. She was his childhood crush, he had watched her for years and knew things about her she probably didn't even know about herself. Holly Paris couldn't kill anyone. She wouldn't even harm a fly—quite literally.

She'd once caught a fly in a paper cup during one of their many high school study halls together, and instead of squishing it, she had released it out the classroom window. Her friends had teased her, but Dan never forgot the mercy she had shown to that insect.

"Let go!" she screamed.

Dan hung on with all his might, as Holly resisted violently. Soon Agent Perez was at his side grabbing for her other leg, and together they hauled her over the railing, kicking and thrashing.

"She's going to kill him! Let me *go!"*

They laid her on the pavement. "What are you saying, Holly?!" he said. "Do you know who has Gabe?!"

She struggled to break free. "Amber!" she screeched.

"We know," said Agent Perez. "We just got the call."

Holly's eyes opened like she was demon possessed. Her body went rigid against their restraint. "SHE'S HERE!"

Perez fought to keep her knee from catching him in the chin. "Where? On the bridge?"

"In the blue car! Across the street! Let go! Let me go!"

Dan's eyes leveled on Perez. "Don't let her go. You let her go and I'll make you pay every day of your life!" He released his grip and climbed onto the car next to them. It was enough to get him above the gathered throng. Four lanes across, he saw a blue car creeping down the breakdown lane. Was that her?

He launched off the hood and pushed through the sea of gawkers. His sneakers slapped the pavement and his arms and legs moved like a machine. The blue car had a ten car lead on him that was increasing with every step, but the traffic at the bottom of the hill would stop her. He hoped.

His lungs burned as he sprinted down the lane after the ever-shrinking car. There was a flash of brake lights as it slowed at the bottom. A squad car had pulled into the breakdown lane, cutting off her escape. The door flew open and he saw Amber scramble across to the other side of the bridge.

Dan cut in front of a crawling SUV and slid over the hood of a mustang that was sitting on the bumper of the car in front of it. Amber was heading for the edge and the railroad dump below the bridge. If she could get in there, it would be over.

He ignored the cramp in his thigh and the explosion of every capillary in his skin as he drove himself harder. She was crawling over the edge of the bridge, and he had twenty feet left to run.

She disappeared from view. He gasped for air, looking frantically over the edge. She had already made it around the area of trees below and was heading into the old train yard.

He climbed over, dangled, and dropped down onto the top of the cement embankment under the bridge. Through the trees he caught a glimpse of her running around a rusted metal barrier used to partition the junk yard. He slid down the concrete embankment and broke into a run. If she remained undetected in the old rail yard, she would probably work her way up behind the casino and attempt to get to the city center.

Dan knew this area; it was his old stomping grounds. It was a long shot, but if he could get around her while she attempted to hide in the rail yard, he could catch her when she came out behind the real estate office. It wasn't the most obvious exit, but it had the best overhead coverage. He could already hear a police helicopter in the distance.

He climbed a grassy hill and ran along the outside of the rusted metal barrier until he reached an access road leading up to the main street. She had avoided the road, because it would have exposed her, but he didn't have that issue—or at least he hoped he didn't. It would have been a terrible miscalculation if some SWAT sniper didn't get the memo that the killer was a woman.

His body was on fire when he reached the sidewalk just past the casino, all he could manage now was a brisk jog. But if he was correct, it would be enough to keep him in front of her. He scanned the junk yard below through the chain link fence that ran along the sidewalk as he jogged down to the front of the real estate office. Sweat poured from his skin as he paced in the shade under the front awning.

She had to come up this way. There was a path below that led up through tall grass to the chain link fence at the back of the parking lot behind the building. There was a good foot of erosion under it, and it was easy enough to climb under. This was the most obvious exit, and to get from the parking lot to the neighborhoods across the street, she would have to have another vehicle...

He ran down along the side of the building and came to an abrupt stop. She was climbing up under the fence, just as he had predicted.

She stood upright, and their eyes met.

Her hand came up instantly. "Dan," she said, panting for breath. "You don't know what you're doing. Just walk away." In her other hand was a phone.

He attempted to hide his exhaustion. "Why don't you explain it to me, Amber?"

She lifted the phone. "If I hit send, Gabe dies. Just let me go, Dan; it was never my intention to kill him."

They circled each other in the parking lot.

"You expect me to believe you? What have you been smoking?"

The sound of sirens and the approaching beat of helicopter blades intensified her stance.

"I don't have time for this! Do you want to be responsible for the death of Holly's son?!" she spat. "This is how this is going to go down. You are going to let me get in this car and watch me drive away, RIGHT NOW, or I am going to press this button and end Gabe's suffering!"

"How do I know you won't press it anyway?" he said, tortured by the thought.

"Because I love him." Her chin tightened and her eyes watered.

Was it true? Did she really love him? Had she planned on killing him but gotten too close? Dan tried to put a hook in reality. His next move could extinguish a little boy's life. He had to make the right call. Amber's thumb rested on the trigger. Time had run out.

He threw up his hands. "Fine! You win. Go! Just don't hurt him."

She backed toward the car, fumbled for the handle, and opened the door. But it was too late. A siren made a quick bleat as a police cruiser appeared from behind the rear of the building.

Amber turned toward Dan.

He could see the defeat written in her dead eyes. "If you had only left me alone, I would be long gone and this wouldn't have happened." She slammed the door and held the phone up where he could see it. "It's done," she said. "He's gone. You killed him."

At first the shock of her words didn't allow him to believe what she had said, but then a wave of nausea kicked him in the gut. She had pressed the button, and, just like that, it was over. There was no chance to leap for the phone, no opportunity for a last minute rescue. Gabe was dead, and it was all his fault. If he hadn't intercepted her, Gabe would still be alive. How would he ever explain this to Holly? She would never forgive him for killing her son.

Amber looked down at the phone in her hand and an odd expression crossed her face. She lifted the phone to her ear. Listened. Then her jaw went slack.

CHAPTER 51

Trees flew past outside the black sedan as Angela Grant raced down a thin country road, scanning each approaching mailbox for the number 1224. According to the directions, the mailbox was white on black, and at its base was a flower pot. There it was, exactly as it had been described.

She punched the brake pedal and pealed up the dirt driveway to a yellow house with brown shutters. The place looked deserted. All the plants on the front porch were dead, and the house looked like it hadn't been tended in months. How had her people missed that?

She strode to the front door, opened the screen and gave the knob a twist. It was locked. It would have been nice to have Perez here; he would have made easy work of the door. But he wasn't, so she had to improvise.

She looked around, grabbed a porch chair, and with one heave, threw it through a window. She blocked her face as glass exploded and wood splintered, then quickly climbed inside.

The dimly lit living room was quiet, and the air was still. She slid her handgun from its holster and listened. There was a noise coming from somewhere, but it was distant and nondescript. She bypassed a search of the first floor and headed straight up the stairs on a hunch. In the video feed, the killer was standing in a room outside of a bedroom. If her hunch was correct, Gabe would be tied up in that room.

Halfway up the stairs Angela heard people talking. She gripped her gun with both hands, and crept down the hall. Her shoulder came to rest against the wall just before a white wooden door; she strained to hear the conversation. It was a man and a woman, and there was music. Suddenly it clicked. It wasn't a live conversation, it was a movie.

She opened the door carefully, for it was not uncommon for kidnappers to leave booby traps to keep out unwanted guests. Usually the traps were rigged to be dismantled from the outside, to provide the kidnapper access in an emergency, so she went slowly, examining the door jam and the ever-increasing crack at the top and bottom of the door for any sign of a thread. It was clear.

Slowly she slid through the doorway, her weapon sweeping the room. The bedroom was empty. She moved quickly to the open door where the sound was coming from and saw light flickering from the interior. She pushed the door open with her foot and peeked around the corner. There was Gabe, in the center of the room, just as she'd hoped he would be.

It had all come together for her when Gary Carter got to the bottom of his laundry list of how he figured out Amber was the Cape murderer. He'd asked Amber about the dead plants around her grandmother's house, and she had claimed it was because her grandmother was too sick to care for them, but Carter was suspicious. Amber's grandmother had been a florist all

299

her life, and if she wasn't able to care for those flowers, he knew she would have called someone to help her. So Carter started poking around and found the grandmother's dead body in a shallow grave in the back yard.

When Gary had said this, Angela knew what had happened. Amber had come back from her flight early in the morning, took Gabe from the apartment, and brought him to her grandmother's house.

Gabe sat helpless in the center of the room, duct taped to a kitchen chair. His face was wet from crying, and the grey tape on his mouth glistened as light from the HD television reflected off the wetness. He immediately started crying again when he saw her. Her first instinct was to run to him and free him from the horrible mass of grey tentacles, but her training kicked in.

"It's okay, Gabe. I'm here to help you." She scanned for traps as she spoke gently to him. "Have you seen Amber recently?"

He shook his head.

"We're going to get you out of here, buddy, but you have to be brave for a few more seconds while I make sure everything is safe. Nod if you understand."

He nodded.

She looked carefully all around the chair. It was so small that she didn't notice it at first. But there it was. A dim red glow shining off the carpet in the direct center under the chair. She got down on her hands and knees and peered under. Strapped to the bottom of the chair was a bomb, and hanging from it was a cell phone. She had seen this type of bomb before in a class she'd recently attended. The phone acted as a trigger. There were many variations, and some were wired to go off if tampered with.

"It's okay, Gabe," she said as she snatched her Leatherman from the case on her belt. "I'm just checking everything before I cut you loose. You're doing a great job, just sit still a little longer." She wiped the sweat out of her eyes, and peered up at the device. The phone was dangling from two wires that ran into the main casing. If this was a homemade job, it was a simple matter of clipping the wires to prevent the current from getting to the trigger. If it was a professional job, there would be an internal trigger that sent a weaker signal through the loop. If that was the case, breaking the signal would detonate the bomb instantly.

Normally she would have called in a bomb squad, but with events unfolding on the bridge in Sunbury, the threat to Gabe's life was imminent. She needed to trust her instincts. The bomb had no official markings, and judging from the use of duct tape on the C4, it was most likely homemade. She opened the clippers on the Leatherman, reached up, and clipped the wires with one quick snip.

The phone fell to the carpet and immediately started ringing. This was never mentioned in the training. What did it mean? She picked up the phone and looked at the caller ID: Unknown caller.

She put the phone to her ear. "Hello?"

301

Through static she heard a car door slam and a distant female voice. "It's done. He's gone. You killed him."

Angela's body spiked with adrenaline. Had she clipped the wires at the precise moment of detonation?

She spoke louder into the phone. "Hello? This is Special Agent Angela Grant with the FBI. To whom am I speaking?"

CHAPTER 52

Holly watched as Agent Perez scratched his final notes onto the official record with his fat, brown hand. She'd been thoroughly checked out by medical, and given something to calm her nerves. But now the debrief was taking forever, and there was still no sign of Gabe. How long did it take to get from Dedham to Sunbury? Certainly not an hour. She was tired of being in the police bull pen, and tired of being the focus of morbid curiosity. The police knew she was innocent, yet they still whispered and cased her with dispassionate glances. How much more intrusive would the stares of the uninformed be? Her face would be forever synonymous with a killer of children, even though the world now knew it was all a lie. Would people be able to forget her standing on the edge of that bridge baring the soul of a psychotic butcher as though it were her own?

Perez looked up through his bushy black brows. "Do you have anything you'd like to add before we seal this thing up?"

"No. But I have questions."

He rested his forearms on the table. "What kind of questions?"

"Where is my son?"

"I told you, he had to be checked out by medical and debriefed, but he's on his way."

She scratched her wrist. "What's going to happen to Amber?"

"Dr. Carter has agreed to testify..."

"You found Gary?"

"Yes, and with his testimony and the evidence found at Amber's grandmother's house, we have enough to put her in prison for the rest of her life without parole."

"How did you find Gary?"

She could hear the gears turning inside his head. What was he allowed to tell her? What did the standard operating procedure dictate?

Some things never changed.

"We got a call from his sister's neighbor," he said. "He was hiding out at his sister's camp and the neighbor noticed light coming from the basement window."

"So, was he involved, you know, in taking Gabe?"

"No. She tried to recruit him, but he refused."

"The way they acted around each other, I thought they were really close, you know, crazy for each other."

"They might have been at one time, but usually when your girlfriend plants condemning evidence in the filing cabinet at your place of work, the relationship is pretty much over."

Holly was dumbstruck by the transparency of his statement. These official people never shared anything they didn't absolutely have to. Why then was Agent Perez sharing this so willingly? Did he know she was the one who had planted the evidence? Was he baiting her for a reaction?

"Evidence?" she said, attempting to sound only mildly curious.

"DNA evidence from the victims."

DNA evidence? It wasn't a bomb? Amber was trying to frame Gary...? Holly tried to reconcile this new information. "But—why would she plant evidence to frame Gary, and then make me pretend to be her? That doesn't make sense. Why frame both of us?"

The gears were going off in his head again.

"Please," she said, I need to know."

"My guess is, it was all a head game she was playing with you. You said she told you she wanted her story told, right?"

"Yes."

"And if you told her story, your son would live, right?"

"Yes."

"That's how she got inside your head. This was all a game to her. She never planned to let Gabe live— he had seen her face. He wasn't afraid of his kidnapper because he knew her and trusted her, that's why he was playing so peacefully in the video; and since he knew who she was, there was no way she was going to let him live."

Holly frowned.

"My guess is, she wasn't content in killing children from a distance. Apparently she wanted to get close and feel the pain she was inflicting on her prey.

She wanted to destroy you and your son. Then once the dust settled, Gary Carter would take the fall."

Was it true? Was it all a lie to convince her to jump? Her belly twisted at the thought of how easily she had been manipulated. Holly's shoulders slumped. "I bought into all her lies. How could I have been so stupid?!"

"Don't beat yourself up, Holly," he said with a surprising measure of kindness. "It could have happened to any of us. We all have doubts and fears."

She gave him a self-deprecating look.

"Hey," he said, putting his hands up in defense. "I'm afraid of mice. You give me one mouse and I'm like no problem. But you put me in a tank full of them and my consciousness is going to exit my body." His eyes flared for effect.

"Everyone's afraid of mice, but thanks for trying."

"All I'm saying is, you know, don't be hard on yourself. Anyone would have cracked under that kind of pressure, and I gotta tell you, you got some fire, girl! The way you ordered me to unlock those doors, and the way you were so willing to give your life for your boy—that's something to be proud of. You just remember that when you look in the mirror, not what that psycho chick tried to put in your brain."

She had misjudged Agent Perez. He wasn't just another cog in the machine doing his job like a mindless automaton. He saw where she was hurting, and instead of casting judgment for all the mistakes she had made, he saw her as a hero. She didn't have to look in the mirror and see a weak person, easily overcome by the troubles of life. Now she could see something more, something stronger. His words had given her a precious gift.

She reached out and held his hand in both of hers, startling him slightly. Tears breached the edge of her lids and slid down her cheeks.

"Thank you," was all she said.

But the message was received. She could tell by the way he pursed his lips and turned his head to the side that he was fighting back his own urge to tear up. He slid his hand out from under hers, and said, "What are you trying to do, ruin my reputation?" His eyes darted to both sides.

She offered him a smile as she leaned back in her chair and wiped the tears from her cheeks.

He folded up the paperwork and got to his feet. "I'll go see if your son is here yet."

She thanked him with a silent gesture.

He walked away through the desks and partitions, leaving her to re-process the last two days with a new perspective. Who would have imagined she, Holly Paris, would have the courage to break into a doctor's office and plant a bomb, or stand on the edge of a ten-story drop and allow the whole world to see her as something filthy and pathetic? Truly, there was no end to the lengths she would go to in order to save her son.

A new confidence began to bubble up inside her soul, and suddenly she felt sure that she would never return to the life she had allowed herself to sink into.

She owed it to her son to give him a better life, and now she felt she had the strength to do it.

She stood and looked over the partition to see Dan sitting in the lobby. He had struck up a conversation with an elderly man, and of course they were laughing. She left the makeshift cubicle and walked down the aisle of the bull pen and into the lobby.

When he saw her, he politely stopped his conversation and stood. His eyes were attentive and innocent. "Is everything okay?" he asked, stepping closer.

How odd for him to ask that. Couldn't he see how she was looking at him? Couldn't he tell how much she had fallen completely in love with him? She stepped in close, and suddenly it was only the two of them; the background became a buzz of noise.

She tilted her head up and found his sweet caring eyes. "I have a problem, Dan," she said defiantly.

His eyes widened. "Only one?"

She punched him on the arm. "I'm serious, Dan." Her eyes grew soft again. "I don't think I can live without you. Can you handle that?"

A big beautiful grin spread across his handsome face. "I don't know; you're kind of a hand full."

She gripped him by the front of the shirt with both fists, pulled him down, and their lips met. It wasn't a long kiss, but a kiss that said thank you for being here for me, and a kiss that promised more to come if he was willing to stand by her through whatever storms life threw at them.

They parted gently and he rubbed her arms with his strong hands. "Is this you thanking me again for the pizza?"

She smirked. "It was good pizza."

"Hey, if you liked that pizza, I've got some really good bread..."

Suddenly a little scratchy voice filled the hollow lobby. "Mommy!"

Holly looked past Dan to see Gabe running in bare feet and pajamas across the hard shiny floor of the police station lobby. Her heart swelled. Never in her life had she seen anything more beautiful. She crouched down and he flew into her arms. His soft blond hair brushed against her cheek and his tiny hands pressed against her back. She was whole again; her son was safe.

"They let me play with the siren in the police car!" he said, pulling back more quickly than she had hoped. How odd, after all he had been through, that those would be the first words he said to his mother.

"Didn't you miss me?" she said.

He looked up confused, as if to say, "Well duh."

She gripped his arms. "Well I missed you!" She pulled him in and hugged him tight again.

He rubbed her back with his soft little hands and whispered, "Sorry, Mommy."

"What do you have to be sorry about?" she whispered back.

"Sorry I went with Auntie Amber."

She pulled back. "I'm just so happy you're back! Don't you ever leave me again, okay?"

He gave a stoic nod.

She looked up at Agent Grant, standing quietly in the background. "Thank you for rescuing my son. I don't have the words to tell you how grateful I..." Her voice cracked.

Angela adjusted her posture. "It's not necessary, Holly. Seeing you back together is all the thanks I need."

CHAPTER 53

Jake tried to get comfortable on the jailhouse cot. But it wasn't the physical discomfort of the abrasive synthetic cushion that kept him shifting position, it was the tempest going on in his heart and mind. Jenna's words plagued him, playing over and over in his head: "I can't wait another day. I can't let it grow inside me and become something..."

Had she gone through with it? Was Aiyana gone? Or had he planted enough doubt in her heart to make her question her belief that Aiyana was just a blob of undeveloped tissue? He remembered the disgust on her face, the outrage at what his words implied. She could never knowingly kill a baby. But had he convinced her?

That opened another wound in his heart. Could he ever love her again if she did kill their child? Could he forgive her for her blindness? He wished he had never seen Aiyana. He wished he had never been given the ability to hear her thoughts, and see her precious little face. It was a face that would haunt him forever. If he had never experienced her very real and tangible presence, he could have forgiven Jenna, and, to his shame, might have even felt relief and gratitude. But not now. How could he?

A face appeared in the window of his jail cell door. The lock clicked and the door swung open to reveal a man in a dress shirt and suit pants. He might have been a detective; there was a badge on his belt. "You have a visitor, Mr. Paris."

Jake rolled to a sitting position and cleared his throat. "Who?"

"Your girlfriend, but we've detained her for a moment to get the rest of her statement. I figured I'd give you a chance to gather yourself."

"Thank you," said Jake, taking an inventory of his disheveled appearance.

The detective grabbed the handle on the door. "She'll be down in a few minutes, just hold tight."

He watched the door seal shut, and that's where his eyes stayed. Watching the door. Waiting to see if Aiyana would appear. He hoped with all his heart that Jenna had changed her mind.

After what seemed like an eternity, he heard foot steps approaching. His eyes stayed locked on the sliver of a window. But the shadow of a guard soon passed, and his heart sank. If Aiyana had come with her mother, she would have connected with him by now. The weight of the thought crushed down on his heart, threatening to turn it to powder.

What if she were dead? How could he bear knowing that she had existed, but had never taken a single breath of life? It seemed more tragic to him than if she had lived and died by some other means. At least then her existence would have been real to others besides himself, and not just a...

Suddenly her sweet innocent face appeared through the door, followed by the rest of her. She looked like she wanted to burst—but she didn't say a word. She didn't have to; her love for him was written in the tightness of her brow and those quietly observant eyes of hers.

He fell to his knees and gripped her arms. "You're okay! Oh, thank God you're okay!"

Her lip trembled, and tears threatened to fall. She threw her arms around his neck and pressed her cheek against his. "I love you, Daddy," her voice squeaked.

"I love you, too, honey," he said, hugging her tighter. It surprised him how good it felt to hear her call him Daddy, and he wondered—how long had she known?

"Aiyana," he said gently, "did you know I was your daddy all along?"

She pulled back and shook no. "Not till you picked me up in your arms to chase Mommy. That's when I knew for sure."

"How did you know?"

She shrugged. "When your daddy holds you, you just know I guess."

His face tightened to fight back the onslaught of emotion about to take hold of him. He had to keep it together. He couldn't let Jenna see him all teary-eyed and blubbering. How would he explain that?

Aiyana put her hands on his shoulders. "You have to make up with Mommy. She didn't mean to..."

"I know," he said. "I'm not angry with her. She didn't see the beautiful and talented little girl that was shown to me. She only saw a piece of tissue. If she had seen you, she could never have let you go."

"So you'll make up?"

"I hope so."

"And we'll be a family?"

"Honey, I should have married your mother two years ago. If I had, none of this would have ever happened."

He heard a click, and the door opened. The detective gave him an examining look. "Am I—interrupting something?"

Jake considered his posture on the floor of the cell and squeezed his eyes closed. "And so that's about it—Amen." He got to his feet and brushed the dust from his knees.

The detective opened the door wider. "Come on. She's in the waiting area below."

Jake stepped out onto the elevated metal grating and immediately saw Jenna through the steel railing sitting at one of the picnic bench style tables below in the communal area. The detective led him down, and Jake sat across from her. Aiyana tagged along and hopped up on the bench beside him.

Jenna played with the strap on her pocketbook, unable to decide what to say first.

"This is my fault," said Jake.

Her head lifted sharply, her face revealing her heart. She felt guilty for what had happened. She had expected to be the one to apologize; she opened her mouth to speak.

"No. Wait. Hear me out." Jake held a hand up. "I've been living my life in fear, fear that I would end up like my mom. I've been so afraid to make a decision because I didn't want to face the consequences of making the wrong choice."

She reached across to touch his hand. "You don't have to do this..."

"Ma'am," said the guard by the door, "no contact."

She glanced his way, then back at Jake. "We don't have to jump into this."

"Do you have a stick of gum?" he asked, holding out his hand.

"A what?"

"Gum, you know, the Big Red you always keep in your purse."

She gave him a look, then dug the pack out of her purse.

"Slide me a stick."

She pulled one out and pushed it across the table.

He picked it up, tore the paper and silver coating off, and put the stick in his mouth. "Mmm-mmm, that is de-licious," he said.

"I'm glad you like it," she said, baffled by his behavior.

He took a couple more chews, then leveled his eyes on her. "Jenna, I have loved you from the first moment I saw you playing hacky sack in the college courtyard. I have never been more sure about anyone in my life. This is not about the baby. This isn't about being pressured to marry you. This is about me saying I should have been a man and married you years ago. It was my childish fear that drove you to that clinic. You didn't want me to choose you because of a baby. You wanted me to choose you because I love you, and this is me telling you—I love you, Jenna. Even if there was no baby, you are the only person I could ever see spending the rest of my life with."

Her fingers squeezed on the strap of her purse, and the tears began to flow.

He brought up a silver ring he had made from the tin foil of the chewing gum wrapper. "I realize this is silver, but it's all I have to work with, and I don't want to let another day go by without asking."

She brought her hand to her chest, and gasped for air.

"Jenna, will you marry me?" His own eyes were watering now as he held the ring up, pinched between his thumb and index finger.

"Yes," she squealed. "Yes, I'll marry you!"

He held the silver ring out exactly half way between them and said, "No contact..."

She reached up and slid her finger slowly through the hole in the wrapper ring.

The officer at the door didn't say a word, only gave a subtle nod and a pressed smile.

CHAPTER 54

Angela Grant followed a uniformed officer down the cell block of the local county lockup, feeling strangely apprehensive about her impending visit. This was the last place on earth she expected to be. The Sunbury authorities had everything well in hand, and Perez was already on a flight back to Washington. A visit like this was highly unorthodox and even mildly frowned upon. The case was closed, and any continued involvement on her part showed an emotional investment which might cast a shadow on her ability to be objective with this or future cases.

"This is it," said the officer, swiping his keycard on the door lock. He opened it a crack and gave her the handle.

The door opened slowly to reveal Jake Paris sitting on the edge of his bunk. He gave a sheepish smile and a limp wave.

"This better be good, Mr. Paris," she said, stepping into the cell. "I'm supposed to be on a flight to Washington." His eyes looked down by her leg, and then flicked back up. She looked down to see if perhaps there was something on her pants.

"I was never a man who believed in coincidences," he said, "but I had one phone call to make, and your business card was the only thing in my pocket."

She assessed the implication of his statement. "I don't know how you think I can help you. You were caught breaking into a private facility..."

"I know, but I was thinking if you knew why, you might consider putting in a good word for me."

"I'm sorry you wasted your phone call on me, I'm afraid I can't help you." She turned to knock on the cell door.

"Wait. I need to ask a question. Just one question." "And that would be?" She made an attempt to mask her irritation, but not much of an attempt.

He was looking at her leg again. "What were you supposed to tell me?"

She squinted at him. "I wasn't supposed to tell you anything." She paused. "Mr. Paris, my eyes are up here."

He pulled his eyes up and stammered. "Sorry." They went back down, up, then down again.

"What did you think I was supposed to..." His erratic behavior made her pause. "Are you all right?"

A big grin stretched across his face. "I knew it!"

"Listen, I don't have time for games. If you're looking to plead insanity, you have to convince your lawyer, not me."

"You're gonna fwee me." His eyes widened and he cleared his throat. "I mean, free me."

Agent Grant stared at him, incredulous. "And why would I do that?"

He thought for a second, then his face grew bold. "Because your daughter says you will."

She squinted. "What? I don't have a... "

"I know this is weird, but please, just hear me out."

She shifted position like a caged animal.

"I know you're pregnant with a daughter, because I can see her. She is standing in front of you right now."

Her eyes narrowed. "You're insane."

He looked down again. "She says she's sorry about making you sick."

Without realizing it, Angela's right hand slid off her hip and rubbed her belly. "A lot of woman have morning sickness," she said defensively.

He listened. "No? Not morning?"

Her heart started to pound. "Okay. Whatever you're doing, stop it right now."

"At night? It happens every night at the same time?"

"Mr. Paris!"

"Listen, I'm not making this up. She's right here. She has curly blond hair and penetrating blue eyes and..."

Angela turned to leave. "This is over..."

His voice intensified. "She looks just like a little Cabbage Patch girl. She's wearing a yellow dress and..."

The room began to shrink around her. "What did you just say?"

He looked back up. "What? She looks like a little Cabbage Patch girl?"

She could hardly believe her ears. "My father..." Her eyes took on a faraway look. "He used to call me

his little Cabbage Patch girl—when I was very young."
Her voice trailed off.

Jake looked down at her leg again. "She says she's taking good care of Grammy's bunny." His eyes fluttered as if he were studying the imaginary thing. "She carries him everywhere. She says she loves him; he's her favorite."

Angela was utterly speechless.

"What?" He leaned in to listen to her knees. "He has a name? Mr. Hairs?"

Angela became rigid. "Okay, that's enough. How do you know that name?

"So, it means something to you?"

"Yes, it means something," she snapped. "My mother had a stuffed rabbit named Mr. Hairs. I used to play with it as a child. It's sitting in a box in the attic. But how could you have possibly known that?!"

His face grew exasperated. "She's telling me..."

She rolled her eyes. "The baby inside me is telling you this?"

"I can see her standing right in front of you," he said. "For some inexplicable reason, for the past two days, I've been seeing unborn children, including my own. That's why I broke into that clinic. I met my unborn daughter, and when I found out my girlfriend was going to the clinic, what else could I do but try to rescue her?" he pleaded. "Wouldn't you have done the same?"

Angela explored his face for deception, but saw instead an undeniable sincerity. "I have to admit, whatever scam you're trying to pull..."

"It's not a scam, Agent Grant. I'm telling you the truth. I'm just an ordinary guy trying to make sense of all this. I have a beautiful fiance who is carrying my little girl, and I just want to be with them. If what your daughter says is true, and you can help me get out of here—please—I'm just asking that you try."

She heaved a deep sigh. "I can't believe I am about to say this—but—who am I to argue with my unborn daughter? I'll see if I can persuade the clinic to drop the charges. Under one condition."

"Anything."

"Never bring this up again. Are we clear?"

"Crystal."

CHAPTER 55

Jake held Gabe on his lap as he sat chatting with Holly and Dan in the waiting room of the maternity ward. He couldn't believe it. They had managed to stay together long enough to see the birth of his daughter. He never would have called that one. There had been times when he thought for sure they were finished, but somehow they'd managed to make it work. In some strange way they seemed to enjoy fighting, or maybe it was the making up they enjoyed. He didn't know, but it was good to see them still together.

They were good for each other. She hadn't touched alcohol or drugs since the crisis with her son, and he had stopped spending every non-working hour in his living room engrossed in frivolous entertainment. There were even rumors that they had done family things together, like, picnics in the park and miniature golf. If Jake didn't know better, he might have thought Dan had finally grown up—but that perception quickly vanished when Dan opened his mouth.

"So, what's the return policy here?"

Jake laughed and Holly stabbed Dan with her elbow.

Dan looked at Gabe, "Not that we would ever think of returning you, even though you are a little defective."

Gabe produced a playful glare. He liked it when Dan teased him, or when Dan did anything for that matter. Gabe was still young enough to attach himself to a father figure, and he had latched onto Dan with everything he had. Jake hoped his friend had the good sense to marry his sister and make things official, but that was for them to decide.

"Jake?" In the doorway of the waiting room was a young freckle-faced boy whose lip was too short to cover his top teeth. "The contracthions are clother now," he said with his subtle lisp.

Jake looked at Dan and Holly. "I better get back to Jenna, if she'll let me back in the room." He smiled.

He left them and followed the boy down the hall, through the double doors, and to the doorway of the room where his wife lay with Aiyana by her side. A man he knew as Joshua sat in a chair in the far corner near the curtain-drawn window, and the nurse was placing a clipboard at the foot of the bed. Jake motioned for Aiyana to join him in the hall, so she hopped off the bed and followed him out.

He crouched down. "I know we've already talked about this, but I'd like to say one last goodbye," he said softly.

"It's not goodbye," she said, "It's hello."

"I know, but it feels like goodbye."

She rubbed his shoulder with her tiny hand.

"Will you even remember all the fun we've had hiding you from your mother these last eight months? Me reading you stories before bed, or staying up late watching old television shows together?"

Aiyana thought for a moment. "Well, at first I'll remember." She thought again. "But by the time I can talk, it'll just be a good feeling, in here." She put her fingertips on her heart.

He took her hands into his. "We've already had such an amazing journey, it's hard to believe this is only the beginning. I know you've told me a hundred times in a hundred different ways that you'll still be the same person, but it's going to be different. For one thing, I'll probably walk you into a pole or something, you know, forget you can't pass through things."

A tear formed in the corner of her eye.

"And you'll probably wonder why I pick things up for you, or ask you how you want me to arrange your room—because you won't remember that I used to do those things for you when you couldn't do them for yourself."

The tear trickled down. "You can still move things around for me if you want. I won't mind."

He kissed her little fingers. "I love you, my pretty little flower."

"Jake?" Jenna's voice carried out from the room.

Aiyana stiffened. "It's time."

Jake climbed to his feet and went in to his wife's bedside.

"She's coming, Jake." She said with a mixture of concentration and excitement.

The nurse slipped out of the room and returned with the doctor. And for almost an hour the room was alive with the sound of a new life coming into the world. Aiyana and the little boy with the overbite watched from the raised platform in front of the curtain-drawn windows. And the man Jake knew as Joshua stood near them in the corner.

Aiyana's hairy little head popped out first. The doctor reached in and turned her shoulders, then a moment later she was laying on the medical sheet. The nurse wiped her off and suctioned her mouth and nose, and the doctor looked at Jake. "Would you like to cut the umbilical cord?"

"Yes," he said, wiping tears, "of course."

The nurse handed him a pair of scissors, and the doctor moved so he could reach. Jake smiled at Jenna and clipped the cord. Aiyana never made a peep.

He looked over his shoulder for her, wanting to share the moment, but only the little boy stood near the window now. He had to remind himself that she was here with him now, real, in the flesh.

He watched as Joshua leaned in toward the little boy. "Do you know what Aiyana means?" he said in a gentle voice.

"No." The boy looked up at him with bright eyes.

Jake heard the response.

"Eternal blossom."

Jake caught his breath, remembering the old woman who had come to his door so many months ago with her strange request: "Don't let the flower die, Jake."

Without knowing it, he had fulfilled that request. He had kept the flower alive. But until this moment, he had not realized who the flower was. It was his own daughter, his precious Aiyana.

Jake turned to thank Joshua for reminding him of the flower and revealing its connection to his daughter, but the man was gone. He looked back at the window —and his heart grew heavy. The little boy, who had teeth too big for his lip, was slowly vanishing.

And then he was gone.

It was over.

With the birth of his daughter, the ability he had been given was taken back, and he was once again his old self, only richer now—much, much, richer.

He went to the head of the bed and hugged his wife, and together they stared at their daughter's pudgy cheeks, puckered mouth, and tightly sealed lashes. She was the most beautiful thing he had ever seen in his life, and she was finally here. A long full life awaited her, and he intended to make it the best one ever.

Jenna's face was a pool of happy tears, but a conflicting set of wrinkles developed on her forehead as she gave him an incredulous look. "You really want to name her after my grandmother?"

He rubbed the baby's hairy soft head with the palm of his hand." Her name is Aiyana. How could we call her anything else?"

CHAPTER 56

Jake stood in front of his neighbor's door, building up the courage to knock. What would he say to her? What could he possibly say that wouldn't make him sound like a complete loon? In the best case scenario he imagined the fiery redhead slamming the door on him. He didn't want to think about the worst case.

His hand shot out and knocked before the signal could get from his brain to his hand to stop it. There was a shuffle, a pause, and then the door opened a crack. "Can I help you?" she said, defensively.

"Yes," he said." May I come in?"

"I'm a little busy right now." She started to shut the door.

"Please," he said, "it's about your daughter Abby..."

Her face twisted. "What did you say?"

"I need to talk to you about Abby." This is it. Here it comes. She's going to slam it right in my face.

"Are you a private investigator or something?"

"I wish it was something that normal."

"Then how do you know my daughter's name?"

He tried to stop the words from coming out. "Because I spoke with her..."

Her face went flat and her hand slid down the door and fell to her side. "Are you a psychic?"

"I honestly don't know what I am, but if you'll just give me a couple of minutes, I'll explain."

She examined him a moment longer, then pulled the door back and led him down the short hall into her living room. Her apartment looked a lot like his, only the furnishings were different.

She turned, and he held out his hand. "Sorry, we've never properly met," he said, "I'm Jake Paris."

She hesitated, then took his hand. "I'm Liz."

"Nice to meet you, Liz."

She nodded. "Ah, would you like a drink?"

"I appreciate the offer, but I don't want to take too much of your time."

"Then please, have a seat."

He sat uncomfortably on the edge of the cushion and took a deep breath. "First, I want to apologize for putting my big fat foot in my mouth. I didn't know you had, well, visited the clinic."

She chewed her lip, studying his face. It was clear the topic was still uncomfortable.

"I'm going to be completely honest with you, and if you decide to throw me out on my ear, believe me, I'll understand." He took another deep breath. "Okay, here goes. Over the last several months, I have been able to see the unborn."

Surprisingly, she gave no reaction.

"When I met your daughter in the elevator she was standing right next to you, and I didn't know only I could see her."

There was still no reaction as she listened intently.

"She introduced herself to me as Abby."

Liz folded her arms uncomfortably.

"Does that name mean something to you?"

She pressed her lips together, then nodded. "I've been attending," her eyes watered as she searched for the words, "grief classes." She spoke softly and with great apprehension. "In the process we were all told to give our baby a name. By recognizing our baby as a he or a she, and giving it a name, we're better able to put it to rest. Last week..." Her face trembled. "I put my daughter to rest in a shared funeral service with the other ladies in my class. On the certificate I gave her the name Abigail, but I call her Abby." She put her hand to her mouth. "So when you said her name..."

Jake waited a moment and let her compose herself. "I understand this must be very hard for you. But I've come with a message—a message from Abby. Do you want to hear it?"

Liz bit her lip. "Yes, yes of course."

"When Abby said this to me, I didn't understand what it meant. I thought maybe you and her father were fighting over custody or something, and I didn't think it was my business to interfere. That's why I didn't come sooner. I just didn't understand. But recently my sister made a comment about seeing you at the clinic last summer, and it all just sort of clicked."

Liz listened intently.

Jake stood and looked her in the eye. "Liz, your daughter wants you to know—that she forgives you."

It was horrible to watch the agony on her face as she fought to keep her composure. Tremors of emotion tightened her cheek and chin and she looked to the side. The silent assault on her heart was most noticeable in the energy with which she wrung one wrist like a towel. It was clear she had no desire to cry in front of a man she barely knew. Yet his words had found a soft target deep inside.

He felt helpless to ease her silent torture. He had hoped his words would bring comfort and some semblance of peace, not worsen her pain. "I'm so sorry," he said, standing. "I meant to help..."

"No," she gasped, "No. It's okay. Thank you. Thank you so much."

"I'm sorry. I don't understand."

Liz discreetly dabbed at the liquid gathering in the corners of her eyes. "There was so much guilt. I didn't realize the depth of it until I started taking those classes. I needed to hear those words. I didn't realize how badly I needed to hear them. Thank you so much for telling me."

He didn't know what to say. Part of him felt like it would be appropriate to describe her daughter and let her know more about her. And the other part of him was screaming at the first part to keep its big mouth shut. She didn't need to know more about the child she had aborted. It would only drudge up more guilt. Wouldn't it?

He stood awkwardly, painfully aware that he was ill-equipped to be of any more use to his grieving neighbor. And as he did, his eyes came to rest on a photograph sitting on a table next to the television. His eyes narrowed. The woman in the photo bore a remarkable resemblance to the mysterious old woman who had given him the white flower all those months ago. She was younger in the picture, and the nose looked a little different, but that was her. He was sure of it. He stepped forward to get a closer look, then looked back over his shoulder at Liz, who seemed a bit more composed.

"Who is the woman in this picture?" he asked.

She moved next to him. "This one?" she said, pointing. "That's my grandmother."

"Does she visit you often?"

Her shoulders sank slightly. "No, she passed away three years ago."

Three years ago? How then had she paid him a visit last summer? He reached to pick up the picture. "May I?"

Liz nodded.

There was a gold plated inscription on the bottom of the picture frame which read: *Margaret Annette Atwater.* As he examined the photo closer, he couldn't help but notice that it wasn't the nose alone that was different. The woman in the photo had brown eyes. That was odd. He was sure the old woman who had visited him had green eyes. He remembered them because they were so bright and vibrant. He'd never seen anyone with such brilliant green eyes before.

Wait. That wasn't actually true. He *had* seen brilliant green like that before—in the eyes of a little strawberry blond girl named Abby.

------O------

Do you have questions?
Would you like to hear when new books are released?
Feel free to contact me.
JohnMichaelHileman@gmail.com

Other books by John Michael Hileman:

MESSAGES

As of this publication, MESSAGES has been in the top
ten of political fiction every month since January 2012.

VRIN: ten mortal gods

Bestseller in the category of Christian Science Fiction

Also check out
Miracles: 32 True Stories
by Joanie Hileman
As of this publication, *Miracles* has enjoyed nineteen
weeks on the top-ten list in the Inspirational category at
Amazon.com.

www.ingramcontent.com/pod-product-compliance
Lightning Source LLC
Chambersburg PA
CBHW051334250626
47155CB00007B/2593